PRAISE FOR *BOY PARTS*

'Eliza Clark is unflinching in this witty and shocking excavation of female rage and desire, and is sure to gain a cultish following. It is unlike anything I've read before, and it left me utterly invigorated and repulsed.'
—Elizabeth MacNeal, author of *The Doll Factory*

'Clark has created a wholly original monster and a sickeningly compulsive novel. I absolutely inhaled this book.'
—Julia Armfield, author of *Salt Slow* and *Our Wives Under the Sea*

'A funny and intensely readable spiral staircase down into the mind of a woman who wears a waist trainer under her clothes and who may or may not be a keen purveyor of ultra-violence.'
—*VICE*

'It's delightfully and deviously rooted in the now with its delectable internet and culture references and evocative and real-feeling portrait of women.'
—*Dazed*

'Boundaries are for breaking and if anyone can crash through and reinterpret the fear of our time, Eliza Clark can.'
—*MsLexia*

'Even at its most transgressive, it all feels effortless. Dark, funny, bold, it's an exceptional debut.'
—*The Skinny*

'The main protagonist will prove to be one of the most alluring, infuriating, and complex characters in modern British literature.'
—Niall Griffiths

'An impressive, fiercely current debut . . . delightful and addictive.'
—*i News*

BOY PARTS

ELIZA CLARK

HARPER ● PERENNIAL

NEW YORK • LONDON • TORONTO • SYDNEY • NEW DELHI • AUCKLAND

HARPER ● PERENNIAL

HarperCollins books may be purchased for educational, business, or sales promotional use. For information, please email the Special Markets Department at SPsales@harpercollins.com.

FIRST HARPER PERENNIAL EDITION PUBLISHED 2023.

Library of Congress Cataloging-in-Publication Data has been applied for.

ISBN 978-0-06-332892-1 (pbk.)

24 25 26 27 28 LBC 11 10 9 8 7

For my mother and father. Please don't read this.

Images which idealise are no less aggressive than work which makes a virtue of plainness. There is an aggression implicit in every use of the camera.
— Susan Sontag, *On Photography*

DEAN/DANIEL

I'm sick in my mouth on the bus into work. I swallow it down; the sandwich I ate at the bus stop is still identifiable by texture and flavour.

When the bus pulls over, I wobble on my heels. I imagine going over on my ankle, the bone snapping and breaking the skin. I imagine taking a photo in A&E and sending it to Ryan; *yikes, guess I can't come in!* But I can't make myself fall over. It's like trying to keep your head under shallow water; you just can't.

'You alright there, petal?' asks the bus driver.

'Just about,' I say.

I get to the bar half an hour late. We were supposed to open at twelve. Ryan won't be here till one, at least. I press my forehead against the cool glass of the door, repeatedly miss the lock with the key, and leave behind a smear of pale foundation.

I do the bare minimum to open, and carefully sip water till Ryan gets in. He whines at me for getting makeup on the door (again) and for failing to take the chairs down from the tables on the mezzanine. He calls it *the mez*. My head throbs. He asks me what time I got in (four a.m. – I say two) and if I'm hungover ('no'), then leaves me alone at the bar while he fannies on in the office.

I chop fruit in peace for an hour; I kill six lemons and flay a pineapple. I leave the limes, the taste of my last shot of tequila is still sour on the back of my tongue.

I hear them before I see them. Men in suits, marching down the street, twelve of them. They burst in, shouting, red-faced, thoroughly impressed with themselves, and I'm stuck mixing Old Fashioneds for half an hour.

They complain I'm taking too long. I offer them a Manhattan as a quicker alternative, and the leader of the pack scoffs. His designer tie is loose, and he flicks open the top button of a monogrammed shirt; an enormous watch cuffs his thick wrist. Great pains have been taken to appear visibly wealthy. Probably 'Aal fur coat and nee knickers', as my mam would say.

'A bit *girly* for us, darling.'

'It's basically the same as an Old Fashioned, it's just a bit quicker to make,' I say, each hand twirling a bar spoon through two glasses. His eyes are fixed on my tits, so he doesn't catch me sneering.

'They're pink, aren't they? Aren't those pink?'

'No, it's bourbon-based.' I think he's getting it mixed up with a Cosmopolitan; he doesn't want it, regardless.

They ascend to the mezzanine and complain loudly about how long they waited. They don't tip. Of course they fucking don't.

I'm praying it's just going to be the one round, but they buy two bottles of Auchentoshan and I am in hell. It is *an effort* not to stand with my head in my hands, or sit down on the floor, or vomit into the bucket of ice they make me bring them. I try putting a Merzbow album on over the sound system to chase them out. It's funny for about three tracks, but they just think the speakers are broken, and the noise makes my headache worse.

The leader separates from the pack. He comes downstairs and leans against the bar. I wait for him to buy another bottle, but he just starts *talking* to me. Talking, and talking, and *talking*. His slicked-back hair is thinning, and a strand of it keeps flopping in front of his eyes – he slaps it back into place as if he's killing a fly.

'I'm a partner, you see,' says the suit. Received pronunciation – he can't be local. A Home Counties transplant. A coloniser. He probably lives with all the footballers up in Northumberland and brags to his city-boy friends about how his Darras Hall mansion only cost him a million, how he lives next to Martin Dúbravka, and how, really, quality of life is just so much better up here, as long as you keep away from the rough bits.

'My time is very expensive,' he says.

'So is mine,' I say. He misinterprets this, and slaps a twenty-pound note on the bar, his meaty hands spanking the granite surface like it's his secretary's arse.

A woman has appeared behind him. She's skinny, middle-aged and alone. Her fake tan is a nut brown, her dye-job is much too dark, and her teeth are stained. She's shaking. I take her for an alkie.

'Excuse me,' she says. The suit ignores her – maybe he doesn't hear her.

'There you go, then, a nice little tip for you.' Demeaning, but I pocket the money. 'So, you're mine for the day now, are you?'

'Maybe the next five minutes.' Another twenty on the bar, in my pocket. 'I'm just going to serve this lady,' I say.

'How much to get you to sack this off and come home with me?'

'It's too early for this,' I say. His expression has darkened in the time it took for my eyes to roll.

'*Excuse me.*' The alkie is barking now, but the suit blocks her out with his bulk.

He leans over and grabs my wrist, his belly pressing against the bar top. He snorts, his tiny, piggy eyes narrowed and bloodshot from an afternoon's drinking.

'You're shaking,' he says. Charming that he thinks the shaking is down to him and not the result of what I had presumed to be a visible hangover. He tightens his grip; I watch my skin turn white beneath his fingertips. The room is spinning. He'll regret this when I vomit on him. It's a shame I can't make myself sick without sticking my fingers down my throat – it'd be a perfect way to get out of this without moving. I could scream, of course, but my voice is raw with the residue of last night's cigarette smoking. 'Are you frightened?' he slurs. He is drunker than I initially suspected.

'Let go of me.' He doesn't. I can't reach the fruit knives. There is a line of pint glasses in front of me, and I grab one with my free hand. 'I'm going to count to three,' I tell him.

The alkie pounds the bar.

'How old do you think my son is?' she asks. The suit lets go, dropping my wrist like my skin has burnt him.

'Gary, what the fuck?' Another suit descends the stairs, wobbly and embarrassed, in a cream summertime suit. He's the same age, but better kept, though still red with too many tumblers of scotch and too many holidays without an SPF. 'Sweetheart,' he begins. The woman interrupts him. She isn't an alkie, I suppose, just a rough mam.

'How old do you think my son is?' She thrusts her phone into my face. My website is up on the screen. She is showing me a black-and-white photo: a boy kneeling, his tongue between my index and middle finger, my ring finger digging into his cheek.

Ah.

'He's twenty. He signed a consent form and brought ID. I can show you.'

'Bollocks,' she says. 'What a load of bollocks. Hew.' She taps Gary on the shoulder. Cream suit asks what this is all about – Rough Mam ignores. 'How old does this lad look to you? Does he look twenty? Does he fucking look *twenty* to you?'

Gary looks at the mam, looks at me, looks at the photo.

'I think we should leave,' says Cream Suit. 'Chaps,' he calls. 'Chaps, it's time to go.'

But Gary is still thinking. Gary is still looking at the photo.

'He had ID,' I say. I pull out my phone and retrieve a scanned copy of his passport. I show it to Gary first. 'See. Twenty. Now go,' I say.

Rough Mam wants the men to stay. Rough Mam wants a

witness. But they're gone in a puff of expensive aftershave, the smell so potent it makes my head spin. Rough Mam wants to see the ID.

'That's my *older* boy. That's *Dean*, you stupid bitch, that's my older boy's passport. *Daniel* is *sixteen*. I'll call the fucking police if you don't take that down.'

I'd scouted him on the bus and suspected he *may* have been in sixth form. He'd been wearing a suit. He must go to one of those colleges with an officewear dress code, but you couldn't expect me to know that just from looking at him. I've seen blokes in their thirties who look twelve. That's why I ask for ID. That's why I keep records.

Plus, no court could possibly convict me. The similarity between the brothers is so remarkable that only a mother could really split hairs over that passport photo. I can't imagine a jury taking against me either: people always conflate beauty with goodness. I'm more Mae West than Rose. I can just cry a bit, talk like I'm daft, tease my hair up like a televangelist: the higher the hair, the closer to God, you know?

'Well *Daniel* lied to me and brought false ID. And I took these on a school day, so maybe keep a closer eye on him?' I boot the backend of my website in front of her (which takes ages on mobile) and delete the single photo of him from my main portfolio. 'Gone.'

'I want to see a manager.'

'Hello.' I gesture to myself.

'I want to see *your* manager, then.'

'It's just me in.'

'Right,' she says. 'Well then.' She just stands there and glares at me. I come out from behind the bar, with the intention of opening the door for her, then she hits me. Like, *hard*.

She runs out of the bar, and I make a half-hearted attempt to chase her but I'm in a stiletto pump. As quick as I am in boots or platforms, I haven't got a chance of catching her in these.

I spit after her. I'm fairly impressed with the distance, but it doesn't hit her. She disappears around the corner.

I clomp back into the bar, out of breath, feeling sick as a dog. My face aches.

'Are you okay?' asks Ryan. 'What the fuck was that?' Maybe it's the sight of him that tips me over the edge. He's one of these short men that compensates by being extremely muscular. He's got this big thick neck, and this teeny tiny pea head; thinning hair, bleached teeth, weak chin. Grotesque. If I open my mouth, I'll vomit. I run to the disabled bathroom, and I smack my head on the toilet seat as I fall to my knees. The sandwich I have already regurgitated once today works its way back up my gullet, escaping in full this time. It lands in the water with a splat, like a slice of bread hitting soup from a height. Carbs are rarity for me, and, upon reflection, I should not be surprised that my body has rejected this floury Tesco baguette like a mismatched organ.

'I just caught it on the CCTV,' Ryan says, entering the bathroom and closing the door behind him. 'You said you weren't hungover,' he says, betrayed, like he didn't sell me coke about twelve hours ago.

'No,' I say. 'Just got a fright. Did you see her hit me?' I ask. I retch. He did see. He wants to know why. 'What do you mean *why*? You saw her, she was just a mad alkie. I was talking to one of the suits, I wasn't serving her, she lost her shit.' I spit. I stick my mouth under the tap, and rinse. My body quakes, my skin flushes, and sweat oozes from every pore. I feel my hastily applied foundation begin to slide off my face, my cheeks streaked with mascara. There is vomit dripping from my nostrils, and I'm fairly sure that's bile leaking from my eyes. 'Give me some gum.'

He tosses me a little packet of bubble-mint – barely better than vomit.

'You know, if someone who's *actually* disabled comes in—'

'Fuck off,' I say. 'Fuck off, Ryan. I'm not going to the customer toilets. I was *literally* just assaulted.'

Ryan wants us to piss with the customers, like animals. Ryan always thinks someone with a limp or a chair or IBS is about to barge into the bar, with the entirety of Scope's advocacy board behind them.

'I'm not ringing the police,' he says. 'FYI.'

'Fine, whatever,' I say. 'You're sending me home though, aren't you?'

'No. We're short today,' says Ryan. 'I'm not sending you home for a hangover. How hard could she have gotten you? She looked skinny as fuck.'

'Are you joking?' I say. 'She was wearing rings. *And* I'm *not* fucking hungover. Text someone. The new girl, with the pink hair. Carrie.'

'Cassie,' he says. 'And no, it's her day off.'

'She won't fuck you for this, you know,' I say. 'And you might want to knock that craic on the head. She looks pretty *woke*.' I make air quotes, and sneer. 'Time's up, Ryan.'

I nod towards the 'Shout Up!' poster we have on the door of the toilet; the one that labels us a sexual-harassment-free zone. Ryan looks outraged. Ryan thinks it doesn't count as harassment if you're good looking, and Ryan thinks he's good looking. Before he can argue, before he can remind me he *went on the Shout Up! training day and everything*, Ergi appears behind him. I didn't know he was in today. He's never in. We're one of three trendy city centre bars he owns, and I think he often forgets about us.

'What's going on?' he says, throwing an accusatory look at Ryan.

'Nowt!' says Ryan. I burst into tears. It's easy for me to cry when I'm tired, when I'm poorly, when my eyes are already streaming.

'Some mad woman hit me, look.' I point to the red mark on my cheek. 'And I got such an awful fright I was sick. And Ryan won't let me go home.'

'Why won't you let her go home, man?' he asks. His accent is strange: a mishmash of Albanian and broad Geordie-isms. 'Call your new lass – pink hair. Carrie?'

'It's her day off, and Irina is out of sick leave.'

'She just got fucking hit, man,' says Ergi. 'Are you okay? Why'd she hit you?'

'I didn't serve her quick enough. A man was grabbing me. It's all on CCTV. It was awful.'

'I'll get you a taxi. I'll sort it out, don't worry,' he says. He asks for my postcode, and orders an Uber for me. He says he's going to check the CCTV and write an incident report, and that Ryan is to get me a glass of water and some tissues.

Ryan glares at me. When Ergi leaves, I stop crying.

'It's fucked up how you can turn that on and off,' Ryan says, handing me the water, the napkins.

'It's fucked up that you sell coke,' I say. 'That's all wrapped up in child slavery and shit.'

'Is it now?'

'Google it.'

He walks me out, seething, assuring me he *knows* I'm hungover. He tells me he's going to tell Ergi. I tell him I'll dob him in for dealing; people in glass houses and all that.

Then the taxi is here, and I'm out.

While I'm in the Uber, I get a flurry of apologetic texts from Ryan. *I'm sorry I was being weird, just sat and watched the footage properly, hope you're okay, please don't tell on me*, etc., etc. I respond with some emojis. Pizza, shrug, smiley, facepalm, sunshine. Interpret these glyphs how you will, Ryan.

It doesn't take long to get back to mine. Flo is still here. She's wearing my pyjamas and hoovering. She beams when I get in, her teeth stained with coffee, her choppy bob in disarray.

'I didn't expect you back so soon!' she says. 'What's with your face? Oh my God, have you been crying?' I grunt, and kick off my shoes, landing on my sofa with a thud. I bury my face in my hands. The bubble-mint gum has gone sour. I recount the story to Flo, who gasps and OMGs as required, like a panto audience.

'You could literally sue,' she says. I left out the bit with the boy, the photographs. I say I can't be arsed. 'You know, if you get attacked at work, you're meant to get six weeks off. Paid, and everything,' Flo says.

'No shit?' I say. 'Well, that's a silver lining. Get my pyjamas and a makeup wipe.' Flo does.

'I've cleaned the kitchen,' she calls from upstairs. 'And I've scraped all the coke off your coffee table. I managed to salvage at least a bump, so I put it in a baggy for you.'

She delivers my only pair of tracksuit bottoms and an old jumper – reserved for the most desperate of hangovers.

I change in front of her, dropping my clothes on the floor of my otherwise immaculate living room.

'Cool,' I say. I can almost guarantee she'll be beating herself up about this on her 'private' blog later. Private, because it's just for her and two hundred of her closest internet friends. It took me about five minutes to find it.

'It was just minging in here, and I thought I might as well tidy while you're at work.'

I groan as I wipe off my makeup, my skin stinging as I scrub.

'That's better,' says Flo. She plucks the dirty wipe from my hand, and holds it up, examining the impression of my face wrought in foundation, mascara and brow-cake. 'Ah, look at that. Like the Turin Shroud, that is.' Her phone is ringing; the right pocket of my pyjama bottoms is lit up. She picks it up and cancels it. 'It's just Michael. I've told him I'm at yours. He's probably just wanting to know about dinner. He's so fussy sometimes! Like, *chill out Michael*!' Then she turns her phone off, which is really a once-in-a-blue-moon kind of thing. 'Do you want some ice for your cheek?'

I do. I get her to bring my hangover kit, and two glasses of water. The kit is a Tupperware box full of over-the-counter painkillers. Flo brings it to me, then the water. Boots own-brand effervescent paracetamol and codeine (with caffeine) in the first glass of water, Dioralyte in the second. I drink the Dioralyte while the painkillers dissolve. I wash down two antihistamines (they're an anti-emetic, and a life-changing addition to the hangover remedy), two 342mg ibuprofen lysine (the good stuff, the period stuff) and an Imodium. By the time I've swallowed the paracetamol and codeine, I feel almost human again. Flo presents me with a handful of ice wrapped in a tea towel, which I press to my cheek.

'Do you want me to nip to Tesco? I could get us some hangover wine? And better food? I went into your fridge. All you have is a big bag of ice and some salad.'

'Yeah, okay,' I say. She toddles off to the shop, still in my pyjamas.

The remaining bile in my stomach curdles at the thought of putting more wine into it. I take a second Imodium.

I sit with my laptop and scroll through the pictures from Dean's shoot. Daniel's shoot. Whatever his name was. He was very cute and very excited that I approached him on the bus in front of his friends, very excited to get my card and very excited when he emailed me twenty minutes later asking when he could come to my studio.

He came in his underwear during the shoot and thought I didn't notice. Honestly, I did have an inkling he wasn't twenty, but he consented, you know? He signed his forms, and he gave me a very convincing passport.

The photos are cool. Kind of grungy. Black-and-white, but he still looks flushed. The freckles on his nose and his shoulders pop. I already sent some preview shots to a few private buyers – the few big spenders who like large-scale prints and originals. No one has responded, so far, but I figured he was going to be a hard sell. He's not the best-looking lad, bless him – a big nose, and a lot of pitting on his cheeks. I think he has character, but I'm a broad church.

I'll hold off on deleting them, for a bit. I probably should, but what's his mam going to do now she's clocked me on CCTV?

Flo is back, announcing her return in a sing-song voice, accompanied by the telltale rustle of bags-for-life. The ice in the tea towel has melted, and I fling it into the kitchen.

My hand is numb with the cold, and I wedge it between my warm thighs.

'I got you some carbohydrates and tins and stuff while I was there.' She walks past me (shoes on my carpet), picks up the wet tea towel as she goes, and starts putting the shopping away. Carbs. I curl my lip.

'Gluten is the *literal* devil,' I tell her. She never listens to me about food and she'd still be skinny if she did. She posts on her blog about my *disordered eating*. How it bothers her, how she's always trying to feed me bread. 'And take your shoes off.'

She apologises. She tells me about a new boy at the Tesco. The same handful of staff have worked there the entire time I've lived here, so he stuck out to her. She tells me he's really cute, but she has such bland taste in men. She likes the men she thinks she's supposed to like. Her boyfriend has a big beard and an undercut, because when they got together that was the *in* thing. The boyfriend she had when we first met was this NME-cut-out, landfill-indie looking cunt with a porkpie hat and a huge fringe. She liked Harry Styles a few years ago, and now she likes that white-bread, absolute fucking baguette of a lad from *Call Me by Your Name*.

'I swear to God, he's adorable,' she says. 'He looks like the main guy from *Mr. Robot*, the one you fancy.'

'Rami Malek.' I roll my eyes. Flo thinks every short, ambiguously-brown man looks like Rami Malek.

'I promise he's cute. You'll know him as soon as you see him. Trust me.' She brings me a glass of wine and sets down bread and hummus that she must know only she will eat. She picks up my ankles, sits down next to me, and places my feet in her lap. 'Do you want to watch a film?' she asks.

I nod. I hand her my laptop, and she compliments my photographs before going to my downloads folder. If she notices anything amiss, if she thinks the model looks young, she doesn't say anything. She flicks through the films I have on my laptop and googles a few.

'Oh!' she says, pointing at the screen. She turns to me with her bottom lip jutting out. '*Fritz the Cat*! Oh my God!'

She's pointing at the file for the film *Fritz the Cat*, but she means *our* Fritz.

When Flo and I lived together during uni, Flo fed a stray cat. A big, ugly, ginger tom, with the biggest pair of balls I've ever seen on a cat. I named him Fritz. Flo bought him a collar with this annoying fucking bell on it and everything. I lost him when I was living by myself during my MA. Flo saddled me with him and fucked off to an internship in Leeds.

'I miss Fritzy,' she says.

'Well, you should have taken him with you,' I say, shrugging. 'I take it you won't watch the film *Fritz the Cat*.'

'Absolutely not.' She gives the laptop back. 'I'm not watching any of these.'

'Your taste is so basic.' She won't watch anything remotely challenging. She made me turn off *Nekromantic*, *Vase des Noces* and *Irreversible*; she even made me turn off *The Poughkeepsie Tapes*. And that's just a found-footage horror, you know? Practically mainstream: with a linear story, and no subtitles and dialogue and everything. She asks if she can flip through the dusty case of DVDs behind my television.

'Don't,' I say. She asks why not. 'We've been over this like... *fifty* times. I'm hanging on to them just in case. Nothing in there is HD and they all look like shit on my telly.' I stab a finger at my downloads folder again. 'Look, *Pretty Baby* is quite normal.'

'Isn't that the Brooke Shields paedophilia film?'

'Anything would sound bad if you put it like that, Flo. *Oh*, Jurassic Park, *is that the Jeff Goldblum dinosaur necromancy film*?' I say, doing my impression of her. She puts on this nasal, babyish voice, and a little lisp. Even with me. Sometimes, when she's drunk, she forgets to put it on. I don't know why she does it.

'Christ, can we just watch *Moana*, or something?'

'I haven't got it. Can you be bothered to wait for a download?'

She can, but I can't. I talk her into *Blue Velvet*, because she knows she's supposed to like David Lynch, even though she doesn't. She cringes and hides her eyes during that first scene with Frank. She tells me it's horrible.

'It's not that bad.' I elbow her. 'Drink your wine.'

I get a text from my mam, who wants to meet for lunch tomorrow. I agree. She knows I'm off (scheduled, not because I got hit), and there's no point in arguing, or trying to get out of it. She came to my house the last time I said I was busy without an airtight excuse – I was literally just sat in my pyjamas and I had to pretend I was ill. The quicker I respond, the less shit I get when I inevitably have to see her again.

Flo complains every time Kyle MacLachlan speaks ('he's so slimy!') and whines like a stuck pig whenever Frank is on screen. Though she sings under her breath when 'In Dreams' plays – having somehow managed to arrive at Roy Orbison's back catalogue independently.

I drop off to sleep at some point and wake up to an empty house. Flo has sent me a text.

> Forgot I had to go home, lol! Couldn't stay all night, bae was getting lonely. Had a lush hangover. See you soon x

I'm checking her blog in the morning in case she's feeling confessional. I genuinely don't trust her not to brush my hair and finger me while I sleep.

● ● ●

Ugghhhh coming at you all with a SadGay (TM) post again. I'm really struggling with Rini. I felt like I'd weened myself off and I'm rlly trying to focus on Michael and how well that's going, but I think about her all the time. It's hard to tell if this is just like something my brain is cooking up as self-sabotage or if I'm still fucking pathetic and in love with her like I was during foundation and in uni. Jeeeeeezzz it's been nearly 10 years now.

I wonder if I'm just literally never going to get over her or what and I know I'm about to cue like 10 of you coming in like SHE SOUNDS TOXIC yada yada yada and I swear she isn't as bad as it sounds on here sometimes!!! but there's just loads of shit in her past I'm not going to share on here, and like she is really really not this awful like Monster i think sometimes you all seem to think she is.

I *really* think she has undiagnosed bpd and she doesnt have many real friends, she's like INCAPABLE of healthy relationships and she really needs my help?? I did her shopping for her yesterday when we were hanging because if I didn't do it for her she'd lit just live on water and salad. This isn't a problem with Rini it's a problem with me, but I appreciate that you're all so concerned for me and that you'll listen to me vent.

I read it on the bus. Flo's theory about me having Borderline Personality Disorder is this weird long-standing thing, and I'm sure if someone else tried to give me a diagnosis without being qualified to do so, she'd be the first person to jump in with accusations of ableism.

Plus, if anyone's borderline out of the two of us, it's her. And I hate it when she calls me *Rini*. Jesus. Mam is texting me to tell me she's already in town, and I get an email.

Dear Irina,
This is Jamie Henderson - junior curator at the Hackney Space gallery. I had the pleasure of meeting you at one of your MA shows a few years ago (while I was still a student myself haha!) I've been keeping up with your website, and we'd be very interested in showing some of your newer work as part of an exhibition on Contemporary Fetish Art. We have a couple of other artists of your calibre on board already (Cameron Peters, Serotonin, Laurie Hirsch to name a few!)

We'd be interested in showing a collection of 5-6 of your photographs, large scale and preferably stuff you haven't shown before. No pay, but we'll cover expenses and we're expecting a lot of buyers to attend, and I'm sure your work sells well.

We've also had a look at some of the older

films of your MA shoots (those are really
buried on your website ha ha!) and we read
your interviews in Vice and Leather/Lace.
Groundbreaking stuff. We think your shoots
sound really amazing and we'd actually be
really interested in showing a film of your
process to show as part of the exhibition, if
that's something you're still interested in.
If you don't make films anymore, it's fine.

We're also producing a limited run of
photo books for the photographers included in
the collection. A print run of no more than
a hundred or so, but it'd be great if you
could dig through your archives and send us
originals/copies of a broad selection of your
work, from your earliest stuff to the works
you'd like to include in the main exhibition.
Looking forward to hearing back from you,
Jamie

I have zero recollection of this bitch, but I grin. From ear
to ear, it splits my face. My heart flutters, and stomach flips.

I take a moment to collect myself. I mean, of course they
want me – who else would they get?

Hi Jamie,
It's great to hear from you! I'm very
interested in taking part in the exhibition.
I also have some recent film work I can send.
I've worked with Serotonin before, actually,
a six-week course of it.

Seriously though, I actually have, we were
at the RCA together (older than me, obvs)
used to go out together all the time. Is she
performing? Or just showing film.

Photo book should be fine as well, my
personal archive is v extensive.

Irina

I read the email again. Groundbreaking. I like that. I send
a screencap of the email to the group chat Flo and I have
with my various hangers-on.

Night out soon to celebrate plz!!! I say, and the congrats
start pouring in. There are three of them, aside from Flo
herself – her ex-students from the college. They're awful in
a very specific art-undergrad way, but you can only drink
alone to a point.

I get off the bus and Mam is waiting for me. We look
nothing alike. She is a literal foot shorter than me.

'For goodness' sake, Rini,' she says, pulling me down,
smearing a sticky lip-glossy kiss on my cheek. 'Do you
really need to wear heels? It's no wonder you're single if
you spend your life looking about six foot four. You could
at least have your hair flat; you don't need the extra height.'

It takes her a moment to notice the bruise on my cheek. I
tried my best to colour correct it; I used an industrial grade
foundation in the hope of covering it. It's the foundation
she goes to complain about first, asking me if I'm going to
my own funeral, before clocking the red mark on my cheek
glowing through the makeup.

'What on *earth* have you done to your face?' she glares.
'You are *far* too old to be getting in fights, Irina.'

'A drunk woman got me at work. I was trying to throw her out.'

'What, yourself?' I try to walk a few paces ahead of her, but she always catches up, even with her daft little legs. 'That was *stupid* of you, Irina. You're not a bouncer! Where were your bouncers?'

'Well, I was in on my own. It was yesterday afternoon, Mam. We've not got any bouncers during the week, never mind during the day.'

She's not satisfied. On the walk to the branch of Ask Italian she likes to eat at, she says I shouldn't get involved with unstable people. She complains that it's embarrassing her: me, walking around, with a bruise like this. She says I look like I've been fighting, or battered, and either way that's *common*.

At the restaurant, she's unhappy with our seat by the window; she doesn't like being seen to eat. We share an antipasti board; she eats the meat and cheese, I eat the vegetables. She tells me she hates my nails. They are long, red and filed to a point.

'Now they *are* common. With the bruise, as well. People will think you're a working girl. And a *sad* one, one that gets hit.' A beat of silence, while I watch the gears turn in her head, searching for a final critique. 'Plus, you'll take your bloody eye out.'

I imagine myself as a sad, one-eyed working girl. Mam says my name. She demands a response, like there's anything I can say to that she won't use to drag me into an argument.

'Well, I just had them done, so I'm keeping them like this.'

'I didn't say you can't have them, I just said I hated them. Am I not allowed an opinion?' she asks.

'I didn't say you weren't. But they're *my* nails, and—'

'I know they're *your* nails, I just *hate* them, Irina. Why are you arguing with me?'

'I'm not fucking arguing with you!'

'Well, there's absolutely no need to lose your temper. You're spoiling lunch,' she says.

I feel warm, and jittery. I stammer, and fail to say anything, knowing that trying to get the last word in will just make it worse. I nod, and I sneak my fork under the table and jab myself in the thigh with it. My breathing evens out. I change the subject.

'How's Dad?'

She rolls her eyes.

'Sunderland were relegated last week, so you can imagine.' We laugh at him. 'He threw one of my good candles at the telly.'

'Serves you right for marrying a Mackem, doesn't it?'

She agrees with me, and does not speak for a moment, instead treating me to a glimpse of that glazed, thousand-yard stare she sports when she remembers she's going to die having only ever been married to my dad. Sometimes, when she drinks, she tells me about the other (poorer, but better looking) bloke she was seeing when she first started going out with Dad. She refers to it as her *Sliding Doors* moment, even though her relationship with my father significantly predates the release of the film.

I fiddle with my belt. Mam snaps out of her fantasy timeline with the handsome husband.

'You should have gotten the next size up in those trousers. I thought before, they look really tight on your bum,' she says.

'They're supposed to be tight. And if they were looser on my bum, they'd be very loose on my waist.' She doesn't admit that I'm right – she has been distracted by a woman she has seen out of the window, limping out from a Brexity pub called The Dame's Garter with a vape dangling from her puckered lips, which are as brown and wrinkled as an unbleached arsehole. Her hair is scraped back from her forehead, silver roots and brassy red ends, which are thin and stringy. A clown dangles from a gold chain on her leathery neck.

'Did you see her?' says Mam. 'I went to school with her. She's younger than me. Can you believe it?'

'Really?'

Mam is well preserved, well dressed, and skinny. She sports a permanently unmoving forehead, and lips as plump as my own. She had worry lines for about a week in 1997, and put a stop to that very quickly.

'That's what happens when you smoke, and you don't moisturise,' Mam says. 'She was always dead common – the whole family. They lived on my estate. Even by our standards, they were scum.'

Mam is rude to the waitress when she brings our salads, and I pierce the fabric of my trousers with the fork. She complains about everything in front of her. The salad is too oily, her lemonade is too sugary, her friend has cancer and keeps posting about it on Facebook.

'Wow, what a cunt,' I say. I'm too exhausted, too irritated, to keep a lid on it now. I drop my calm-down fork.

'*Irina.*'

'No, I'm serious Mam. What a *cunt*, talking about her cancer on Facebook. She should just fuck off to Dignitas and get it over and done with, shouldn't she?'

'You always have to *escalate* everything, don't you? You can never let *anything* lie; it always has to be this big drama with you. You're very *extra*, Irina.'

I'm extra. *She's* extra. And if I'm extra *she's* the reason I'm so fucking extra. I no longer want to eat my own salad (which is, admittedly, far too fucking oily). She has this shitty look on her face now, like *Ooo, I've got you, that's shut you up!*

'*Anyway*,' she says, 'how's work?'

'Fine.'

'And the photography stuff? How's that?' she asks, sounding bored. I smile. 'Well, don't just sit there looking smug, Irina, what is it?'

'I got invited to take part in a pretty big exhibition today. Hackney Space want my photos and a film as part of this big retrospective they're doing on UK fetish art. So, you know, all that hard work *finally* paying off I suppose.'

'Is that what they call hard work nowadays? *Fetish* art.' She rolls her eyes. 'Honestly, Irina, I wish you'd take some photos I could hang up.'

'Lots of people hang up my photos.'

'Yes, lots of strange *gay* men, and sorry if it makes me a homophobe for not wanting photos of willies all over my house.' I feel like I'm at lunch with a fucking *Daily Mail* comments section. 'I miss when you did your nice drawings, Rini. You're so good at drawing.'

This is something she's totally made up: that I used to do *nice* drawings, and that she ever liked them. She told me once that a picture I drew of Galadriel looked like a burns victim (I was, like, twelve). She told me if I was naturally gifted, I'd be better at drawing, and you can't really do anything with art if you're not naturally gifted with it.

I grafted my arse off through GCSE, and she was shocked at how much I improved. Like yeah, no shit, when you put loads of work into something you get better at it. She was always like, *Irina, you just give up if you're not good at something straight away*, as well.

The shit with Lesley absolutely would not have happened if I'd had a little bit more encouragement at home. My therapist at the time said so, more or less.

'Yeah, well, Hackney Space is a pretty big deal, anyway. It's good news.'

'I suppose. It's been *years* since you had an exhibition. I've never heard of them, though.'

'I have print sales. I don't *need* an exhibition it's just… Well, it *is* a big deal.'

'It can't be that big of a deal if I haven't heard of them. I'm not *stupid* just because I don't know all the weird little galleries in London.'

'I never said you were stupid, I just said, it is a big deal. Because it *is*.' I hiss, 'What is your problem, Mam?' I'm furious again, and she's just sat there. She lifts an eyebrow, with great difficulty.

'Problem? I'm happy for you, darling. You needn't take everything so personally! I just said I haven't heard of the gallery.' I sulk in my seat.

She offers to buy me an outfit as a treat. I accept, begrudgingly. A lifetime with this woman has taught me that I can be bought. Quite easily, in fact. She treats me to a little black dress from the sale at the soon-to-close-down branch of Westwood, and I'm just as giddy as a schoolgirl by the end of the afternoon.

I get off the bus a stop later and go to Tesco. I imagine I

cut a strange image, with my Westwood bag and my basket full of red wine and bag salad.

There's a new boy. He's sitting behind the counter – staring.

Eddie
Customer Assistant
Checkouts
Joined the team in 2012.

He must be new to this store. Perhaps they were hiding him in Kingston Park or Clayton Street.

He has a gap between his front teeth – his tongue winks through when he smiles at me. It's awkward. I smile back, but I'm not good at smiling off-hand like this. I generally need more prep, a moment with a compact mirror to practise.

He has curly black hair, brown skin, freckles. An earring – I love girly shit like that. He's a vision in polyester, a checkout movie star; he's the Oscar Isaac of random boys who work in Tesco. He reminds me of someone else too, an old model.

Eddie from Tesco has a little anime clip on his keychain, one of the characters from *Madoka Magica* – which I remember Flo being very into.

I drop some phallic vegetables into my basket, for the sake of it, and approach him at the counter. He says *hullo* and stares directly at my tits. He doesn't make eye contact, and his eyes flick from my tits to my lips, to the boxes of tampons over my shoulder. He makes pleasantries, and he has quite impeccable manners, but he is still looking at my tits every few seconds.

I'll scout him. I'll be able to get him to do some weird stuff – beta males like this are usually nasty. When you don't get any pussy and spend your teens falling down the free porn rabbit hole, you end up like one of those freaks with an *ahegao* profile picture on Twitter and an internet history that's seventy-five per cent bukkake, twenty-five per cent tragic Google searches.

How do you know if a girl likes you?

How to casually flirt with women.

How to make a lasagne for one person.

How to feel less lonely.

Gokkun schoolgirl.

How do you get semen out of your carpet?

I realise he's just asked me a question.

'What?'

'I asked if you live nearby,' he says. Which is a good sign. It's definitely a weird thing to ask a customer, so that implies he fancies me enough to risk asking me inappropriate shit. 'Sorry,' he says. 'I just feel like I've seen you around.'

'I'm in here all the time. I live just round the corner.'

'Cool,' he says. 'I— I like… your shoes.'

I hope he doesn't have a foot fetish. Maybe he's just into high heels, or huge women – possibly both. I hand him my business card, give him my spiel – *blah blah blah photographer, blah blah blah street scouting.*

'I don't pay, but, if you're interested, I need models for a new show I'm doing. Heard of Hackney Space?'

He has heard of it. Which surprises me, on account of the fact he's about my age and he works in a fucking Tesco.

●●●

I have an email from Mr B when I get in. He's one of the private buyers I sent the previews of 'Deaniel' to. My best customer, in fact. I groan. The subject line reads: *More?* And he's asking about *the little redheaded creature*. He has noticed those same teaser shots are gone from my website. I groan again.

Mr B just popped up one day – he got my personal email, and I still have no idea how. His custom is always generous, if slightly sporadic. He buys originals and large-scale prints, and he always tips. The more explicit the image, the more open his hand. He likes younger men, feminine men. He likes it when I'm in the photos. It was stupid to think he might not take me up – Deaniel's photos tick all his boxes.

    B,
    Yeah, about him. Found out he gave me a
    fake ID. Already dumped the files and the
    stuff's obvs off the website, (even the stuff
    behind the paywall) ((especially the stuff
    behind the paywall)). I'll hit you up w my
    new shit soon. Sorry.
    I have an exhibition coming up soon -
    Hackney Space. Very exciting.
    Irina x

His replies are automatic. My phone buzzes before my shopping is even away.

    Dearest Irina,
    First of all, my darling, let me congratulate
you.

Now, let me decry this sudden showing of a dark-ages morality. We should align ourselves with greater men than fuddy duddies in robes and wigs. Hadrian, Confucius, da Vinci. Why deny Zeus his Ganymede? Olympus is so heavy with treasure.

Alas, it is illegal. I will mourn for my Antinous.

Mister B

B,

Sorry. I'll send you some freebies? Outtakes from some of the experimental webcam photos i took w that blond, skinny, girly looking boy frm April? Can't remember his name but attached as an apology. Panties! V cute.

Irina x

Dearest Irina,

As lovely as you are fair. You are an artist in your photography as much as your seduction. Remember: Mister B is an omnivorous creature, and he delights in your participation as much as theirs.

Mister B

● ● ●

I sort out ten prints. Flo sneaks me into the college after hours, and lets me use the big, fancy printers there. I handle the photos with a pair of latex-free gloves, and post them on my way to the bus. I'm sending it first class to his 'contact' address: a *Benjamin Barrio* in Belmopan, Belize. Stupid. He generally pays as soon as he knows something's in the post, so I drop him a cryptic email.

I shop around for a while and end up giving my card to a Hot Dad on the bus.

It's a slow evening otherwise. I aggressively encrypt Deaniel's image files, and store them in an encrypted folder, deep in the bowels of my laptop, where all of my other dodgy shit lives.

● ● ●

I'm woken up early the following morning. B sends me a fat wad of cash by special courier, who leers at my dressing-gown-swaddled chest (despite my unbrushed hair and teeth) when I accept his package. At least B didn't try to pay me in fucking bitcoin like last time.

I also get a text from Ryan, about midday – a pissy one, with no 'x's or emojis, asking me to ring him.

I'm on a six-week paid sabbatical as of today – Ergi insisted. No police, but I'll have to sign an incident report. Ryan doesn't even say bye to me when he hangs up.

● ● ●

The group chat arranges the night out for Monday – student night. Flo switches her day off to Tuesday. The students have a Tuesday morning seminar that they decide to skip, on my behalf. For about twenty minutes. Then they drop out, so it's just going to be me, Flo and Finch. Finch is the least obtrusive hanger-on from that group, anyway. He's quiet, he always has MD and tobacco, and he always shares.

I'm having a coffee at Pilgrim's and looking through some old photos. I'm trying to decide what to do for Hackney. One of my models works here: Will with long, wavy hair and a pretty face. He's a little more conventionally attractive than my usual boys, but he's just enough on the feminine side that I'm still into it. A lot of fat on his thighs, which I like. Flo once said she thought boys' bums look like they've been shrunk in the wash, and I haven't been able to un-see that since. I photograph a lot of men other people think are ugly, or weird looking. But, I *always* try and find a proportionally sized backside – it just makes me sad otherwise.

Will brings me my usual before I get the chance to order it — black americano, two extra shots of espresso. He hovers at my table, trying to force some 'flirty banter'. He's asked me out a few times, and I always say maybe. Sometimes I bump into him on nights out, and he gives me drugs and buys me drinks.

I slag off his new beard. He has a sharp chin, a face shaped like an oval – the beard squares his jaw, and makes him look butcher, and older. He has big lips too, like a girl's, and the moustache covers the sharp points of his cupid's bow. I imagine this was quite deliberate.

'You look like a proper bloke,' I whine.

'Yeah. Like a Viking, with the hair, don't you think?' he asks.

'I don't know,' I say. 'I don't think Vikings wear side ponytails.' He's got his hair pulled into a pink scrunchy. It swings down from the left side of his head, to his shoulder. He makes a face.

'It's a joke,' he says, as if he'd forgotten. He goes to pull it down.

'Leave it. It's adorable,' I say. 'When do you finish?' I ask.

'In half an hour.'

'Come play dress up with me.'

I make him drive me home – barista to go.

He drives us back to mine in his new car, a black Beetle he seems very pleased with.

'You can't afford a new car.' He's a postgrad student. I can't remember what he studies.

'It was a birthday present,' he says. When he's drunk, his accent is very neutral – I think he's from the Midlands, or something – but sober, he has a forced, cockney twang. I imagine he thinks it makes him sound more exotic, more working class, but he often over-eggs it and goes a bit Oliver Twist.

We get to mine.

'Let's just go straight to the studio,' I say.

'You mean your garage?'

'No, I mean my studio,' I say, with a sneer. I *converted* it when I got rid of the car. Garage. Fuck off.

He sits on the sofa – this kitschy vintage loveseat I picked up from the British Heart Foundation – and I start picking through the rail of clothing I keep for them. I have to keep a lot of costumes. Most men dress like shit, you see. I've had them turn up to shoots in cargo shorts and ask what's wrong with what they're wearing and I'm literally, like, *lmao*. I pick out a thin cotton vest, and a pair of shiny polyester short-shorts for him. He looks sporty, so I fold him into yoga poses, ignoring the cracking of his bones and the popping of his joints. I change into a sports bra and yoga pants and take a set of timed photos with me in them, snarling as I bend his soft/stiff body into improbable, uncomfortable shapes.

'Where'd you get that bruise?' he asks.

I'm surprised he can tell through the makeup.

'I was trying to chuck out this drunk lass on the close, and she clocked me. It's pretty cool, actually. I get paid leave,' I say.

'Really, a drunk woman did that?' he says. He looks up at me, while I try and push his ankles to his ears. 'You know, if a feller did it, you can tell me,' he says. The bruise must be darker than I thought. Still, that was spoken like a man who has never gotten into a fight with a girl in a Bigg Market takeaway at three a.m. A lass half my size knocked out one of my canines when I was nineteen. My parents had to buy me a set of veneers.

'Are you fucking kidding me?' I say. 'I don't know what you want to hear, mate. She was wearing rings.' I snort. 'What's the rule about talking while we're shooting?' *Don't speak unless spoken to.*

'Sorry,' he says. I don't know what the fuck he thinks he'd do about it, if a bloke had hit me. Beat him up for me? Console me? Will is soft. I do press-ups every morning, and advanced yoga and Pilates twice a week. I push his left ankle closer to his ear, and he grunts, his glutes twinging against my stomach. I make sure he feels how strong I am, how easy it would be for me to keep him knotted up like this.

I let him go and get him to kneel. I wrap his hair around my fist and wrench his neck back.

'That hurts.' The timed flash goes off.

I tell him not to be such a baby while he dresses. He

invites me to a party at his on Monday night. I tell him I might see him, and I kick him out.

The photos turn out great. I *do* love his hair. I've told him before, if he cuts it, he'll never work for me again.

I go through his book. I met him when I moved back up north after my MA. Years pass as I flip the pages; I watch his hair get longer, and his outfits get skimpier. I watch him get more and more desperate to please me.

The shoot-comedown hits me a bit harder than usual, and I find myself slinking off to Tesco, after going through Will's photos for another hour or so.

Eddie from Tesco is, thankfully, here (he wasn't yesterday) and while he rings up my vodka, I tell him I'd really *really* like it if he modelled for me.

'That's not funny,' he says. He's red from scalp to collar. He checks over his shoulder, as if he's nervous someone will hear. There's a big, older woman arranging frozen food an aisle away. The manager, I think.

'Do you think I'm taking the piss?' I ask, lowering my voice and leaning close enough for him to smell my perfume. 'I'm not. Look at my website. I'm serious,' I say. 'I always am. I literally have no sense of humour.'

He laughs.

He stares when I leave.

I think about Eddie from Tesco at home. Will he be pudgy? Slim? A surprise gym rat? Would his chest be hairy? He looks small. I can't tell *how* small, though, as he's always in a chair behind the cash desk.

He's my favourite kind of boy to shoot, I think. A *nice* boy. A boy who works a demeaning job and has the subtleties of his beauty overlooked by glamorous women, and the industries of the aesthetic. The kind of boy who's bewildered, and grateful, and will gaze down the barrel of my camera and do *anything* for me.

It's like discovering a new flower no one else has noticed. Pressed in a photo; preserved and filed away forever, ageless and lovely and all mine.

I think about him all evening. I even pull out a sketchbook and scribble some ideas for photos. I try and find him on Facebook, and fail, without a last name.

I text Flo.

U were sooooo right about the new boy at tesco omg

Gave him my card the other week

Basically totally besotted

> Yeah ha ha i thought you'd like him

> See what i meant tho he is cute isn't he??

I'm gunna see how his shoot goes but i actually get a really interesting feeling from him.

Might let him take me out for dinner, who knows?

> Oh?

> I thought you werent dating atm

I'm not

But maybe I'll make an exception this time.

We'll see.

> Hmm okay.

> Be careful, i guess?

About an hour later, I check her blog. She's posted *I fucked up*, in isolation, and does not respond to her concerned orbiters.

Occasionally, she needs a wake-up call. I can date anyone I want. I can make friends.

JUVENILIA

Hackney Space want a little bit of everything for the photo book – including old work I think might serve as an 'interesting artefact' to accompany the short biography at the start of the book.

I pull out my entire archive. Albums and portfolios, sketchbooks wrapped up in tissue and plastic, kept in boxes beneath my bed, in my wardrobe, and stacked up in my studio.

I have a digital archive as well, but that's more of a *best of*. It's a lot more recent, too. There are things I've deleted, things I've forgotten about and, at the end of the day, it's a good excuse to look through my work. It's good to get your hands on a physical archive, sometimes, to rip it to bits, and put it back together again.

I remember being six or seven and getting immense satisfaction out of lining all of my My Little Pony dolls in order by colour – starting with the red and pink ones, ordering them as close to the rainbow as I could, and finishing with the purples. I feel just like that, almost giddy, as I get the boxes stacked into chronological order.

I sit on the floor in front of the oldest box, labelled A-LEVEL/FOUNDATION, 2006–2009. I don't know if I'll end up pulling anything from here – it's a lot of drawing, of greatly varying quality.

The early AS stuff is ropey – really ropey. There's a lovingly rendered watercolour of Galadriel in there, and a lot of drawings of Brigitte Bardot, and, later, Pamela Anderson in *Barb Wire*. I did a whole project where I tried adapting *Barb Wire* into a graphic novel without realising it was a comic first, and the upward quality curve in my drawing is surprisingly steep.

My second sketchbook for that year opens with women but closes with men. I open the book – Barbarella, Dita hanging from her prop Martini glass, Jayne Mansfield and her impossibly tiny waist. Wishes – *Wife Goals, or Life Goals?* as Flo is wont to say when confronted with a beautiful woman. It's funny the way my work changes – like a switch flipped. I turn a page and find a study of a grown man's chest – headless, flabby and spattered with hair – next to a chest which is young, and androgynous. Typical for me, the line work is very good, but the shading is a bit half-arsed.

I had fumbled with boys before Lesley. Over the summer, I had made an effort to dress for my new shape, to dye my red hair black, to fill in my eyebrows, to apply winged eyeliner and red lipstick – and to change my profile pictures, and make sure I was *seen* in places I knew the in-crowd hung out. They started adding me on MSN, inviting me to things. And I'd turn up, and I'd buy everyone alcohol because I never got carded, and get blackout drunk, and wake up with my underwear around my ankles, or my skirt pulled up over my stomach. I remember stumbling out of someone's spare room after a house party, and their indulgent mother telling me, 'Your shirt is on inside out, petal,' and her lending me a thin, silky scarf to cover a love bite on my neck the size of a fist.

I went back to school popular. Girls who used to pick on me liked me, because I could get fags and vodka, and I'd held their hair back while they were sick. When I'd started sitting with the pretty girls, when the boys snapped my bra straps, and hung round my worktable – this was when Lesley noticed me.

My mam told the school he'd started grooming me at GCSE, which was bullshit. Lesley was a shallow man; he didn't pay any attention to me till everyone else did. He held me back after a lesson in late September and told me: *You have a lot of potential, Irene.* (It's Irina, sir.) *You haven't done much over the summer – you mustn't let your modelling career distract you.*

Of course, at the time I thought he'd gotten me mixed up with Molly Jones, who I sat with. My new friend had been a six-foot-tall netball player: pretty as a picture and thin as a rake, she'd spent much of the previous school year bragging about signing to a modelling agency. We both had bottle black hair – but she was flat as a board. I'd been the exact mix of flattered and offended that I assume he was shooting for. I'd corrected him, shyly, and swallowed that compliment like a mouthful of the ice cream I'd sneak while Mam had me on a diet.

I know he was negging me, now. At the time, I was stupid enough to believe he'd genuinely mixed me up with Molly. But I wasn't quite so stupid that I didn't realise he was trying it on with me. I can't remember what he looked like in any detail, which annoys me. I don't have any photos of him, or even sketches. I sometimes google him, looking for a social media profile, or a tabloid news article. '*Sex-pest teacher allowed to work in school again*', or something. But he's off the grid.

He was in his forties, with thick, black hair, and he wore glasses. He was slim, and taller than me, but none of his facial features stick out in my mind.

I remember finding him very attractive at the time; though any man who pays attention to you, at that age, can transform from frog to prince in the time it takes to tell you he likes your hair.

I leant into being stupid for him. I giggled for him, and I smiled bashful smiles, as he edged further into my personal space with each passing lesson. He'd make up reasons to hold me back; a few minutes for *oh, hang on, is this your jacket?* then fifteen for *I just think you're very talented, and we should talk about your future.* In late October, he gave me an arbitrary detention for an unfilled sketchbook page (I'd done three rather than the requested four). The detention was administered at half past two, and by four thirty his dick was in my mouth. He didn't tell me when he was about to finish, so I choked, and coughed, spraying cum from my aching mouth all over his crotch. It was disgusting: the unexpected smells, the presence of a distinct flavour and the texture of wiry hair in my teeth, and flesh (somehow hard and squishy at the same time) bumping dangerously close to my throat.

I got used to it.

The sketchbook descends into a wall of hairy limbs, flat chests and comedically large bulges in jeans – Tom of Finland, eat your heart out. I put it down, and flip through the others, finding more men, and escalating tastes. This was around the same time I got into extreme cinema, and with my palate whet for the violent, disturbing and bizarre alongside my new-found interest in grown men, my artwork becomes a twisted mash of flesh, hair and bodily fluids, rendered in pencil and sickly watercolours.

A birthday card with a pressed flower taped to the inside falls from my AS-level exam sketchbook. The smoking gun. A large number seventeen glitters on the cover. The badge is still attached.

I move a couple of sketchbooks and find a fat wedge of birthday cards banded together in the bottom of the box. They're all different, all seventeenth-birthday cards and all from M&S. Must have cost him a fucking fortune.

Lesley did this thing where he would get his A-level students birthday cards, and tuck them into our sketchbooks without telling us.

This one reads: *Happy birthday, I hope you enjoy your party on Friday evening, I've heard the food at Princess Gardens is delicious!* So I'd get this, and I'd know to meet him at Princess Gardens on Friday evening. If my mam found it and was like, 'What the fuck? Your birthday's in November and it's January,' I could just tell her he'd gotten me mixed up with *Molly Jones* whose birthday it actually was, and that he got Molly and I mixed up all the time.

My mam is a lot of things, but she's not stupid. Upon reflection, I don't know how I managed to get away with it for as long as I did. She'd pick through my sketchbooks like a rat picking through the bins whenever I left the house: silent, but increasingly disturbed by the content.

He told me once that she'd rang him. She wanted to know why he was letting me draw stuff like that. Lesley said it was just me expressing myself, and that teenagers were macabre, unpredictable creatures. I was hazy with wine from our date and thought I should move my stack of birthday cards out of my art stuff, and under my mattress, or something. I forgot about it promptly, and I giggled, and told him not to talk about my mother while he was fingering me.

The following week Mam turned up to one of our dates, birthday card in hand, and caused a scene. She physically dragged me out of the restaurant by the sleeve of my dress, berating the staff, screaming about nonces and CRB checks and calling the police.

She tells it differently, of course. As far as her friends, my late grandmother, my father know, she cracked the code in the birthday cards, and calmly collected me from the restaurant. I collapsed into her arms, weeping, like a little girl. She makes sure to call me her little girl whenever she tells it. *People forget she was just a little girl – because she's tall, and so well developed*, like I was twelve and not seventeen. *She was covered in bruises*, she'll say, tearing up.

They tried to keep it quiet, but everyone at school found out eventually. I always say everyone *knowing* was more traumatic than being with him. Because: I did like him. I liked the way he made me feel. I liked learning how to fuck – I liked having my hair pulled and being bitten and the way his big hands felt on my skinny neck. I didn't like my dad, my nana and her cancer, my head teacher, Molly Jones, looking at me and seeing a raped child where Irina used to stand.

The flower taped to the card is a single white rose, stem cut short and pressed well. I used to press them all the time in high school and college, but I stopped doing it when I picked up photography.

When you get into theory, you find the flowers aren't miles away from the photographs. They're impressions of living things – like fossils, pressed and preserved, the way an image impresses itself onto a roll of film. I mean, fuck me if I can remember my early photography seminars, but that sounds about right. It's always interesting when these genetic connections pop up in your work.

A book of pressed flowers was the first thing I handed in to my college tutors, once I'd specialised on my foundation course. When you do art at uni, you normally have to do a foundation year first – a year at your local college, or a uni, where you decide which kind of art you actually want to do. Like, are you an illustrator? A fashion designer? A graphics wanker? An erotic fine art photographer? You do a rotation of different disciplines, then pick one. I did Fine Art, because I hate being told what to do. If you get the right Fine Art course at any level, you're essentially just set free to do fucking anything you like. And that's what Colin and Kevin, the veteran tutors, offered their charges: anarchy, with bi-weekly hand-ins.

This is also where I met Flo; where I caught the social equivalent of a nasty case of herpes, if you like.

Colin took a look at my delicate, lovely flowers (the life expertly squeezed from them) and asked me if I liked to collect flowers – if I liked to make little collections like this. I said yes. He asked me if I had penis envy, in front of everyone, like that's a yes or no thing.

He quoted the Baudrillard essay *System of Objects* at me and explained that collectors are either children, or sexually dissatisfied adult men. So I was either a child, emotionally, or I must have a strong case of penis envy to still be making collections at my age. He pointed to the wristwatch I was wearing, which I would check with compulsive regularity. He told me that was more evidence to support his theory. More Baudrillard: the watch was a masculine comfort object, something to check habitually, dispel 'temporal anxiety' and provide a constant 'organic pulse' in its ticking. I told him to fuck off and stormed out. I stopped wearing a watch around then. I suppose I've replaced it with the constant vibration of a smartphone, like a heartbeat in my pocket.

Next, I did this project where I drew gay porn, and I titled it *XXXtreme Penis Envy*. As I look through the pages of this particular sketchbook, I realise this was the last time I did any extensive drawing. It's very good, anatomically, proportionally speaking. I spend a good few minutes admiring my delicate shading on a pair of swollen testicles.

Colin said he appreciated the defiant nature of the project, but I'd *more* than proved his point by doing it. The shock value of dirty drawings was clearly non-existent at this level, and the frequent accusations from a sixty-something-year-old man of being cock hungry on a deep-seated psychological level got very tiresome, very quickly. I decided to give photography a go.

I have a little book of test shots, which is small, and blue, and surprisingly heavy in my hands. They're all photos of Flo and myself messing about in the college studio, when she was still skinny and faux-ginger with her Boho Chic + the Machine aesthetic. She's modelling very hard for me in them; borderline blue-steeling her way through and doing some twisty shit with her hands like I imagine she'd just seen Florence Welch do in *NME* that week. There are a few photos of us together, which is beyond hideous. I'm still a bottle-black brunette, filling my eyebrows in with black eyeliner instead of a brow pencil. I have a blue ring on my forehead where the dye (clearly fresh) has leaked and formed a compound with the thick, white stage foundation I was trowelling on to cover my freckles. Red lipstick bleeding all over the place because this was before we had liquid lips and YouTube tutorials, and before I knew lipliner was a thing that existed outside of 1996 in a dark brown. I'm also wearing this ridiculous tea dress. It flatters my figure but, it's just like… ugh, that rockabilly goth bullshit, it's… so *basic*.

These photos are shit, but I loved taking them. I loved telling Flo where to stand, and what to wear. I loved fiddling with the settings of the cheap DSLR I'd been given for my birthday during the last year of my GCSEs. I loved the way the slightest nudge to the aperture or the white balance totally changed the quality of the image, the mood. I loved playing with lights and costumes and makeup.

I was hooked.

I'd visited London between terms and had come home with a bag full of those cards that sex workers use to advertise their services in phone boxes. All women. I had this idea to recreate them, but instead of advertising sex, I'd photograph the people on my course advertising their artwork. I had a tough time getting everyone into the various costumes I'd acquired for the project: the skimpy school uniforms, the cut-offs and construction helmets which matched what the girls on the cards were wearing. But I managed, with varying degrees of success, in the end.

In this first proper photograph book, I have pasted next to a real calling card reading, *Naughty School Girl Needs Detention: Red Cheeks For Louise? Genuine photo*, a photograph of a boy named Luke, similar outfit, but his caption read, *Straight White Male Painter Thinks Rothko Rip-Off Revolutionary: Original Ideas For Luke? Genuine hack*.

I was such a cunt in the captions. Colin thought it was exceedingly funny, but Kevin was not amused. Kevin was a gentle man who'd spent the majority of his career teaching in private schools, unprepared for even the light brutality of the Fine Art foundation diploma and degree students he taught at the city college. He covered his mouth when we swore, and seemed genuinely distressed when he'd walk past Flo and me smoking outside the building, or when we'd complain about hangovers on a Tuesday morning.

Irina, this is exceedingly mean spirited. To embarrass your fellow students in such a way after they did you a favour is cruel. See me in the office on Monday please?

It's written in red pen, torn from the feedback form and glued to the title page – beneath it I've drawn two stars, and written Kevin's name, like a bad review. I recall getting into a huge argument with him in the office, with Colin sniggering in the corner.

This is my art, and it's transgressive and I'm sorry if that offends you: I can hear my own voice in my head, girly and shrill.

Colin was on my side, and he and Kevin bickered in front of me like an old married couple. Someone had complained; I needed to be dealt with. Then Colin let slip that Luke, specifically, had complained. I hadn't even been that mean about him, compared to the others.

I find a page with a picture of a girl called Georgie, who had let me photograph her holding a pair of toy handcuffs, and that was as racy as she'd let me go. I've written, '*Insipid posh bitch, will paint your nana's dog for a tenner*'. Next to her, a photo of Tessa, who's a full-on-Flat-Earth-Facebook-racist now. She's dressed as a sexy builder, duck-facing, glossy lips shrivelled and pressed to the head of a hammer. I've written, '*Hot Charva! Get her before she's pregnant (please contact ASAP)*'. It's funnier with hindsight, now she's a proper racist and stuff. And she *did* get pregnant about a year after the course finished.

She tried to fight me, for this. She told me to meet her round the back of the building after the tutors left. She was all bark and no bite, in the end. She squared up to me, and I came at her with a lit cigarette. The tip had barely brushed her cheek, before she scarpered. She wouldn't come near me afterwards.

She didn't tell on me, though. Not like fucking Luke. I reckon the comment stung because he *loved* Rothko, in that very genuine way only teenagers can admit to loving artists they love – it's a cardinal sin by BA. I had to apologise to him in a letter, *and* his dad shouted at me at our final show. Kevin hid in the studio while a grown man screamed at me; my parents weren't even there.

I peel Luke's photo out of my sketchbook, and drop it into a plastic wallet marked, *To include?* That's the only certainty at the moment. Maybe a couple of drawings from *Xxxtreme Penis Envy*.

About halfway through foundation they started telling me I needed to experiment and try something away from erotica and the *erotic inspired* (trying to push me to that conceptual installation bullshit tutors always cream themselves over), and when I complained they were still letting Luke repaint Rothkos, they said they weren't and he'd gotten the same advice.

They made us do this transformation project, where we had to do something that was more or less the polar opposite of our current work. Well, they didn't *make* us. I just followed their suggestions out of, like, intellectual curiosity. And, you know, you want to get into a good uni, you have to play the game a bit, don't you? So, fair's fair, I had to do some abstract bullshit, and I did some reading on Dada and German Expressionism and watched the first twenty minutes of *Painters Painting*.

Unfurling from an A3 sketchbook like a Dead Sea Scroll falls my result: an enormous ballpoint drawing of a penis, captioned simply with, *je suis not un le penis*, which Kevin hummed at with a thoughtful, 'I think it's a breakthrough,' and Colin had responded, with a great sigh, 'I think it's a breakdown.'

Luke painted a naked lady instead of a Rothko.

Flo took over Kevin's post when he retired properly, and Colin's desiccated corpse is still there. We have a pint with him on occasion. He still thinks I have penis envy.

therabbitheartedgirl:

Me and Michael had another fight about Irina last night lol. She's coming round for pre-drinks and he was just like being weird about it again. He knows we had a thing during uni, and he's never been cool with it like as soon as he found out. I told him flat out he was being jealous and honestly???? Kind of biphobic????? Like he thinks bc me and irina r both bi and we had the briefest thing in uni like there's something going on there????

Unreal tbh. Told him to fuck off down the pub and cool off. Like my feelings for her aside, I WOULD NOT CHEAT ON HIM and it's not like he knows about it so wtf. Like where does this come from and why does he have this HUGE PROBLEM all of a sudden w my best friend who happens to be another queer woman. He swears its not a bi thing n he just doesnt like irina or 'how she speaks to me' but like,,, she never tried to police who i hang out w.

So he was on the sofa tonight but i let him come back to bed. Still annoyed tho.

WILL

Flo shrieks along to the entirety of Lizzo's 'Good as Hell', and I wince. Her 'THIS IS A GAYS ONLY EVENT, GO HOME' playlist, finishes, then loops, and takes us back in with 'Cool For The Summer', which I just *hate*. The homoerotic over-current of the lyrics while we're both in sat in the living room in our bras and curlers is just… It's a lot.

'Come and do my eyeliner for me,' says Flo.

'Come and do my eyeliner for me,' I repeat, with a sneer.

'I never get it as good as you do. You're baking, you have time.' She's got me there; powder is piled up on my cheekbones and cannot be disturbed for at least a few minutes.

'Fine.' I shuffle over to her on my knees and sit between her thighs. Nothing gay about this. Just a pair of regular gal pals here. Her lips are slightly parted.

I rest my hand on Flo's shoulder for balance, and there's this sharp little intake of breath down her end. Demi warbles in the background. I tell Flo to stay still, and gently sweep the liquid liner from the corner of her eye, so it almost meets the point of her eyebrow. Always looks a bit daft when I do that, but she likes it.

I'm almost waiting for her to lean in and whisper, *Oh, Irina, remember the summer that we were 'cool'?* Flo licks her lips. I could slap her – she's posting about it on her fucking blog again. I can practically see her having flashbacks. For the record: *we* were never *cool for the summer*. We were more… lukewarm for the September/October period.

I hate that she tells people. I hate that she fucking blogs about it, like my sex life is just fucking Tumblr discourse for her. You know, for someone who claims to be woke, she truly does not give a flying fuck about consent the second it comes to flapping her skinny lips about my personal business.

'Did I tell you Serotonin is going to be at the Hackney thing?'

'No,' says Flo. 'She's quite big now, isn't she? Like, doesn't she live in New York?'

'I think so. It'll be nice to see her again. I used to be—' I move from Flo's left eye to her right. '—*so close* to her. Weird we didn't really keep in contact.' Flo hums. She fucking hated Sera. It was very transparent – a lot of 'I suppose you're busy with *her*' when I told Flo I couldn't speak to her on the phone. I always assumed making exactly one new friend was one of the main reasons we stopped speaking for a bit while I was in London and she wasn't.

Ariana Grande kicks in next. 'Greedy'. Flo's eyeliner is finished, and I shuffle back to my corner of the room.

'I'm not doing your falsies for you,' I tell her, and I brush the powder off my cheeks. When the chorus to the song kicks in, I sing 'greedy for cum' instead of 'greedy for love'; I do it every time that line pops up, and I do it specifically because Flo thinks it's disgusting.

I've gone for a bronzy eyeshadow look – everything else tends to be a bit clashy when you're ginger. Flo's hair is bobbed, and bleached to shit, but it does mean she has a lot more by way of eyeshadow choices. She's gone for purple tonight.

'Should I do a red lip?'

'If you want to look like a slapper, then aye, absolutely,' I say. Flo has no taste; she just copies. If left to her own devices, she'd wear total trash. And not trash in a good way, like when I do trash.

'Don't you think it'll look quite editorial?'

'Not on your bone structure, no,' I say. Flo is... cute. Like, she's pretty but she's not *stunning*, she's not *beautiful*. 'You've got those round baby cheeks. You'll just look like you've made a mess with your mam's makeup.'

'Hmm. You're probably right,' she says. 'Nude lip?'

'If you pair it with, like, a lilac and wear a blush with kind of a lavender tone... that'd look... like, *editorial* without looking super OTT.'

'Genius,' she says. I don't think she has the bone structure to pull off a monotone makeup look either, but I'm wearing a nude lip tonight, and I'd rather we didn't match. She's always trying to match me. I never tell her what I'm wearing.

A knock on Flo's door – probably Finch. She sticks on a dressing gown before she trots over to answer.

I'm right. He looks cute tonight. Concealer on his acne, and a half-open shirt. He's been very determined to be as shirtless as possible since his recent top surgery. Fresh haircut too. Short back and sides, heavy on top. Not very exciting; I think that's the only haircut barbers are doing at the moment. I've offered to let him model for me, but he said no, even though he's a bit of an Irina Sturges fanboy. I think he caught on I was just interested in the novelty factor – or maybe he was just shy. This was years ago, though, early transition. His skin's been consistently garbage since he went on testosterone; I've fully lost interest.

He's holding a bottle of prosecco, which I loathe. Flo immediately pops it open, firing the cork out of her front door, into the garden.

'You look nice,' Finch says, Flo dangling on him.

'Oh my God, he is *such* a ladies' man,' says Flo, to me. Finch gives her an uncomfortable smile, his lips rolling back into his mouth.

'I'll grab some glasses,' he says, plucking the bottle from Flo's hand and slinking into the kitchen. Flo mouths, *So cute*. 'Have you picked up?' he calls.

'About a month ago. Hang on, I'll go and ask the old ball and chain what we've got—'

I cut Flo off. 'I'll ask, I'm going for a drink anyway.' I cut through the kitchen and bump past Finch on the way. I pluck a glass of bubbly piss from his little hands.

'I like your top,' he says.

'It's a bra,' I say. It's longline and sits just above my

waist. I didn't want to get makeup on my top. I'm heading
to Michael's 'man cave', a small room off the kitchen where
Flo keeps him. There's a recliner, a huge desk and this big,
loud gaming PC with a three-monitor setup. He's playing
some crunchy looking medieval RPG on the centre screen,
with football and *Archer* on either side.

The PVC of my skirt squeaks slightly as I nudge open the
door to his room.

'Hey.'

'What,' he says, pulling off his headphones. There's no
need to perform pleasantries without Flo here. He gives me
a look, sullen and lascivious. Scowling at me, sneering, while
he looks at my thighs, my tits, the bare sliver of stomach
between my bra and the waistband of my skirt.

'Flo wants the drug box,' I say. He sighs, and begins
digging through his desk drawer. Michael is not unattractive,
but his urban-lumberjack look is very 2015. He's heavy set:
fat but solid, you know? I like his arms, but he always wears
long sleeves. He holds out a Tupperware box for me to take,
opens his mouth to speak, then doesn't.

'What?'

'Nothing.'

I wink when I take the box off him. I'll get Flo to do
a slightly suggestive snapchat to send to him later, when
she's getting sloppy. Cry-wank and a Pot Noodle for
Mikey tonight.

Flo labels her drugs with little stickers, which is dorky,
but it is a massive time saver. Michael's weed lives in a
separate Tupperware box, so we have here only powders,
and a few scattered dud pills rattling around beneath the
baggies. I knock back my drink and return to the living

room where Finch tops me up. Flo has removed her curlers and is combing her hair out with her fingers.

'Doesn't she look *just* like Marilyn Monroe with her hair like this?' says Finch. She doesn't. She looks up at me, expectant, like a dog after fetching. I hum, non-committal, and perch on the sofa, cracking open the Tupperware with my thumbs.

'You have, about—' I begin lifting each baggie, holding it to the light, giving them a shake so the powder settles at the bottom. '—like, two grams of coke? A gram of MDMA, and a mostly empty thing of ketamine. Like, less than a third of a gram?' There's also a small, unlabelled wad of tinfoil in a bag, which I hold out for her. 'What's this?'

'Acid. We bulk-bought the last time we picked up,' Flo says. 'We have, like, ten tabs if anyone's interested in going halfsies with me on one tonight?' Acid is Flo's new thing. Acid and ketamine. She keeps banging on about how she's gone off uppers, and she's into dissociatives now, even though she can't physically say no to coke when it's stuck under her now highly unfashionable septum piercing. Tomorrow, she'll be picking dried-up coke off it, I'd put money on it.

'No thanks. Acid isn't a club drug, IMO,' says Finch. Flo protests – she thinks it can be. Finch shakes his head. 'I just feel like I'm three when I'm on it, like everyone's scary but I fucking love shapes and textures? Like, no thanks.'

'Suit yourself,' Flo says. Flo and Finch bicker for a moment about whether or not Flo should take half a tab. He tells her it's antisocial, I say I agree with Finch and point out how unpredictable her little trips can be, so she pouts and says, '*Fine*. I'll just stick with MD.'

'Good lass,' I say. About eighty per cent of the time she's fine on LSD. She says it's a way she can be up without a comedown, without a risk she'll throw up, conveniently forgetting the occasions I've had to put her in a taxi because she's gotten paranoid over nowt.

I drink my shitey prosecco, and I tuck the cocaine and ketamine into my bra, in the slit where my chicken fillets are currently stuffed.

'Is that a push-up bra?' asks Finch. 'Your tits look cracking.'

'No,' I say. 'So you know, I'm holding the coke and ket. We should be fine.'

'Should we make some bombs?' asks Flo. I shrug.

'I'm just going to stick with coke,' I say. Flo makes a face.

'I've gone well off coke.'

'No you haven't.'

'I mean, like, *morally*,' says Flo, smugly. I sneer at her and tell her to shut the fuck up.

'I'll make bombs,' says Finch, 'Better to have them and not need them.' I throw Flo's MD at him, and he starts making up a few little bombs with cigarette skins. I'm not into MDMA – I always end up with a harsh comedown, the kind they report on anti-drug sites for teenagers, full-on *everything's-shit-I-might-as-well-just-top-myself* comedowns. 'Do you want one?' Finch asks, looking at me.

'No thanks,' I say. I pat my tit. 'I'm good with what I've got.'

'Oh, don't let me smoke tonight, guys,' says Flo. Finch and I exchange a look.

We finish hair, makeup and dressing, and opt to walk, rather than taxi. Flo lives slightly closer to town than I do, and it's a warm night – close and sweaty. My damp thighs rub together beneath my skirt, and Finch rolls up his shirt sleeves. Flo complains about her heels and asks Finch if she can have one of his rollies, before changing her mind.

She makes us stop in a Sainsbury's for gum and comes back out with gum and a pack of Marlboros. She immediately lights one up, her eyes rolling back into her head when she takes the first drag.

'Gimme one,' I say, and she does, handing me her lit cigarette, and lighting another for herself. Finch is already on his second nasty rollie, complaining his baccy has exploded in his pocket.

I walk ahead while they faff about. Flo stops and tries to stroke a ginger cat she says looks just like Fritz. She tries to get me to stop and look at it, but I just keep walking.

'So.' Finch appears at my side, trotting along like a puppy. 'Hackney Space? Holy shit.'

'Yup,' I say. 'Big deal.'

'It is,' he says. 'I hate to be this guy, but can I send you some of my photos on Monday? I could really do with some crit. It's like… photos documenting my top surgery, but everyone on my course just keeps telling me I'm *so brave*.' He takes a drag of his cigarette.

'Oh my God,' I say. 'I *hate* that shit. I used to get it all the time.'

'It's fucking obnoxious,' Finch says, puffing smoke from his nose. 'I swear down, I could come in with an out-of-focus photo of a dead pigeon, and be like, *the pigeon represents my dead name*, and everyone would be like—' He tucks his cigarette into the corner of his mouth, goes '*Ooo*' and applauds. I snort. 'Like I just want to know if the photos are *any good*. And right now, I have no idea.'

'Yeah,' I say. 'Send them over. I'll be brutal.'

'Thanks,' he says. 'I know you will. That's why I'm asking you and not—' He nods his head back at Flo. 'You're honest. I appreciate it. I really do… Um… If you need, like, an assistant for hanging your show, or anything, I'd really like the experience. If you need someone.'

'Can't afford you, babe.'

'I'll work for free?' he offers.

'I'm not comfortable having anyone doing unpaid work for me. Plus, they do have people at the galleries who do that.'

'Yeah. Of course. Fair enough. Um. Well, the offer's there just… in case.'

We get to town for around ten, and head to BeerHaus, where the manager gives me a free drink. Everyone else pays.

We find a table in the corner. I'm drinking a negroni; Flo twists her face over the top of her piña colada and wonders aloud how I can drink it.

'More refined palette,' I say. 'Plus, less sugar.'

'Ugh, I don't want to talk about calories and sugar content,' whines Flo – spoken like someone who was a size six till she was twenty-five, then ballooned to a fourteen over the course of a year and a half. I raise my eyebrows at her and sip my drink. Finch sighs into his pint and complains about the prices.

We'll have one more drink here, then move on to Universal Subject (or UnSub, as people have taken to calling it), where we have tickets to the 'alternative' club night *Big Deal*. It wasn't my choice. I'd rather go somewhere out-and-out naff than somewhere trying so hard to be 'alternative'; it swings back around to being naff. It's aimed at the kind of people who get really, *really* excited when a DJ plays The Smiths. I suspect it'll be full of nineteen-year-old Home Counties student girls in vintage Adidas tracksuits – if it's unbearable, we can fuck off to Will's party. He texted me the details this morning, and I didn't even know he had my phone number.

I talk Finch and Flo into shots before we leave.

We end up queueing for UnSub for ages. Flo smokes two cigarettes, I smoke one. Finch clears the loose tobacco from his pockets, trying to salvage what he can. He and Flo drop while we wait, which means Flo will be gurning and wriggly in an hour. Alcohol tends to leave her maudlin and solipsistic without the intervention of MDMA, so I'm guaranteed a low-maintenance night with her. She might chuck up, but there's a low risk of crying, or her rehashing being bullied at school.

There's a group of underaged girls behind us muttering about IDs. It sounds like one of them has her sister's old passport, but the rest are going to blag it. I never get ID'd. It was a huge boon when I was younger, but in the last few years… I mean, the rule is challenge twenty-five now. It's absurd not to ID me.

When we get to the front of the queue, the bouncer only asks for Finch's. I recognise him – the bouncer. We chit-chat for a moment (*Yes, I do work with Ryan! Aye, he is a tosser, isn't he? Ha ha!*) and I tell him he should make sure he cards the girls behind us. I hear them whining while I get my hand stamped.

It's gone midnight by the time we get in. I head straight to the bathroom. There's an unreal number of posh girls buzzing about. I hear one call her friend Pollyanna, genuinely, *Pollyanna*. A name someone chose to give their child in Britain in, like, 1998. Pollyanna is being asked for toilet paper, and Pollyanna can't find any. She knocks on the door while I'm pissing.

'There's none in here either. I'm just changing a tampon,' I say.

'I can hear weeing, though,' she says.

'It's the pipes. I'm not gunna lie about having no loo roll. *Pet*.'

'Soz babe,' says Pollyanna. *Soz*. Like she's not from Surrey. That'd get her decked in another club.

There's a whole spare roll in here; I hope she gets a UTI. I have a bunch of texts from Will when I check my phone.

Hey.

R u coming tongiht?

What do u drink I'll pick smth up befro the family shopper closes

*before

I'll just some spare vodka n hide it 4 u ;)

**get some

Sorru im quite stoned

U bringing firneds?

Its rlly cool that ur coming

All my friends think i made u up

Lol

> We're at Universal Subject now!
>
> Seeing what the vibe is like.
>
> If it's shit we'll be at yours for 1-ish

He texts back before I've even wiped.

> Yaaaayyy
>
> Idk if your into it but the vibe here is quite geary
>
> Like
>
> Drugs and stuff
>
> I'm sure we'll fit right in 👍

Patronising little shit. He texts me his address again, just in case I've lost it when it's, like, two scrolls up.

I can't be bothered to rack up a line. I also have, as a general rule, a policy against doing drugs off toilet seats. It's tragic for one, but for two, I've gotten stomach bugs before, and there's nowt quite like a bout of the shits which you *know* you've gotten from taking coke off a dirty toilet seat.

I pull the baggy out of my bra and dig a lump of coke out with my index fingernail. There is something particularly visceral about sniffing drugs off your fingernails. It's like eating rice straight out of the pot with your fingers. Like the bit at the start of *Temple of Doom*, where Steven Spielberg's wife and Harrison Ford are getting fed by the 1980s racist-caricature Indian villagers, and she's all like, 'Eww, eating with my hands, disgusting,' and he's like, 'This is more than these people eat in a week.' An apt comparison, because I bet what I've just taken is three, maybe even four, times the amount of cocaine oppressed movie villagers get.

You can't really romanticise a drug you're sucking off your fingers alone in a toilet stall. I'm doing it like this because I need it to be here, not because I'm going to especially enjoy it.

It does occur to me after I'm done sniffing and rubbing the remnants onto my gums, I could have just used a key. I have a second bump, off my fingernail again. I've committed to it now.

I deposit the baggie back in its hiding place, and exit the cubicle, finding the bathroom more or less empty when I attend to my nostril in the bathroom mirror. I brush it gently, trying not to wipe the makeup off the tip of my nose.

There's a girl looking at me. She's wearing those tracksuit bottoms with the buttons up the sides, a cheap satin cami and heavy hoop earrings. I'm still bewildered by this act of appropriation: rich white girls pretending to be poor white girls (who I assume were originally appropriating 2000s hip-hop culture?) pretending to be rich black women. It's bizarre.

I'm staring at her, and she's staring at me. Not sure who started it.

'What?' I ask. She finishes washing her hands, I start washing mine. 'What?'

'You're beautiful,' she says. Her pupils are huge.

'Thanks pet.'

'Your hair is so nice.' She blinks at me. 'Is it… extensions?'

'Nah, just good hair. Coconut oil and hot rollers, you know,' I say. She nods, and repeats *coconut oil*, dreamily, tripping on her gleaming white Nike Airs as she walks out.

I look for the others, giving the dance floor a sweep. Busier than I thought it might be. All students. What did I expect from a Monday night? All students, and mostly boys. Like a school disco, a few small groups of girls are clumped, or coupled off already, while the remaining single men shuffle-dance, clutching warm bottles of Beck's and scanning the doors to the entryway and the toilets and the smoking area, as if any moment a whole horde of women could pour in and correct this dire ratio. I go to the bar. They're playing The Smiths, on purpose, in this post-racist-Morrissey economy. I mean, there's an argument to be made that he's been racist for fucking ages, and shit for even longer, and I don't know why we're all just deciding *now* that it's bad.

I watch the young white people dance badly to the bloated old racist's music while I wait to get served. This is a white-as-fuck club, and I like… I know I'm white, but there's just a lot of white people White People-ing in a very small area, like it's just some very, very densely packed mayo, you know? Densely packed mayo, jiggling about, doesn't know what to do with its arms, doesn't know what to do with its feet, undulating loosely, barely in time to the rhythm.

'HI. HI THERE. WHAT YOU DRINKING?' asks a man. He's standing more or less eye to eye with me. He has a bun. Buns went out almost as soon as they came in, didn't they? It's weird to see one out in the wild in this day and age. He doesn't even have a beard. Maybe he's just hot; it's a reasonable thing to do with long hair if you're hot. He's okay looking. Big. Muscular. I try to stick with men I imagine I could physically overpower if push came to shove. 'DO YOU WANT A SHOT?'

'I'M GOOD,' I say. He either mishears me, or wilfully ignores me, and he hands a shot to me, which he watches me drink very, very closely (white sambuca, cheap) and then he indicates that he'd like to high five me when I'm done. I leave him hanging. His pupils are enormous – but aren't all of our pupils enormous?

'I'LL FIND YOU LATER. I'LL FIND YOU IN THE

SMOKING AREA, OKAY? I'LL GIVE YOU MY NUMBER.
IMAGINE HOW TALL THE KIDS WOULD BE! RUGBY
PLAYERS, MODELS, THEY'D BE. I LOVE THIS SONG.'
The Cure is playing now. He scampers off, a lightness to his
feet despite his size. I watch him swing around to 'Just Like
Heaven' as if it was techno. Still no sign of my quote-unquote
friends, who I assume are in the smoking area. I finally get
a drink. A string of texts from Will on my phone, and one
from Flo, which simply reads *SMOJKING OUTSDIE*, and I'm
delighted, because they just started playing the Weezer cover
of 'Africa', like, as if it wasn't lame enough in here already? As
if the vibe couldn't get any whiter? And like I said, I'm aware
I'm adding to this deluge of whiteness, but at least I'm local,
and I'm not from the Home Counties, which is the whitest
kind of white. Geordie girls are up there with Irish girls and
Scottish girls; the black women of white women, you know?

I'm outside. Strange mix of cigarette smoke and fresh air.
Quote-unquote friends huddled in a corner, Finch smoking
and rolling at the same time, standing awkwardly beside Flo
while two studenty-looking blokes chat her up. Beta males,
the pair of them, but the *alpha* betas, the most confident of
their jittery, sweaty friends who like *Star Wars* and think that
that's a personality trait. That's not even a guess – there are
three more lads stood to the side of this interaction, and two
of them are wearing *Star Wars* shirts. A Darth Vader design,
and one simply reading 'Han Shot First'.

'Hi,' I say. I point at Flo, 'She has a boyfriend.'

'What about you?'

'I'm with him,' I say, pointing at Finch. He glares at me.
'Watch out, he's very jealous. He'll kick the shit out of you.'
Finch is 5'6, and skinny, and the idea of him kicking the shit

out of any one is laughable. So laughable that I snort, my hand beneath my nose to cover it.

'Shut up, Irina,' says Finch. 'She obviously isn't my girlfriend, and I'm obviously not going to fight anyone.'

'Can you believe what I have to put up with?' I pout and walk over to Finch. I pluck a recently rolled cigarette from his fingers and wrap my arm around his shoulder. 'Light me up, babe.' Finch lights the cigarette, still frowning at me. 'Go on, shoo,' I say to the *Star Wars* boys. They scuttle back to the club, their obedience to being shooed like dogs, proving both their weakness and my alpha beta hypothesis. Beta male in any form fucks off when I tell him to. Finch gives me a look. I say, 'Well, I got them to leave, didn't I?'

'You're so awful on coke. I'm going for a piss.' He rolls his eyes at me.

'Don't fucking roll your eyes at me,' I snap after him. He just ignores me. 'Hey!' And then he spins on his heels, with a clenched jaw and a scowl. He takes a deep breath, then seems to decompress.

'You know what? Never mind,' he says. 'Doesn't matter. They left. Well done.'

'That was quite mean, Rini,' says Flo. 'You know how insecure he is.' I roll my eyes at her.

'Oh, come on, I was complimenting him. It's not my fault he's never had a girlfriend, is it? There are some men who'd literally snap their fingers off to pretend to be my boyfriend in front of some other blokes,' I suck on my beer and my cigarette. 'He's so fucking overly sensitive.'

He'll be back. I down my drink.

I drag Flo back inside, where they hoot and clap, because David Bowie is playing; the DJ knows his audience very well. I scowl.

'YOU'VE GOT A FACE LIKE A SMACKED ARSE, RINI.'

'WHAT?'

'I SAID, YOU'VE GOT A FACE LIKE A SMACKED ARSE.'

'THERE'S A LOT OF WHITE PEOPLE IN HERE, ACTING LIKE THEY DON'T KNOW THAT THEY'RE WHITE PEOPLE, BUT THEY ARE AND THEY LOOK STUPID.'

'WHAT?'

'I'M GOING FOR A PISS.'

Flo follows me. She makes a beeline for her own stall, but I grab her by the wrist.

'Flo,' I say. 'Hey, Flo.' And I beckon her into the stall. 'Step into my office.'

'What?'

'Step into my office. Business meeting,' I say. She comes in and I slam the door shut behind her and lock it. 'You'll be wanting a line, then?'

It's a tight squeeze; there's a lot of woman for such a small space. I'm crouched by the toilet – the floor is a bit wet – and sprinkling coke on the seat, chopping and pushing and fixing it into lines with my National Insurance card, which is always my card of choice. My mam found it once, on the floor of my house, and said, *why's your NI card here?* And there's no explanation for that really, no legitimate reason it could possibly be there. Like, *yeah I just leave it on the floor. That's just where it lives, Mam. On the floor. Put it back. I'll lose it.*

'Aye, go on,' says Flo. Flo wants a line of coke. Of fucking *course* Flo wants a line.

'Do you have a note?'

She does. She has a fiver. I feel safer with the plastic money, I feel less like I'm going to get hepatitis. Cashing up at work with paper money, you feel like you could shake the notes off and salvage a bump, at least. Plastic money, though, it just bounces off. And if you have a nosebleed, it's not like you've ruined a note; you can just rinse it off. I make Flo go first, because she has the note, and I watch her hoover up that line like the sesh gremlin I know she really is. Fuck morals. Fuck ethical drug consumption. What's that fucking bit in *Trainspotting* from the posters, you know, from everyone's room when they're sixteen, *Choose Life*, *Choose A Job*, and all that shit. Choose fucking up. Choose to come into my office and take cocaine because I told you to. Choose to follow me back out to the bar, after we've had a line, and drink a shot of tequila.

The thing with Flo, with a lot of people our age: she's so fucking quick to blame everyone else for her shit, you know? And you do *choose* these things. You choose to make yourself feel like an absolute fucking spineless, easily led pile of shit with a steaming hangover tomorrow morning. Maybe even tomorrow evening. The night is young, and I have so much cocaine in my bra.

When Finch turns back up, I buy another round of shots, and tell him it's apology tequila and he *has* to drink it.

I realise I forgot to piss.

●●●

Tequila makes my fingers numb, so I keep dropping my phone in the Uber. We're heading to Will's presumably squalid house in Heaton. Student Village, Flo calls it, every time, like she doesn't live three feet away in Sandyford. I sit in the front, because I'm the only adult, and the only person who can handle talking to strangers for extended periods of time. I order drinks,

I order cabs, I make men go away, I make drug deals happen, I get us into places. In the land of the borderline autistic, the man who can make eye contact is king. I've known Finch for three years and he's never looked me in the eye once.

'How's your night going, then?' I ask. I can't bear the silence. Finch has gone quiet, furiously chewing gum, and Flo is creased; she's absolutely pissing herself back there, stuffing her fingers into her mouth to try and stop herself from laughing.

'Just students and stuff. Back and forth, town to Heaton, Heaton to town,' he says. 'You going home?'

'Nah, house party.'

'Is... Is she okay?' The driver (Iqbal) nods back at Flo.

'She's fine. In fact, I'd be more worried about your man there.' I point at Finch. 'Gurning like an absolute twat. Forgot to take his magnesium supplements, now look at him. He's going to lose a tooth, like that. Have you ever seen Bounce by the Ounce? On YouTube, Bounce by the Ounce?'

'No... What is that, is it a music thing?'

'Sort of. It's a video of this tragic club, somewhere shit. Some shitty town. There's this bald feller, gurning his tits off. Looks like Gollum, Gollum in a really rough extended cut, Gollum in Middle Earth After Dark, like one bump to rule them all, one bump to line them, one bump to... something, and in the sesh we bind them,' I say. Flo screams with laughter, stomping her feet on the floor of the taxi.

'God, you fucking love *Lord of the Rings*, don't you?' says Finch. 'You only ever talk about it when you're off your tits and that's how I know you love it.'

'She still had an Aragorn poster while we were in college,' says Flo, gasping between giggles. 'In 2008.'

'Fuck off.' I drop my phone again. Flo laughs more. 'Hey,

since we're sharing fun facts, did you all know that Flo isn't actually called Flo? Did you all know she was christened *Lauren*.' And Flo's laughter slows. '*Lauren*, and rebranded before she started foundation, and actually named herself after Florence of *the Machine* fame? Changed it by deed poll and everything.'

'Well, I think you should be able to choose whatever name you want for yourself. For instance, Irina, if you decided to change your name to Mrs Frodo Baggins, I would support you,' says Finch.

'That's not funny because it wasn't a fucking *Frodo* poster, it was an *Aragorn* poster, so if you wanted your joke to land, Finch, which it didn't, you'd have said I'd fucking change my name to fucking... Look, he's not short on aliases, is he? Like, I'd be Irina Telcontar, Queen of Gondor or something, wouldn't I? Jesus. If you're going to fucking do this, if you're going to fucking—' I sniff. '—pull this shit with me, pull something I haven't heard before, alright? Pull something less basic than Mrs Frodo.'

'Telcon... what?'

'It's the royal house of Gondor,' I snap. 'Jesus.'

My loose, powdered lips have dug me a hole deeper than any lingering reference to teenaged posters, or spiteful revelations regarding Flaurence. There's no real getting out of it. My face feels warm. Not cokey warm, just warm, and I feel squirmy. I shrink in my seat a little. I have accidentally conjured up a shorter, wider, speckier version of myself, hunched over a battered copy of *Fellowship*.

The feeling is like when someone sees a mark from where you've self-harmed, and you slap your hand over the cut, or the burn, or the bruise. You've tried to hide it and, in doing so, made it even more obvious that mark is not an accident.

Jesus, self-harm and *Lord of the Rings*. My tween years crash back to me in waves.

'Never seen *Lord of the Rings*. Is it much good?' asks the cab driver.

'It's alright, yeah,' I tell him.

He drops us off outside a house with an unkempt garden, an overflowing bin, and trip-hop exhaling from the windows in a marijuana-scented fog.

I dig the coke out of my bra and take a generous bump.

'Is that the right house?' asks Finch.

'Yeah just, gimme a second.' Cocaine replaced in bra, I march up to the door, ring the bell. 'Don't you live round here?'

Finch nods. He's just in the next street over. Good. I can send them home with zero faff when they inevitably become a liability.

Will answers. Nice shirt, unbuttoned, tucked into high-waisted jeans, hair wavy, flower behind left ear, joint behind right. Jewellery. Calculated. Effort clearly made, more than likely on my behalf. He says my name and gives me a kiss on the cheek. I generally wouldn't let him touch me, but he didn't give me enough warning, and I can't feel the lower half of my face anymore, aside from the roof of my mouth, which aches as if all the booze and drugs are building up above my incisors, like they want to burst out of the sockets and take my front teeth with them.

'These your friends?' Will asks.

'In a manner of speaking.' I push past him. There are people talking in the corridor, mostly men, mostly baristas and bartenders and gallery invigilators and the kind of general, miscellaneous artsy people I see fucking everywhere but have never spoken to. They're a rotation of background extras in my life, a handful of unnamed NPCs with repeating models populating the playable areas of the city.

Even with my hair askew, and the foundation rubbed off the tip of my nose, and my lipstick slightly smeared, I turn the head of every bloke in that corridor. I make my way through to the kitchen and immediately grab a plastic cup. The kitchen is disgusting, fag ends and spillages and dishes and cups piling up in the sink.

Flo will anxiety-clean at parties if given the chance. She immediately starts collecting cups and putting them in the bin. Finch starts laughing at her.

'She's real,' says a voice. 'She's, like, actually real then.' Scottish, but posh Scottish. A fat man, standing at six foot two, with a well-kept beard and a boyish, handsome face. Blue eyes. He's sweating profusely, and wearing a top hat, and holding a cane. 'No offence, I just always thought he was, like… lying. Exaggerating. I mean, look at him. My mam always says he's a bonny lad, but *still*.'

'I'm not a fashion photographer, you know. I'm not, like, shooting him for *Vogue*,' I say.

'Aye. I've never seen none of the photos, I just thought… Well, I didn't think anything, because I thought he was lying.' He shrugs. 'I'm Henson. Well, Jack, but. Everyone calls me Henson.'

'I told you she was fucking real, mate.' Will removes the enormous spliff from behind his ear, and lights it up. He lost his flower, somewhere, between the kitchen and the door. 'See?'

'We gunna get to see some photies, then? Some sexy photies of wee Willy?' Henson takes a step towards me and nudges me, and winks unnaturally in a way which screams, *I've been trying to make winking at lassies my 'hing.* I offer to swap a look at Will's photos for some alcohol, and Will promptly produces a bottle of vodka from a cupboard, removing it from behind a bag of potatoes.

'I picked you up some vodka before, so there's no need, babe,' Will says. He opens the bottle, and tips it into my cup, spilling a decent glug on my hand by way of marking his territory. Might as well have pissed on me. 'Oopsy.'

'It's fine.' I lick my wrist. I follow their eyes. Finch drags Flo away from her cleaning, and Will offers her the joint with a 'Smokum peace pipe?' as if this was ever going to be the group of people to impress with a bit of comedy archaic racism. She doesn't take it – PC even when wrecked, she says, 'What the fuck,' so I introduce Finch before Flo can kick off. Finch plucks the joint from Will's fingers, and smokes it easily, letting it dangle from the corner of his mouth while pleasantries are made.

'So, the vibe's like… all night seshy?' Flo asks.

'Oh, it's totally *the vibe*, like, that is deff the *vibe*, yeah, like *heavy*, like, *really seshy.*'

'Aye pal, I think she gets it,' Henson says. He gives me this look like, *look at this fucking idiot, don't have sex with him.* Cute that either of them thinks that's on the cards. The joint has made its way to Henson's hands. He blows a smoke ring.

'Quick poll, as he does this all the time: does anyone find the smoke rings sexually alluring, or do you just think he looks like a tosser?' Will asks. We ignore him. Flo, I think, is trying to convince Finch to drop another bomb. I go to lift the cup of vodka to my lips. 'Woah! We have mixers! I have ice and loads of juices. You don't have to drink it straight!'

Will plucks the cup from my hand. I'd normally fight more, but, alas, tequila fingers.

'My delicate constitution couldn't *possibly* handle a sip of straight vodka,' I say. 'I'd have some tonic water, though.' Will bumbles around the kitchen till he returns with a vodka and tonic, with ice, a scruffy little wedge of lime, and a fucking straw. We watch him. Henson keeps looking at me, elbowing me as if we've formed a bond through shared disdain for our mutual idiot. Henson offers me the joint, and when I say I'm on coke, and I'd rather leave the weed till I'm winding down, he offers me a line. I ask if we can all have a line.

'Aye. Um, aye I can sort three extra lines out. Can't we, Will?'

'Three?' He makes a face, then remembers himself. 'Oh, shit yeah. There's like… I mean we're practically like *Scarface* up in here. Have you seen *Scarface*?'

'Yeah, Will. I've seen *Scarface*.' And I join Henson in a side-eye. Our eyes meet, and he winks again. Will scowls.

'I was just asking.'

●●●

We take the living room for lines. There are two girls in there, pretty girls, girls younger than me, so deep in conversation they seem a little taken aback when Will pulls a record from his neatly organised shelf and drops it on the coffee table in front of them. He takes a baggie from his pocket, and tips most of the powder inside it onto the sleeve. Finch says he should use a black vinyl not a white one. Will says it's too late for that now. The girls get up to leave. Will looks to me, to the girls, back to me, and seems to mentally put all his eggs in one basket. He lets them go, without a line offered, or even so much as a nod of his head.

Flo leaves for the toilet, comes back and says there are quite a lot of people in the rooms upstairs, and Henson explains that their other housemate, Sam, is up there. Sam wanted to 'get ketty' around the time we arrived, so him and a handful of other guests retired to his bedroom, where they'd pulled a load of quilts and mattresses onto the floor earlier in the day, with the idea it'd be a comfy, 'chill' room, for people to go and get a bit weird later on. They must have all thought there'd be more girls here. Including myself, the one I came with, and the two who just left the room, that's four women and probably fifteen or sixteen men, unless there are more women up in the ketamine room, hiding. No women is such a red flag for a shit party, but then no men is a red flag too – you want a fifty-fifty ratio, ideally.

I think Flo might have had her second bomb. If she's sick later, I'm not fucking dealing with her.

Will runs to the kitchen and returns, carefully snipping up a couple of plastic straws with a pair of scissors, distributing them among the group. He assures us we will be kept 'safe at the sesh'.

'The girl to boy ratio here is really off,' I say. I look at Flo.

'I want to dance,' she says. Will sticks some disco bullshit on, and Flo grabs Finch by the wrists, forcing him to dance.

'Ah, do you not have a boyfriend, then?' asks Henson, as if it were a natural segue.

'Nah,' I say. 'I don't do relationships. Never have.' Henson smiles at me, and tells me he's a serial monogamist, but single at the moment. Flo snorts, from her dance.

'What about Frank?' she asks.

'Shut the fuck up.' My face turns red – Frank is a fucking no-go. Honestly, I'd rather she brought up Lesley. Finch wants to know who Frank is.

'*Frank Steel*,' says Flo. 'The photographer?'

'Oh!' says Finch. '*Really?*' A demented little smile spreads over his face, like it's such a shock.

'Shut the fuck up, Flo,' I say. And when she laughs, I throw an empty cup at her. That shuts her up. That shuts everyone up.

'Ladies,' says Will. 'Please.'

'You're so aggro on coke, Rini, oh my God,' whines Flo. I don't dignify her with a response.

'Should I roll a joint after this, then?' asks Will. 'Bit aggro this vibe, like. Plus, I'm nearly out of coke after this, mostly.'

'So much for *Scarface*,' I say. I dump my cocaine on the table.

●●●

It's four a.m., and the sky is getting lighter, like a threat. I complain about it; Henson has a solution, proudly drawing the blackout curtains he bought specifically for the sesh. He's also covered all the mirrors, so we don't have to worry about the way we look. It's like a Jewish funeral in here, but with more class As. We're now out of coke, properly out of it. Flo is wittering on to Finch about gender. Finch has withdrawn; he is sweating and gurning. Will is texting his dealer, but I sincerely doubt he'll get a response.

Will discards his phone. He is in a beanbag, pouting and dutifully rolling joints while I've been talking to Henson. He tried to craic on with Flo earlier, but she just said, 'Boyfriend, sorry,' and he didn't even keep up the fucking *pretence* of wanting to talk to her. He sagged back into his beanbag with a grunt.

I've demoted him. Demoted from better looking, thinner friend to man-in-corner-rolling-joints. The mere act of my speaking to his cute, fat friend has him in a massive huff. It's incredible. Who said masculinity was fragile, eh?

Henson and I have been deep in party chat for ages. He doesn't seem to be the type of bloke who needs to interrupt you with his own hot takes, which is refreshing – maybe he's too wrecked to respond. He's still wearing the top hat. I described *Salò, or the 120 Days of Sodom* to him in full, and explained Pasolini's vision: the way he criticised the voyeuristic nature of film, but the inherent hypocrisy of the cinematography. The way he can't stop his camera from lingering on boys. How he frames the female victims in the film with a cold, detached eye, but his male subjects are filmed with significant *heat*, with the lens lingering, not just on buttocks, but on eyelashes, and soft, floppy hair, and pretty lips. I told him that, *as an artist,* that was *so* influential for me. I could do that, if I wanted, you know? I could train a camera on a man and look at him like a man looks at a woman; boys, too, could be objects of desire.

I pull up some photos of Will on my phone, as an example. I pick out one where he's nude, apart from an open button-down shirt. You can't really see his dick. Mostly pubes – there's a strategic bit of lighting.

'Do you see, though? He looks *soft*, doesn't he? He's looking at you like he wants you, isn't he? Like a… girl in a perfume advert, or something.' I zoom in on his face. Heavy eyelids, parted lips, glimpse of a tongue glittering beneath his teeth. 'Take my phone, have a scroll.'

'Aye. Um… Was his… He never told me you shot nudes,' Henson says.

'Oh. Not as often as my mam thinks I do, but yeah. Will's done loads of nasty shit for me.'

'*Irina*,' Will hisses. He's crawled over to us, scattering a small nugget of weed into his carpet. 'Don't, please.'

'Ah, come on, don't act shy. You're obviously not,' says Henson. He's stopped on a photo of Will in what I call lazy drag. He's wearing lip gloss and delicately applied false eyelashes with a touch of eyeliner, and is dressed in one of my nighties (silk, pink) and a short dressing gown (see-through, pink, marabou feather trim at the hem and the sleeves). His hair is down, and he just… he just looks so *pretty*.

'Don't be embarrassed,' I say. 'You look lush here.'

'Aye, dead bonny, lad.' Henson has a smirk on his face. 'A wonder you're not using these on your Tinder. It'd be a statement of intent.' Will tries to grab my phone from his friend's big, meaty hands. 'I'm still looking.'

'I thought you *liked* my photos,' I huff.

'I do. I just, like, I don't want him to see them.'

'Well don't model if you don't want people to see your work,' I say.

'Most of them are fine! I don't care about him seeing *most* of them, Irina. Do you get me? *Most* of them are fine, but maybe not one or two?' Will is pleading, and Henson is now scrolling furiously. I give him a look like I have no idea what the fuck he's on about. I do assume, however, he's on about the photos I took about a year ago of him wanking.

Again, the lighting is very tasteful. You can only just see the tip of his penis poking out from the top of his fist. He's on his knees, with his forehead touching the floor. I don't think I set out to take photos of him out-and-out wanking, but things escalate, don't they?

'Woah,' says Henson. And my phone is locked, and placed face-down on the coffee table.

'What?' I feign ignorance, unlock my phone. '*Oh.* Ah, shit. Sorry. I forgot we took those.'

Will is bright red. His mouth is twisted.

'Forgot,' he says. 'You're a fucking bitch sometimes, do you know that?' He doesn't spit it at me. He's not angry. It's stated like an unpleasant fact, one he's already dealt with. Global temperatures are rising, Brexit means Brexit, and Irina is a fucking bitch. I crawl over to him and sling an arm around his neck.

'*Diddums,*' I say, my bottom lip jutting. 'I can't remember every single photograph I take, you know?' He shrugs my arm away and lights a joint. 'Gimme one.' He hands me the one he's lit, and lights another for himself, slinking back to his beanbag, still red. Henson grabs one from the small pile on the coffee table.

'Well,' Henson claps his hands. 'On that note, shall we get a bit ketty? After these?'

'Go on then,' says Flo. She's gone a bit green. She gets up, suddenly, rushing out the living room and through the front door. The living room windows are open, so we can hear her throwing up in the garden.

'Christ,' says Finch. 'That's home time.' Once Flo starts vomiting, she's done. No endurance, no dedication to the sesh. She comes back in a moment later, shaking her head.

'Ah, babes. You really shouldn't have started on the coke, should you? Like, *morally.*' I say. Flo nods. Finch has already picked up her handbag, and sighs heavily.

'Let's go,' he says. 'You coming, Irina?'

'Nah, I'm good,' I say.

'Are you sure?' Flo asks, around a burp.

'Um… Yeah?'

'Just… Leaving you by yourself and stuff…' she says.

'Aye, I'm sure I'll get gang-raped the second you leave the house.' I roll my eyes. She flinches when I say *gang-rape*. So does Henson.

They leave, and so do a steady trickle of people from the upstairs bedroom. We smoke a couple of joints between us. I don't normally smoke weed, as it does very little for me; I'm feeling relaxed, but nauseous, less aware of my heart pounding in my chest. The mix of substances has my nervous system confused. Am I relaxed, or wired, or knackered? No idea. Fuzzy, though. Possibly hungry? Haven't spoken in a while. Just managed to drop the K on the coffee table.

'We've got enough, I reckon, for six small lines, or three *rather large* lines,' I say. I flip a coin – heads for little, tails for big.

Tails.

I realise it's been about four hours since I went to the loo, and I leave Will to rack the lines up, while I spend five minutes in the boxy downstairs toilet staring into the crotch of my underwear and pissing like a racehorse. I feel woozy, nauseous. My entire body is blanketed in a thin film of sweat. I give myself a quick once over with some loo roll, my neck, my tits and my forehead; I take with me a great swipe of makeup I'd forgotten I was wearing. I remove the scarf tacked over the mirror. There she is, the undulating reflection, her eyes bloodshot, her pupils a great black sinkhole in the concrete grey of her irises. Her makeup is crusty around her nostrils and her mouth, lipstick is smeared beyond the outline of her lips, and mascara running down her cheeks. Her red curls are now a mass of knots, at some point stuffed into a raggedy bun.

'You're a fucking mess,' I tell her. 'Jesus Christ, bitch.' I tack the scarf back up, and wipe off what remains of my lipstick before stumbling out of the bathroom, back to the living room.

'We thought you fell in.'

Three fat slugs of ketamine are lying on the vinyl on the coffee table. I ignore the men, pick up my designated drug straw, take my K, and flop onto the sofa.

● ● ●

The slug is where it all went tits-up for me. The last thing I properly remember is Will suggesting we break out the laughing gas, and after that, my vision unfastening like a reel of film slipping off a projector. I recall lying down on the floor, and suddenly being aware that years were passing. Henson's and Will's voices were there, and they did not slow or speed up, but years were passing. Decades. And they had no idea, the two of them. I sank down into the carpet, consumed, swaddled, and ascended.

Ascended, in that my vision had not just unfastened from my brain, but this reality itself. I was above time, inside of time, beyond time, the survivor of the passage of millennia.

My memory returns in flashes and echoes. I heard a bell – an incessant, jingling bell. I eventually found myself with my head in the toilet, now a portal into every reality. The bowl of that toilet, the water softly glinting inside; I was Galadriel with her mirror, each and every timeline set before me, inscribed around the bowl. And it was me, in every timeline. Me with my head in the toilet. Thousands upon thousands of me from above, each with my head in the toilet.

I recall Will trying to speak to me, and wrenching my head up, and thus, selecting a timeline. And while I was lifting my head to speak, I was actually diving into one of those timelines, where I would lift my head, and see Will, crouched in the doorway of his downstairs bathroom, trying to check on me.

Of course, the force of shifting away from the high, voyeuristic position above my body and above time itself, made me feel a little queasy, and I would then need to throw up again. Slamming my head back into the toilet bowl would then take me out of time, and back to the place above it.

Sometimes it would be Will in the doorway, sometimes a red cat with the fucking bell. Sometimes, a different boy, younger, with dark hair and scars, choking. I knew him. He coughed, and he spluttered, and he looked so pathetic and lovely that I wanted to fold him into my arms, and squeeze him. I wanted to keep him. But when I reached for him, he flinched, coughed, wriggled away from me. He dissolved around the corner of the small doorway. I couldn't follow him. I went back into the toilet, where I saw his face in the water, swirling away with the flush.

When Will came back, he seemed angry, and the boy did not return. I believe I recall Will pulling my head back, yanking me by my hair and tipping water down my throat, me almost choking on the water and, a moment later, my own vomit. I remember him scrubbing my face with a baby wipe and, when vomiting had dissolved into dry-heaving, dragging me upstairs (possibly with help from Henson?) and brushing my teeth for me. Brushing them hard, hard enough to make my gums bleed, so hard, in fact, that I remember being in pain when I could feel nothing else. My mouth still feels raw.

I returned from Above when he dropped me on his bed. Unable to even flail by way of protest, completely prone, paralysed. I think I remember him lying on top of me, enraged, grabbing my face and squeezing it. I think he didn't take his slug. He called me a cunt, I do remember that, because I remember his spit landing on my face. I remember him taking my skirt off, my lace bodysuit. He couldn't work out my bra, he couldn't quite get me rolled onto my stomach to get to the clasp, so he gave up, and just sort of scooped my tits out of the cups and fiddled with them for a bit, before proceeding to pull off my knickers and try to jam his *completely flaccid* cock into me.

He gave up, seemed to survey his work, then panicked, and redressed me. He popped my breasts back into my bra, stuck one of his T-shirts on me, and put a pair of his own boxers on me, too.

I'm working all of this out after waking up in his bed, in his clothes, with him asleep on the floor. I suspect this is a Xanax-induced sleep, because there is half a tablet on the nightstand and when I kick him, he doesn't stir. I kick him again.

I wonder how I'm going to address this with him. He's not the type of person who accepts being ghosted; it's been made *very* clear to me he doesn't like to be ignored. Like, do I send him a text? Just checking, Will, did you and your useless dick half-heartedly try to rape me last night?

I put my skirt on and gather my dirty underwear. My shoes are at the bottom of the stairs, and so is my vomit. I assume it's mine, anyway. I sneak through the house, and find my handbag on the sofa, where I stuff my underwear. To my sheer delight, my phone still has thirty per cent charge, and I have a series of increasingly panicked texts from Flo. It is nine-thirty a.m., and she is concerned about the complete radio silence. She also assures me that she's okay – like I'd fucking care?

> Got in a k hole but worse
>
> All went wrong
>
> Went to hell like a time travelling hell like
>
> I went to time hell
>
> Still at will's.
>
> Please come get me.

I get an immediate reply

> Stand outside, gettin uber r/n will pick you up!!!

She arrives fairly quickly. The morning is balmy enough that even half-dressed, with bare feet on the pavement, I'm warm.

In the cab, on the way back to hers, I can tell Flo is freaking out. She keeps asking me if I'm okay. I don't reply.

When we get home, I hole up in her upstairs bathroom. I vomit, and shiver, and Flo wraps me in towels. She brings me water and asks questions. I spend the rest of the morning alternating between vomiting and explaining to Flo why I'm not going to call the police. In short: drugs, and the fact I can sort him out myself.

'Do you remember when we watched *I Spit on Your Grave*?' I ask. She makes a face. 'What happened to *all cops are bastards*, Flo? I can deal with it. He didn't actually stick it in me, so as far as I'm concerned…' I shrug. 'I mean, I won't work with him again, if you're worried about that.'

She sits down on the bathroom floor beside me. Her bathroom. Michael is at work.

'I just feel awful. I shouldn't have left you,' she says. She hasn't slept a wink; her eyes stream while she speaks to me. She still has eyeliner smeared around her brow-bone, her temples, and mascara ringing her eyelids. She takes advantage of me coughing and spluttering to speak, uninterrupted for a while. 'You know, you want to think you're… You want to think you're not like other women, but you are, you know. You're still… that's still how the rest of the world, how *men* are going to see you. Like, I know you hate *labels*, but like… You live in a woman's body. You're vulnerable. No matter what you think, you're vulnerable, and sometimes, you'll need other people. Friends. Me.'

'Then why did you leave me?' I snap. 'If I'm so *vulnerable*, if you *knew* it'd go wrong, why the fuck would you let that happen to me?' She starts sobbing. She tries to touch me, and I lean away from her hand, moving closer to the toilet. Which, to be fair, has proven to be a stalwart ally in the last twelve hours. 'Just leave me alone.'

She leaves. I check her blog pretty sharp. At the moment it's just loads of obnoxious seshy bullshit about being on drugs. I'll check back this evening.

When I'm feeling a little more able to move without gipping, I check in on Flo. She's sleeping, face-down on the bed. I leave, get an Uber, no note, no text.

●●●

Is it a little bit crackers to stick my head straight into Tesco when the cab drops me off? Yes.

Have I done it anyway? Absolutely.

In my defence, I only have bag salad in my fridge and I think I'll be badly in need of some potato products by this evening. I'm wearing one of Flo's shirts, my skirt from last night, still, and have all my stuff shoved into one of her many art gallery tote bags. Luckily genetics and La Mer have rendered my skin flawless and youthful, so I'm fine walking in with no makeup. Hair looks a bit... It is what it is. I still *basically* look good. I can crawl out of Time Hell and be a solid 8/10.

I buy chips. He isn't here.

I get home, drop on the sofa and send a text to Will, intending to block his number as soon as I'm done.

Any particular reason why i woke up in your fucking clothes this morning pal???????

And I leave it at that, with the only tangible evidence I have.

therabbitheartedgirl:

Jeeeeeeesussss fuuuuuucking chriiiiiiiiiist Ive had the
fucking worst 24 hours I am fucking..... RRRRRRRRR!!!!!!!!
I'm literally sat here sobbing off the back of a huge fight with
Michael about irina AGAIN. Im really scared we're going
to break up this time. Really really scared, but he just said
the worst things about her. Something really bad happened
to her at the party on Monday night and he said she was
making it up and she was trying to upset me and make me
feel guilty and i was just so angry with him!!!! How dare he
say that about her???? How DARE he????? I know she
has a manipulative streak, and i know when she's upset she
likes to twist the knife and kind of put it onto other people.
lots of people do that, it doesnt mean she's evil and it
doesnt mean she's a fucking liar. So disgusting. And he said
'any one but her, literally any one but her I'd believe it 100%
but shes a fucking monster.' And he tells me he loves me
and he's just worried about me.

   Idk i just feel weird and sick. I love both of them. And i
think w my job being 4 days a week and stuff, I'd probably
have to move back in with my parents if me and michael
broke up. And I just like i dont want to break up with him
and its just such a GROSS thing to say but part of me
wonders if he might have a point you know? Its a fucked
up thing to lie about, and i dont actually think??? She
lied??? But she went from zero to blaming me so quickly
as well??

   Aaah jfc this is sort of messy to explain but ive caught
her in lies before. Ive never told her or pulled her on it but
ive caught her before, just on dumb shit like her fucking

college results like she told people at uni that she got a distinction but she got a merit and that's the deliberate stuff but she'd also always do this thing where like. So all the time in uni she'd get blackout drunk (when i was with her, and not as fucked up as her) and she'd just sort of fill in the blanks for herself and repeat it for people, and I'd literally be with her thinking 'well that's just not what fucking happened???' Like she'd tell this story about how some chavvy girl had shoved her in a club, and that's why her knees were bruised, but she'd just fallen over — shit like that all the time. And granted this is some dark fucking shit to fill in the blanks with but... christ im almost not fucking surprised? Im a shit friend for even thinking it. Shit friend, shit feminist. Urgh.

FRESHERS

I wake up a full twenty-four hours later on my sofa, bag of chips completely defrosted in my lap. I bin them, and promptly head to the shower, where I sit under the spray for a solid half an hour, wedged into the bottom of the bath.

I had one of those horrible post-party dreams. I don't usually have dreams. If I do, they're always these repetitive, black-and-white things, where I'm squeezing through a series increasingly small doors, or chasing something, or losing teeth. That is, unless I've drunk a lot, or taken something.

I dreamt about a boy. The boy from the toilet, I think. He was sitting at a bus stop, and I was trying to speak to him. He started screaming, and I tried to cover his mouth.

My hand slipped inside him, down his throat. His head fell off. Still shrieking, his head was looped around my arm like a bracelet, my hand poking out the bottom of his neck. I flicked the head off my wrist, and it smashed on the ground like a plate. Then I woke up.

The dye I brighten my hair with tints the water a rusty shade of orange; it pools behind me, dammed by my thighs which squeak against the bath when I move. Shampoo, conditioner and three going-overs with the most pungent soap Lush has to offer, and I still feel like the smell of Monday night is on me. My nana, a heavy smoker, used to wash her hair with half a cap of laundry detergent; I bet that'd do the trick for me now. I can't get the smell of fags and booze and weed out of my hair.

I give up after an hour, too hungry for another round of shampoo and conditioner.

The food in my house is limited, but I can't bring myself to leave. I'm not getting a takeaway: the solo-hangover-takeaway is the domain of women who eat their feelings.

Bag salad it is, I suppose. I grab one from the fridge and open it. I drain a tin of tuna and dump it in the bag, giving it a little shake. I chuck in a handful of olives, a spoonful of mustard, give it another shake and it's basically a Niçoise salad. I go back to the sofa and check my phone: two per cent battery and fifty-odd notifications, which makes me want to hurl the fucking thing through the window.

I like partying, but I loathe the aftermath. I need to stop letting people have my phone number. Maybe that's something to do while I'm off – new sim card, new *phone* even. I've got that cash from Mr B burning a hole in a pocket. My phone purrs greedily when I plug it in. Four missed calls from Flo, a series of texts from her, from Will, and one or two from Finch. Finch, I check first; he's just letting me know he sent me his photos, and could I look at them when I'm finished vomming, and later, could I ring Flo back when I'm awake and able. I reply to him first. I don't quite have the strength for Will's essay, or Flo's simpering apologies. I have twenty texts from Flo and seventeen from Will.

Later. I leave my phone in the kitchen, opting to spend the afternoon in the arms of my archive. All my uni stuff is in my studio. I grab the first two boxes and drop them in my living room. I set myself up on the floor with a coffee, a cushion and my *Salade Niçoise dans un sac*.

I crack open the lid of box one, marked CSM, FRESHERS in Sharpie. I only applied to art schools in London, and I got into a few, but went for Central Saint Martins in the end. It seemed like the coolest one, to be honest. Colin told me not to; he said the CSM Fine Art course was more for people chasing shock value than people with any actual talent, that it'd be a different story if I was doing fashion, or something, but I wasn't. He was half right.

We had to bring work to show on our first day, and I've never seen so many swastikas or nipples in my life. Do you remember the lad who was losing his virginity as performance art a few years ago? Bigged it up till he got in a few shit tabloids, then just fellated a banana in front of a (presumably) disappointed crowd? That was CSM.

I could have gotten into Goldsmiths. But there was this whole big cock-up with my application. I don't really know what happened. And the Slade basically only take people from private schools, so whatever. And Chelsea is just... It's boring, there, isn't it? Smug. So, I went to CSM, and it was basically fine. A culture shock, but basically fine. I'm quite posh in Newcastle, practically middle-class up here, but there... State-educated, regional accent, a heavy drinker. The clothing which was fashionable and sexy at home was *so last year* and brassy and showy in all the wrong ways. Someone asked me if my dad was a miner the first day I was there and I wanted to scream.

Flo followed me down. She fit in better – she's from Durham, the city, not the county. Not much of an accent, and after a term to adjust her wardrobe, you couldn't pick her out. She went to Camberwell, which is a banded Fine Art course, and she ended up bouncing from sculpture to painting before changing course and moving to illustration, where she stayed. She went from banging on about how she was going to get a Turner Prize nom by 2012, to crying about how she just wanted to go back to drawing without getting the shit ripped out of her for it. I had no sympathy.

My work doesn't get good till the end of that year, when I realised that I needed to do something a bit different to separate myself out from the YBA Clones, from the swastikas-and-nipples crowd.

And I'll say now, I never actually *deliberately* intended to do stuff just for shock value. I can't really help it if things just bother me less than they bother other people. That really helped me push my work early on. Everyone else is just appropriating iconography they think is shocking for attention, rather than genuinely having an interest in transgressive subject matter.

My first workbook for the year is mostly notes, pages torn out of magazines, images of women posing that I'd later have male models study while I bent their skinny limbs into place like dollies. First year I mostly got boys on my course to work for me by doing model swaps with them; I'll sit for you, if you sit for me, and so on and so forth. There was a lad I got on quite well with, for a bit, called David, who was really into exploitation films. I don't know why I'm being coy – it was David French. As in, Turner Prize nom David French. He was pals with Peaches Geldof for a bit, so I used to see him knocking about in the tabloids, which was weird as fuck.

The first photos I find are of him. They're quite funny, actually. He's on the couch in our halls – which I covered in a pink Ikea throw – nude, feet in the air, lying on his stomach. He's holding a toy telephone I'd picked up at a charity shop, with the red plastic cord wrapped around his fingers. There are two shots side by side, more or less identical, but in one photo David is biting his lip, and looking at the phone, and in the other he's giggling and staring straight down the lens. Smiling at me. Blushing.

I've written underneath, *pic 1 is more what I had in mind but pic 2 is better.* I peel them both out, and pop them in the 'to include' wallet. The next page of the book is just notes, a bit garbled, but you see me work out a good chunk of the driving principle of my practice in two sentences.

Picture 1 is posed and cute and it's fine but he's like interacting with the viewer in picture 2. David is giving me very genuine *fuck me* eyes in picture 2 IMO, and that's why it's better, because then the audience get the fuck me eyes as well?? More engaging. Does this make sense????

It does. It makes perfect sense.

I flip the page, and a print of one of David's photographs falls out, from the agreed model swap. It's a photo of me dressed up as the eponymous character from classic

Nazisploitation film, *Ilsa, She Wolf of the SS*. It's a photograph which, in this post-woke economy, would be a massive embarrassment. I think he's buried all of this stuff, or no one cares too much about his early work, now his shit's all serious and black-and-white and wanky.

I'm not wearing a swastika armband (David has cleverly altered the outfit and replaced the swastika with a penis) but I am holding a huge dildo. To this day, I have no idea how he procured this get-up. The boots in the photograph are mine, but he did the rest, down to the surprisingly high-quality blond wig. I'm standing on his neck.

If I recall correctly, his justification for this was a weird narrative about being a Jewish man and reconciling his identity with capitalism pushing the Nazi aesthetic, and fetishising big blond women. *Shiksa Goddess* is scrawled on the back of the photo in his handwriting.

I remember him getting into an argument with the Israeli girl on our course during the crit, where she just had this massive go at him for co-opting a critique of capitalism and the narratives around internalised anti-Semitism to justify objectifying me, and fetishising the suffering of their people. Or something like that. She also said I should be ashamed of myself for playing along with it, and I remember just being like, *well, good art asks these questions, doesn't it*? Because, you know, we still had a Labour government at this point *and* Obama was in the White House, and that liberal free speech shit went down with a lot less resistance.

I offered to sign prints after the crit, because it's a fucking good photo. I look sick, honestly. The wig suits me. I stripped out the black hair dye shortly after this with the intention of going blond – but I left it natural.

In a later sketchbook from the same year, I've taken a few photos of David mid-coitus; this is harder to execute than you'd expect. Just, like, logistically. I kept dropping the camera, because he just kept fussing and moving and whining. I've definitely captured the physical and emotional discomfort of the situation, but it doesn't quite work. I think what I like most in this set are the close-ups. I have a photo of his hand wrapped up in my ugly Ikea bedsheets, and one of his eyes scrunched up really tightly.

Notes under the photos read: *promise of fucking works better than actual fucking tbh.*

And then he kept pestering me to do it again, which bewildered me for about two weeks until he completely fucked up our relationship, which was very platonic, by the way. From my perspective, at least. I just thought we were two artists who'd clicked professionally. But boys ruin everything, don't they? Everything has to be this *When Harry Met Sally* bullshit, where sex always gets in the way.

We were on the bus together, me and David, and he's talking about this party his friend is having, and she's freaked out about the amount of people coming to her flat, and has suddenly said that all plus ones are cancelled. He was recounting the conversation, 'And I said to her, *can my girlfriend not even come?*' And I was on the bus thinking, *hmm, I wonder who his girlfriend is*? I asked him. He laughed.

And then I could practically hear the *Kill Bill* sirens going off in my head because he meant me. *He thinks I'm his girlfriend.* I must have made a face, because he went from laughing to *not*, and flushed bright red. I got off the bus.

Some lass who fancied him in our year ended up having this big go at me for it in the middle of the studios, while he was standing behind her telling her to leave it, and I sat there, let her finish, then smacked her.

This effectively blacklisted me for about six months at uni. The lass didn't even complain, but I went from like hot, edgy, novelty-northern girl to weird, fighty, state school chav. This idea of me permeated the whole course – I was having tutors referencing my difficult background, and I kept having to correct them.

I drop David's mid-fuck close-ups in the folder as well. They're interesting failures, and very embarrassing for him, if nothing else.

My phone buzzes in the kitchen. I let it ring out, then go and collect it. It's Flo again. I don't ring her back, but I pick up her texts. She's all apologies, and panic, threatening to come to the house if I don't pick up in the next five minutes. I tell her to calm down, and that I just slept for twenty-four hours straight. She replies, *whatever happens, you're my best friend, and I love you*. But then she asks if I'm sure about what happened last night.

The fuck do u mean *am I sure*

You know how you sometimes fill in the gaps?

Because i feel like we both know you do that

And sometimes when you embarrass yourself/get blackout you do like to blame other people??

Especially me???

Oh my god go fuck yourself lmfaoooooo

She doesn't reply after that. I go back to the box. I don't have the strength to speak to Will yet – the number by his name keeps ticking up and up.

I pick up another workbook, containing a number of photos of boys on my course (taken before the blacklisting) which don't quite work, but they're what I ended up putting together for *Barely Legal*. Nighties, glossed lips, a lot of pink. The aesthetically pleasing, retro, pastel erotica stuff with skinny, androgynous boys, selected for being both skinny and androgynous. At the time it felt revolutionary, but everything does when you're twenty. They're silly. If you were going to take the piss out of my work, and people who make work like mine, you'd make these photos. The proper prints are rolled up in a small poster tube in the box, which I'll go through another day with gloves and hands that aren't shaking quite as badly.

This *is* how I booked my first solo show over that summer, however. I put those up for our end of year show, and Anne Werner asked for my details, and rang a week later to offer me a solo show. She owned this little gallery in Peckham (The Werner Gallery, her own house with the ground floor converted into a gallery space), not huge, but it got me some attention, got me pegged as one to watch in a couple of little art magazines.

The show was in November. Anne wanted more work than I had, so she gave me the summer to produce something new for it, but my well of models had dried up. Flo kept trying to get me to photograph her, and I'd gone well off photographing women. I gave her this big spiel about the problem of the female form in visual culture, how it was impossible to divorce or protect it from the male gaze in the context of the western art world, yada yada yada.

My phone continues to light up insistently. There are notifications from social – Finch has uploaded some pictures from last night – but it's mostly fucking Will. Will, Will, will you pay attention to me?

I pick up my phone with the intention of blocking his number. I read the texts instead, my thumbs overtaken with a toxic curiosity.

> I let you BORROW my clothes because you were covered in sick :/

He insisted, yesterday afternoon. 12:32. But when I picked my top up off his floor in the morning, there wasn't any sick on it. Not even sick that had been wiped, or washed off. It was *clean*.

> At 13:04:
> Hey sorry for the tone of that last message, i get that must have been weird to wakeup in my clothes and probably not remember why. Sorry

> At 14:18:
> Hey do you remember much about last night?? Stuff got pretty intense haha
>
> Sorry if i seemed like i got the hump about you and Henson as well. If you fancy him that's cool! He's a handsome chap haha
>
> That scots charm haha. He asked me for your number but I'm not giving it over bc you know privacy and consent and shit

> At 14:36:
> I mean I just sort of thought you were coming over for me but i obviously misread the situation and it's fine so sorry for being weird
>
> Not that you probably even remember

At 14:45:
Im also fine with you showing people my photos and i
suppose i appreciate you might have forgotten about
some of the more intense photos we took. Sometimes
you forget things can mean more to you than they do
to other people

At 15:05:
Sorry to lay all my cards on the table here but i did think
there was a little more going on between us than just a
model/photographer thing but ive been looking at your
website today and it looks like you take those kinds of
photos with lots of different men and hey i guess thats
fine if thats your thing. Kind of stupid for me to expect
loyalty from someone like you, i suppose

At 17:49:
Hey sorry again about that last message my feelings
are just hurt

At 19:01:
I hope youre just sleeping and not ignoring me because
after all the shit last night i think that'd be really bitchy
of you fyi

At 19:26:
Im so sorry youre probably just sleeping

At 20:42:
I really like you?

At 21:12:
Just so weird that youd go off with henson like that its like
you did it just to fuck w me. Im sure you didnt but thats
how i feel. So id really appreciate some reassurance

At 21:39:
Not that you owe me anything sorry. I did a gender
studies module in uni and im aware that men are trash.

Im trying my best and i really hope you dont hate me after this but you probably do :(

At 23:00:
Im really sorry ill stop messaging you now

But he didn't stop. He sent me another text as soon as he woke up this morning, and has kept going in the same cycle of apologies, aggression and self-pity all day. It's almost four, now. I read the texts through again, alternating between a smirk and a sneer.

The first draft of a reply is aggressive, accusatory, (*My shirt was clean you flaccid rapist fuck*), the second is too breezy (*lol it's cool chill out omg*) and I settle on making him feel guilty, delaying gratification, twisting the knife. I think I'm going see if I can get the pic of him wanking in the photobook.

> Okay! Hey it's fine, don't worry about it. Thanks for reassuring me. It's really scary to black out like that, it's all wrapped up in some childhood trauma stuff I don't really want to get in to.

> But yeah, the other night I went to fucking space mate so thank you for looking after me. Soz if it felt like I was being inconsiderate of your feelings, it honestly just didn't cross my mind you'd feel that way about me. If it makes you feel better, I did just genuinely click with Henson, and I'm a little ??confused?? that you'd assume I was chatting him up to 'fuck' with you?? I also don't appreciate being called 'bitchy' even if your feelings are hurt.

> I really was just sleeping...

> I had kind of a rough night, idk if you noticed haha.

> Feel free to pass my number on to Henson.

> No hard feelings?

The response is almost instant, as if he'd drafted it.

None at all! Sorry for all the psycho messages. Comedown and bruised ego. I passed your number on to the big man. He's over the moon, glad you guys clicked! I hope we can still be friends. Honestly if I could delete stuff I already sent... I am such an idiot tbh, I wouldn't fancy me either lmao!!!!

I roll my eyes and reply with a smiley face. I go back to my archive.

I loved my next project. I still love it. It's this video/photography combo project called *What would you do to be my Boyfriend?* I screened the film at uni before Christmas and my tutor had this massive whinge about how the project was really exploitative, and how I'd put my safety at risk, and how she refused to mark it in case it encouraged me to do something like this again. I just asked to be moved tutorial groups. They put me with a good, unscrupulous male lecturer who gave me a distinction for my bold, risky work.

I spent the summer of 2010 picking up strange men, taking them back to halls, stripping them down to their underwear, and photographing them. I filmed and interviewed while I photographed, and asked them various probing questions about their personal lives, finishing on *do you want to be my boyfriend?* And *what would you do to be my boyfriend?* This is when I started experimenting with street scouting and photographing different kinds of beauty in my work. Less traditional models. No out-and-out monsters, mind, but some *interesting* faces, if you will.

The accompanying photobook I made is actually a really beautiful object. I had it printed and bound properly.

I made five copies; four were on sale at the solo show for an obscene price (all of them went, and even after Anne's cut I made about a grand) and one stayed with me. I have three or four photos per page, with the full interview transcript accompanying them; the DVD of the film is tucked into a sleeve at the back.

I flick through the photobook. While I did sneer when my original tutor said I'd put myself in danger to make this, things did get a bit dicey on a number of occasions. I rang building security three times, and on the third occasion, the security bloke came back up to my flat to tell me he wasn't going to throw any more weirdos in their underwear out of the building for me.

I find the diciest bloke on pages 21–30. He was such a fucking serial killer. Credited here only as 'Forbidden Planet', named for the hunting ground where I acquired him.

Games Workshop, Travelling Man, miscellaneous indie comic shops, were all great for finding weird blokes, but I'd actually gone to Forbidden Planet that particular afternoon for personal reasons. I'd intended to pick up Kitty Media's recent unrated Blu-ray/DVD combo release of *Urotsukidoji: Legend of the Overfiend*. They had it in stock, but behind a glass case, *locked*, like jewellery or something. I got a member of staff to grab it for me and ended up talking with him. Tall bloke, *blond*, very blond, *hard* bone structure, his face almost like a skull. With a little more weight and a box of dark hair dye he'd have been handsome, I think. But with that *Children of the Corn* aesthetic, you'd never give him anything past *striking*, and striking would be generous. He had a blue vein which ran from the corner of his mouth to his neck, like a fat drop of ink.

I remember licking the corner of my own mouth, chasing an imaginary vein with my tongue.

He raised his barely-there eyebrows at me, and said, 'Huh, hardcore,' when he passed me the DVD. It isn't a good film, more of an interesting artefact. *Urotsukidoji* was one of the first anime to get an English language release, so there are lots of reports of parents renting the video for their kids, not realising it was super violent and full of fucking.

I remember him saying, 'You do know what this is, right?' I told him to get someone else if he couldn't sell me tentacle porn without patronising me, and he apologised, and started making desperate conversation with me: do I like any other anime? Do I like other tentacle stuff? Am I into comics, etc., etc.; each answered with a shrug or a *not really*.

He followed me out of the shop. He really was sorry. Could he get me a coffee, to make up for it? I told him he could let me take his photograph.

Still no business cards, so I gave him the address of my halls. I found him outside the gate later the same day, grinning, like he thought he'd just stumbled into the meet cute bit of a rom-com that reviewers would describe as *screwball* and *edgy*. Being mistaken for a Manic Pixie Dream Girl has served me well over the years. I'd go out disguised in a non-threatening sundress and flat sandals, slouching and leaning heavily on my left hip, shrinking myself down to a less intimidating height. Drop a niche interest here, and a little sass there, and they eat me up, every single time.

I had the man from Forbidden Planet sit on my bed, in my tiny box-room in halls. I switched on the camcorder I'd bought recently and stuck my brand-new DSLR in his face, both purchased with the small pot of inheritance I'd gotten after my grandmother died. I started taking test shots.

It was an unremarkable shoot; I couldn't even coax him out of his shirt and he went to the bathroom before I got to the uncomfortable questions. The transcript is the driest one in the book, versus some of the absolutely wild shit some of the other blokes said. He went to the toilet, and I remember thinking what a fuck-up this was. He was just a dork, not a weirdo like the others had been. He'd been in there for fifteen minutes or so. I couldn't hear anything through the paper-thin wall, so I nudged the broken door open, and found him perched on the toilet lid, chewing a used tampon he'd fished out of my bathroom bin. One hand in his jeans, eyes half-shut, head tipped back. He didn't notice me till the flash went off on my camera.

He spat the tampon out and lunged, fluff all over his teeth, and I took another photo before cackling and legging it out of my room.

On the DVD, you can just hear him shouting, 'Fucking delete that,' and doors slamming. His section of the book closes with the photos of him with the tampon in his mouth, and then *Subject disappeared to bathroom for fifteen minutes, whereupon I found him chewing a used tampon and wanking.*

I sigh and close the book. I have a text from a new number.

Hey! It's (jack) henson from Monday night.

Hope you're feeling okay/cool with me texting you. Also, I don't know if you remember, but I'm sorry for going to bed and leaving you with wee willy when he seemed so pissy about us craicing on, he was very insistent that I should eff off because you were his guest...

For what it's worth hes harmless? But i think it was just a bit of a shock to his ego, so sorry on his behalf if he upset you. Hes used to me being his fat sidekick/ wingman and he can be really immature when he doesnt get what he wants. I think he has a lot of growing up to do with girls and i hope he didnt make you feel bad. I know hes sent you some pretty whacky shit in the last day or so. Hope youre okay xx

I know I said i hope youre okay twice! I doubley hope youre okay haha xx

Cute. I think about how best to play this.

Hey you!

Yeah will has been pretty whacky... Not sure how harmless he is either.

This is weird, i know you said you went to bed, but do you remember Will doing anything weird to me? I just remember him being a bit rough with me and stuff.

I'm actually a bit freaked out.

Again, sorry if this is weird. Does he have a history of behaviour with women which is... Not great?

I also woke up in his clothes. He said I'd thrown up on mine but I definitely didn't. I'd be able to tell.

Don't tell him I said this.

Henson says he won't. He says he's not aware of Will doing anything bad with women, really, before this. Henson says he's sorry this happened – whatever Will did, he's sorry. He hopes I remember.

No attempt to defend Will, I see. No *he doesn't have it in him*, or *he'd never*.

I talk to Henson for a while and sit up late into the night with my photos, going over and over the first box of stuff. I find myself lingering on *What would you do to be my boyfriend?*. I've read it through a few times now. There was one man who said he'd cut off one of his toes to date me – he was quite graphic about it.

I get an email at two a.m. from a <u>neongenesisedvangelion@ hotmail.com</u>

Hi!

Sorry about my email address I've had this account since 2005 and it's too deeply entangled with all of my other accounts to change now. This is Eddie - from Tesco? I have been thinking about modelling for you, but I'm not sure I can. I like the idea of it, but the stuff on your website is a little blue (which I am personally fine with) but I start teacher training for primary in september. Is there a work around? I like your stuff a lot, but i really really can't impress the importance of how much my face can't be in the photos if you decide to use me. I'd also really appreciate being able to discuss it first. Maybe over coffee, if this doesn't sound too much like I'm trying to take advantage of your artistic practise to hook a date? Feel free to tell me to bugger off! I know I'm being awkward.

I do some (embarrassing) photography as well, but it's mostly just trees. I like a

lot of the stuff you like, though. Arbus,
Mapplethorpe etc. In terms of Fetish stuff,
it is something i'm interested in more
academically than anything for instance i
read the marquis de sade for an essay in uni,
and I'm interested in some ero anime such
as Urotsukidoji and Belladonna of sadness
(which you should definitely check out if you
haven't!). My brother is also a professional
photographer but he just takes photos of food
for magazines and packaging and stuff, which
pays very well so he lives in London now - so
he lets me have his old lenses and stuff for
my daft hobby.

Eddie (from tesco)

Is it weird to reply instantly to an email sent at two a.m.?
Do I care? Shy bairns get nowt, as the saying goes.

Hi Eddie (from Tesco),

Great to hear from you. Not much of an
anime gal myself. Have seen the stuff you
mentioned there, but I'm not really big on
anime. Also not much of a reader. LOVE salo
tho, as you mentioned marquis de sade. I do
like j-horror/pinky violence and I'm big into
extreme cinema in general, if any of that is
your bag.

Anyway, I have a few props I shoot with on
occasion. I prefer to have a clear view of a
model's face for the most part - but masks

and stuff are kind of part of the territory with my work. I have a few options we can look at - I have a giant bunny head (has a tail too - kind of cute!) and a couple of gimp mask things, which are a little cliche; its not really my taste so I try to make those photos a bit more creepy/less sexy in tone. I have some masquerade things too and one of my old friends makes masks with old porcelain doll faces - she sold me a few.

Let me know when you're free, and I'll give you my address. We'll have some fun with disguises.

Seems a shame to cover up such a good face, but oh well :(

I generally get my models to sign a consent form, so I'll make sure there's an anonymity stipulation in yours, if that makes you feel more confident. I'll treat you to a coffee and we can talk it through.

Irina x

When I'm brushing my teeth, cleaning my face, moisturising, etc., I spend a little time in front of the mirror rehearsing. I try to smile, naturally, nicely. I pull the corners of my mouth into place with my fingers and see what it looks like when I show my teeth. It always looks a little smirky or sneery, I think, or like the anxious grin of an agitated chimp. I've never had a nice smile. A shame – you spend all that money on a set of veneers to find out your teeth were never the issue. I try looking sad. I try twisting my mouth up the way Flo did Tuesday morning, forcing my eyes to well up, looking down at the sink, furrowing my brow. I'm better at sad.

I let the skin of my face relax, and gently massage in my night cream.

'Hi, Eddie from Tesco, is it?' I stick my hand out at the mirror. We won't shake hands. 'What do you drink? What do you want to drink?' I try smiling. I think if I smile at him like this, he'll leave. I look like I want to skin him and wear it.

EDDIE FROM TESCO

Eddie, Eddie, Eddie from Tesco, shall I compare thee to a heavily discounted piece of meat on the reduced shelf at the end of the day? Thou art cheaper and, hopefully, fresher.

I smooth my skirt down – the denim is damp beneath my palms. I'm distinctly aware of a rash forming on the insides of my thighs, a combination of razor and friction burn exacerbated by sweat and the day's heat. I squirm. I've gone without foundation today, knowing it would melt straight off my face. Sweat gathers on my forehead, melting my SPF.

I should have worn bike shorts under my skirt, but it's almost thirty degrees outside, and it'd be another layer. I suck on my iced coffee, absently scrolling through some old photographs. I peer over the rim of my MacBook; no sign of him yet. We still have ten minutes, which means he's just not an early bird. Will isn't working today, which is a shame. I was hoping to ignore him, to rub another, shorter, man in his face.

Eddie from Tesco stumbles in, drawing my eye by tripping on the door frame, and going 'Oopsy!' as he enters the cafe.

He's just as sweet outside of the supermarket. I make him five foot five (if he's lucky) and nine stone (if he's soaking wet). I wave, brightly, from my table, with a big, white smile so he knows I'm happy to see him. He waves back and shuffles over. He's wearing a slightly-too-tight T-shirt and skinny jeans. He carries his weight on his tummy, his backside and his thighs, like a girl. His arms are like toothpicks, and his thick thighs taper into calves as thin as a bird's. He has a high waist, and an effeminate swing to his hips. With the freckles, the curls and brown summer skin, I'm smitten. *Dimples* when he smiles, too, and a little chest hair peeping over the collar of his T-shirt.

'Hi,' he says. He can't meet my eye. He's looking back and forth from the chalkboard menu behind me to my tits. Still, he's got this look on his face like he can't believe his luck. He takes a seat, cheeks reddening, and hides his face in his hands. 'Did you see me trip?'

He smells of baby powder.

'Don't worry about it. I'll get you a drink. Any particular milk preferences, or…'

'Oh um. A latte? With full fat milk, if they… I mean, you don't have to buy—'

I shush him and walk over to the counter. There's a girl with dark hair and a lip ring arranging brownies on a wooden serving platter.

'Will in today?' I ask.

'Nah. I'll tell him you said hi, though.'

'Hey, this is going to sound a little…' I clear my throat, lower my voice. 'Do you ever have any problems with him and female members of staff?' Me and this barista chat sometimes – I think she invigilates at the Baltic at weekends. She has one of those haircuts, like she has a Tumblr and runs a feminist Etsy store; you know, those very short fringes? Like Betty Bangs but shorter, like she's seven and she cut them herself.

'He actually keeps, like… bothering one of the new waitresses. Texting her and stuff. Why?' And then, 'Aren't you two friends?'

'We were,' I say, pointedly. 'I'm not telling tales, but you know… Just keep an eye on him, babe.'

'I will *now*. Thanks.' She takes my order, and doesn't charge me for Eddie's drink, with a wink, murmuring something about solidarity.

I sit back down with Eddie from Tesco. He is fiddling with his curls, wrapping one dark lock around his middle finger, and letting it bounce back into place.

'Did you used to work at the Tesco on Clayton Street, or something?' I ask. He shakes his head.

'Oh. No. I worked at one in Leeds, where I did my undergrad. I did my teaching qualification at Northumbria,' he tells me, like I asked for his life story. 'But um… then I worked at this little Tesco Express in High Heaton? Why do you ask?'

'You just look really familiar,' I say. 'Maybe someone I've shot before, or something.' He shrugs and doesn't seem to know what to say. An awkward silence hangs between us, which I break. 'So… your email said you teach primary school?'

'Yeah… I really love kids. I just… This is so cliché, but I'm really just like a big kid myself, you know? Um… not in a weird way, though.' He clears his throat, and trails off, staring down at the table, then back to my chest. 'So, do you, um, do you like kids?'

I shrug. I actually fucking *hate* children. Teaching at a primary school is a personal nightmare. In Irina's inferno, the seventh circle of hell is me doing potato prints with a room full of five-year-olds.

'They're fine. I'm probably not going to have any.' I've been scraped twice: once when I was nineteen, and again when I was twenty-two. A couple of mishaps related directly to my latex allergy. Hormonal birth control makes me go a bit loopy, you see, and no one ever just *has* latex-free condoms. I have since learned that the pull-out method is not effective, and if one would like to avoid bareback accidents (barebaccidents, if you will) one must simply deal with carrying her own special condoms.

'Yeah. I mean I love them, I just… I like being able to give them back at the end of the day? But… I mean, I do probably want them, just… not right now. Well. I don't know. If I had a girlfriend – which I don't – and she was pregnant, I'd be fine with it? I think?'

'*Cool,*' I say. Am I sneering? I scratch the top of my lip, knock it back down to a neutral position. But the damage is done, and the checkout boy has shrunk into his chair, flushed redder than before, with a thin film of sweat on his forehead. 'I promise I don't bite,' I tell him. It doesn't seem to help. 'I know I'm quite intimidating—'

'Oh, oh God, you aren't! I'm sorry, I just don't spend a lot of time with women outside of a customer service setting. I mean, on placement I talked to quite a lot of mums, and some of them were quite attractive, but...' He trails off, and screws his face up like he's just stubbed a toe.

'Stop talking. I *know* I'm quite intimidating. It's *fine*. Don't worry about it. Just... answer my questions. Speak when spoken to, if it helps.'

'Okay.' He nods. 'Speak when spoken to, okay.'

Men get like this with me, sometimes. I find it quite repulsive that anyone could so openly roll over and show their soft parts to a stranger. It's so gross, it's almost captivating – like when people cry on public transport. I'd literally rather die before I acted like this in front of someone. It feels like he's expecting me to mate with him and bite off his head, or perform a backwards traumatic insemination ritual that'll end with a load of ginger spiders bursting out of his chest.

Now we've established that he only speaks when spoken to, we can get on with things. I ask him if he's seen much of my work, and he has. He went through my whole website – he really likes it. I let him go off on one about how great my work is: *ooo the colours, ooo isn't it so revolutionary to see the female gaze, ooo eroticised images of normal men by a woman.* The phrasing is decidedly similar to a *Vice* write-up of a show I did during my MA. I think that article is still the third or fourth result when you google me, as well. But that's fine. Forgivable. A little sweet, even, that he'd try and pass off a write-up from four years ago as his own clever observations. Maybe he thinks I don't read my own reviews.

I ask him if he's cool with doing some more explicit stuff, as a trade-off for the mask. He shrugs – as long as his face is covered, he doesn't care.

I ask him why he's doing this.

'I just...' He shrugs again. 'Just not every day this happens, is it? I mean... I'm not *ugly*. I know I'm not ugly; I'm not fishing for compliments. There's just a big difference between not being ugly – having an *okay* face – and being attractive, isn't there? I'm just... I'm short. I'm really short and... *weird*. And I know it's risky and stuff, I just. You're like... It's really flattering. It's really, *really* flattering.' He's red again.

I'd take his photo now, if I could.

●●●

Yo...

Saw that dude from Tesco today hes going to drop in for a shoot after his shift on wednesday.

So you know. Thanks for the rec.

As hit and miss as your picks for models normally are, he was a good shout.

I quite like him. Like, more than I expected.

I see you watching my Instagram stories

Ugh whatever.

●●●

Eddie from Tesco comes over the day after our coffee date.

He likes my house.

'Spartan,' he says. 'Modern.' The only decorations are prints of my own photographs, a couple of Flo's drawings hanging, and a set of pressed flowers above my mantel. The walls are white, the floors are wooden – slate tiling in the bathrooms and the kitchen. My mam thinks it looks like a hospital, smells like one too. I bleach everything.

Eddie from Tesco settles into my leather sofa with a squeak, a cup of peppermint tea in his hand, and asks me about myself. I do this to walk them through what'll happen in the shoot, get them to sign consent forms, scan their IDs. They normally just sign the paper, and monologue at me for a bit until I ask them to stop talking.

Eddie from Tesco signs without reading, but he asks me what attracts me to a model, and how I get those washed-out pastels when I shoot in colour. How do I know if a photo is going to be black and white? And how do I know if it'll be in colour? Do I just see a model and instantly *know*; I'm going to shoot you like *this* and it'll look just like *this*. Or do I just wing it?

'A mix. Sometimes I see someone and get an idea, sometimes I just like the look of them and want to try some stuff out,' I say. I don't have any explicit ideas for this shoot, just that we'll be working with masks, which is fine. I also warn him my studio used to be a garage, in case he panics at the sight of my dad's box of hammers and saws and power-tools. The nervous ones do, sometimes.

I have a rack and a bin full of clothes in there, and I set about pulling out masks. I have a couple of gimp masks (which I hate, and I should really just bin, but you never know, do you?), one of those weird, leather dog-mask things (pilfered from the toilet of a gay bar during Pride last year) and a couple of porcelain masquerade masks I cadged from Serotonin during MA. They're very delicate, and I've broken one before. Easy enough to glue back together, but I still give Eddie from Tesco a sharp warning when he starts fingering them. There's also the bunny head, a big, mascot-looking thing, but not cartoony. Its face is a bit like Peter Rabbit's, very… Beatrix Potter, you know? Makes it creepier, I think.

'Where did you even get that?' he asks.

'Don't worry about it. It's horrible, isn't it? I love it.'

'Well, if you love it… it's cool, I guess,' he mumbles. 'Cool, cool, cool.'

I get him down to his pants and do a couple of test shots of him with the masks, then in the bunny head. He is more or less as I imagined. Thick thighs, soft stomach and a flat, ribby chest. He's not as hairy as I thought he'd be.

I'm surprised by how into the bunny head I am. Like I said, it's creepy as shit, and the previews on my camera are just like… gross. But like, sexy gross. So wrong it's right? I don't know.

I have a cotton tail, which I pin on him. I clip it to the waistband of his briefs (tight, navy blue), and he clears his throat when I brush my knuckles against the fuzzy small of his back

I get this great shot of his arse, with the little tail – and it's round and fat, and the tail is so fluffy and cute. It's like a peach; I could bite it.

He's clearly uncomfortable, but he asks for direction, and he does everything I say – which is weird, because normally the models are stiff and ignorant, too busy panting and dribbling to think too much. They don't think they're performing – they have mistaken my critically acclaimed artistic practice for a prelude to a fuck. Eddie from Tesco hasn't, though. Maybe he gets the work, maybe he doesn't think there's a world where I'd ever want to sleep with him. Maybe it's six of one, half a dozen of the other.

I want to touch him. Not just to look, but to actually reach my hands out and touch him. My fingers slip on the buttons of my camera, because my hands are so sweaty, and the plastic in my palms is a stand-in for his hips. I squeeze the lens and imagine it soft beneath my fingertips.

'Stretch,' I say. 'Arch your hips, roll over, put your hands on your stomach, get on your knees, touch yourself.' He's a good listener.

After half an hour, we're done. He takes off the rabbit head, and I find him red-faced, with his hair plastered to his skull. I'm looking at him like a piece of meat. Any man, any proper man, would be on me like a rash, but Eddie from Tesco just sits on the floor of my garage and starts getting dressed, knees lifted to disguise the semi I've already photographed.

I ask him on the spot if he wants to be in a film. For Hackney. I tell him he's great – he's perfect for it – responsive, engaged, compliant; he was made to be shown in two dimensions. He smiles at me, all pretty, all flattered.

'It'll just be a test run, though. I don't know if it'll work with the masks.'

And the smile drops, though just a little.

Instead of packing up my equipment, I watch him while he puts his clothes back on.

I see him out, then I am alone with his pictures. I cycle through them on the preview screen of my camera. I'm glad I didn't shoot on film – instant gratification. My thumb trembles as I click down the tiny left arrow on my camera. The display ticks through two hundred images, and I don't delete a single one. My hand drifts to the inside of my thigh, the crotch of my underwear.

It's bad when it gets like this. It's been a while since it's gotten like this. I made a rule for myself – when I moved back up here, when I finished the little break from photography I had after my MA: don't touch the models. I was under the misguided impression that touching was what pushed me over the edge, you know? Touching made my hands wander and my knickers drop. And I broke that, because you have to touch them sometimes, you have to put them in the right places, you have to physically arrange them. Sometimes the photos work better when I'm in them – a hand, a high-heeled shoe, a dramatic silhouette – a powerful female presence, a phantom dominatrix.

So now the rule's more like 'Don't shit where you eat' with 'No touching' applied at my discretion. I probably shouldn't touch Eddie from Tesco, because I clearly want to, and if I can't obey my only vague guideline I'm fucked, aren't I?

I sit, for a moment, with my hand wedged between my thighs. I'm wet, and uncomfortable, and the lace of my bra is irritating my hard nipples. My cunt flexes.

I decide to have a cold shower. I decide to ignore the yawning, drooling hole, the way I ignore my treacherous growling stomach or my aching thighs a mile into a run. I catch a glimpse of my naked body in the mirror, and look away like I've made eye contact with a stranger in a gym's changing room.

I quite often take cold showers – they're better for your skin. I don't often spray icy water straight onto my crotch, though. I cringe, but I feel better, colder, cleaner. More human. More than human.

But when I get out of the shower, I'm still thinking about him. I slap my face. I imagine the two of us fucking. I try to bash the thought out of my skull, but it comes in intrusive flashes, almost violent. I try to change the thought, squash it, kill it. I imagine my hands around his neck but that tangles with the thoughts from before. His neck flexes beneath my palms in the daydream, and my insides flex along with it.

I can only ever ignore my stomach rumbling for so long before I have to eat something. I might want bread, grease, red meat, but I can ease that off with bag salad, and a teaspoon of olive oil, half a tin of tuna. So, if my twat is my stomach, and Eddie from Tesco is a cheeseburger, I'll go get a salad. If Eddie from Tesco is shitting where I eat, I'll go shit somewhere else.

I get dressed to go out. I curate an outfit that's sexy but not desperate. A short, white wrap dress, cute and kind of sixties looking. A daytime dress, to match the light summer sky, the long warm evenings. Light makeup, *date* makeup: a gentle, sparkly eyeshadow, and baby pink lip gloss; the kind that irritates your lips, makes them swell a little for that just-sucked look.

I go to BeerHaus, where I consider taking home the manager, the one who's fully given up charging me for drinks. I tell him I'm meeting someone, but they're late.

'Who could ever stand you up?' he asks. I shrug.

I'm casting a wide net on my phone, sending the slightly more sophisticated equivalent of a 'U up?' text to a few ex-models I have no intention of photographing again. To Henson, too, who replies, but doesn't seem to pick up the vibe I'm putting down. We end up chatting about *Raw* over text, and that's fine. I'm always happy to chat shite about films, and I refuse to ask for sex. They ask me. They beg. That's how it works.

I get chatting to this suit. He's patronising. I forget his name as soon as he tells me, so let's call him *John*. He's broken away from *work drinks* to tell me about his job. A plastic surgeon, from London, talking about merging practices with someone up here. I'm supposed to be impressed.

He tells me: if I ever came in to get work done, he'd send me away.

'Some girls are just born lucky,' he says. 'You're one of them.' I bet he says that to every cunt; I bet he says that to girls with tiny tits and bent noses. My mam actually had my ears pinned back when I was twelve – and then there's my teeth. While I always had a good waist-to-hip ratio, what I have now is the product of years of dedicated waist training and exercise. My hair is dyed, and I have extensions. I smile, with my teeth, and he tells me my veneers look very natural. I tell him another girl knocked my tooth out, but in this version of the story, I was playing hockey, not getting lippy with a rough lass in a takeaway.

'Has anyone ever told you you look just like Priscilla Presley?' he asks.

'They have,' I say.

'When she was young. Before all the bad work.' He snorts. 'Obviously.' Then, with a squint. 'You know, if you ever want anything done in the future... Those fuck-ups almost never happen, now. That Meg Ryan shit.'

I keep my hair over my ears.

We talk a little more about that Meg Ryan shit. About how everyone has lip fillers nowadays, and they always take it too far. We talk about the Kardashians – our theories. I think Kim's had her nose done and her hairline taken back, maybe some lipo around her jaw to get it sharp.

We talk about her arse, at length, and I'm arguing in her favour. It was always big, and she's had kids, you know? Kids, waist training, squats, illusions. She had it X-rayed. In season six of *Keeping Up with the Kardashians*. She had it X-rayed, and she didn't have implants.

'Fat transfer,' he says. 'She wouldn't have injections. They're risky. Fat transfer, and maintenance. Corsetry, squats. Tits are done as well.'

'I know the tits are done. She's had two kids; the tits are obviously done. The arse is more of a mystery, though, isn't it?'

John disagrees. Fat transfer. He buys me another drink.

It gets a little blurry. I'm drunk enough that moving from point to point feels like teleporting. We're in the alley outside, by the bins. I can hear a rat. I can hear John breathing.

He touches me surgically. I feel him weighing my breast in his palm, searching for resistance, or something. He slips his hand under my dress, and squeezes my arse, seemingly satisfied when his fingers find a dimple on my left cheek. And he pulls away from me, with a satisfied hum. *It's all natural*, I think to say. I don't. It isn't, really. It's yoga and corsets and salads and hours of my time, to wake up in the morning and wake up like this.

'I've got a hotel,' he says. And we walk together. He's staying somewhere expensive, by the river. I ask him if he always looks a gift horse in the mouth. 'Sorry about that. That fake shit ruins it for me. It's like... What do you do for a living?'

'I'm a photographer.'

'I meant for a job.'

'*I'm a photographer.*'

'Oh,' he says. 'Well... It's like when... It'd be like seeing a photo that's... So, you think it's a photo of a beautiful woman, *man.*' He waves his hand. 'Whatever you're into. But actually, it's been photoshopped. Can't enjoy the photo then, can you? If you know it's not real.'

I kind of get what he's saying. It's sort of like if you condensed all the academic craic out there on the 'presumption of veracity' people ascribe to photography, all the resulting authority and seductiveness, into a common tweet. I don't know if 'that take is so basic come back to me when you've read some Sontag or Derrida' is good foreplay, though.

'I kind of get you,' I say. I am feeling drunk, and charitable. 'It's a bit like... So, I heard that people who photograph food – like, for adverts, and packaging, and that – to get that fresh rising steam effect on, like, chicken, and mashed potato, and shit. I hear they soak tampons in water, then pop them in the microwave till they steam. Then they either put it just behind the food, or, like, just bury it in there? Ever since I heard that, whenever I see the packaging on an M&S curry, all I can think about is the fucking soggy microwaved tampon that's probably stuck in it.'

'Yeah. That's fucked up,' he says.

I decide to let him know I'm allergic to latex. John is a pretty man: he's tall and slim, with green eyes and thick, honey-coloured hair, but the sneer that twists his pouty, pink lips is plain ugly. He asks me if I'm fucking joking.

'I carry my own condoms. Jesus.'

We arrive at the hotel, and he's already back-pedalling, insisting he's not a wanker, he's just had a long day, he promises. I roll my eyes when his back is turned.

John tells the front desk to send champagne to his room. Champagne makes me sick like nothing else, but who am I to turn down a free drink?

The room is nice: plush carpets, clean, mini-bar, king-size bed. I perch on a loveseat in the window and look out to the river while he complains about how long the champagne takes, and de-suits, removing his jacket, his tie, and unbuttoning his shirt to reveal a chest which must be waxed.

A knock at the door. He opens it wide enough to make sure the male member of staff can see me, and makes that member of staff open the bottle and fill our glasses, which have strawberries skewered on the rim.

John brings me a champagne flute, and I give him a condom.

'How big is this?' he asks, immediately, his nose wrinkled.

'It's just normal. I carry a big one?' A girl can dream. 'And a *trim* one, FYI.'

'I'll try the normal one… I'm on the *big* side of average, you see, so…'

'Do you need the big one, or not?'

He waggles his eyebrows, and undresses completely.

He does not need the big one. I swig heavily from my champagne flute, while he strokes his spectacularly average dick, like I'm supposed to be impressed. Eddie from Tesco, bless his heart, seems like more a trim kind of guy. But I'm no size queen. I'm a broad church.

It's funny to see John with his clothes off. His body is perfect. It doesn't do a lot for me. It's fussy, and fake, one of those display bodies, built for gym selfies and thirst-trap Instagram pages and Tinder profiles. Not unlike my own, I suppose. He has abs, and he's as waxed and buffed as I am. I've gotten so used to tummies and body hair and stringy limbs that I've almost forgotten there are men who look like this in real life. I've forgotten there are other Salad People who exist outside of glossy mags and Instagram. I wonder how many protein shakes he drinks, how many hours he spends at the gym. All that money, all that time, and I'm going to spend the next three and a half minutes thinking about some chubby, short-arse checkout boy. I snort, and I imagine him lusting after a Forbidden Planet shop girl, with dimply thighs and scabby lip rings.

The heart wants what it wants. I take off my clothes. Now my shoes are off he's a little taller than me. He points it out, says he has the upper hand. I duck away from his lips when he tries to kiss me on the mouth. I touch his stomach; there's no give at all, my fingers don't dent it. His thighs are hard, and slim. His arse doesn't look like it's been shrunk in the wash, at least, but I bet he's done a lot of squats to get it this way.

I kneel on the bed, tell him to go from behind. I don't want to look at him. I don't want to touch him. I want to bury my hands in the generous hotel pillows and pretend I'm grabbing a handful of pudgy boy-thigh. No foreplay. He runs a cursory hand down my side, he checks if I'm wet, then sticks it in. It stings. I haven't done this in a long time.

He huffs above me. I don't particularly want to look at him, but there's a big mirror on the wall. I see us both looking at ourselves. John is watching his dick go in and out of me, and I'm just staring at the girl in the mirror. The bored redhead and the plastic surgeon, pulling at the flesh of her flank. She looks posed, and so does he, like a little girl is doing something obscene with Barbie and Ken.

'Let's switch,' I say. He ignores me. 'Hey, let's switch.'

'Why? Am I keeping you awake?' he snarls. 'Didn't take you for a pillow princess.'

'Let me get on top,' I say. But he ignores me, and reaches around to touch me, and tells me to scream for him. It hurts. He hurts me on purpose. The pain makes me stick my face into the pillow and moan; makes my toes and my spine curl. I struggle. He yanks my head up, taking a merciful fistful of the hair growing from my scalp, rather than the Russian shit I paid £200 to get sewn in. I tell him, if he's not going to let me get on top, he could put his back into it. He asks me if I like it rough.

'Sure,' I say. 'Whatever.' That winds him up. I can see the veins bulging in his neck, his face turning angry red. I close my eyes, try to ignore the wet slap of skin on skin. I try to focus on the abstract, on the tangle of pleasure and pain. I think about Eddie from Tesco. I think about shooting him without a mask. I think about his eyes filling up, his face going puce because my hands are around his neck. I think about filming it. I think about watching the film. I think about putting my fingers in his mouth.

I come, but I'm quiet about it, glad not to give John the satisfaction of a scream. He slaps my side, and gloats, and I smear lipstick and mascara all over the hotel pillows. He goes limp on top of me a moment later.

'Off,' I snap. He rolls over, and snuggles into his crisp, hotel bed, cuddling up with the quilt when I stand, immediately dressing. He prattles on about how much fun I am, how he likes a little play-acting, all the while yawning, curling and uncurling his toes like a cat relaxing in a sun puddle.

'I'm in Newcastle for a few days. My phone's on the bedside table,' he says, yawning. 'Call your cab from my Uber account, and stick your number in my contacts, yeah?'

I try to tell him that I can pay for my own cab – I don't want to give him my address – but he's asleep. Out cold. I shout, but he doesn't stir.

'I wanted to fucking switch,' I say, and I throw a champagne glass at the wall behind the bed. It shatters, tiny shards landing all over the hotel room.

Three pieces in his face: cheek, forehead, eye. He doesn't move. His chest rises and falls steadily, while little rivets of blood leak from the wounds.

I take some photos. Just on my phone.

And then I'm in the taxi. Thinking, thinking: did I enjoy that? Did I even properly consent to that? Do I care? I haven't been raped before. Well, I've never been *raped* raped: no bag over my head, no knife to my throat while I screamed and fought. Nothing *traumatic*. Even Will the other week, that was nothing. But it's all the little shit. He wouldn't switch; I passed out; I don't remember it; he's way older than me. *Do you like it rough?* I think so. I think I must. Men *are* rough, aren't they? Have I always had a taste for rough stuff, or did I acquire that? In the back of Lesley's car, on the floor of a friend's house, half-conscious with my underwear around my ankles? Was it my idea to have him hurt me, or did he just let me think it was?

And that gets sewn into them young, doesn't it? Violence. I've had to go to some fairly extreme measures to defend myself.

I used to think about older men, even before Lesley. I had an imaginary sugar daddy; I had affairs in my head with actors and musicians thrice my age; I had intentional and prolonged eye-contact with my dad's friends. Whether I'm in control or losing it, I've always had a power thing, I think.

I never do things like this with women. I never did anything like this with Frank.

There's a soft part of your brain. A place where you're still just a child. Once someone's poked the soft spot, the dent doesn't go away. Like sticking your fingers in wet concrete.

I catch my reflection in the wing mirror. There she is, with her smudged eyeliner and her messy hair, the tracks of her hair extensions on display, lipstick on the tip of her nose and her chin. She's wet concrete gone hard, full of dents, reshaped into this *thing*, which burps and pisses and has to be washed and fed and fucked.

I look in the mirror and think: who the fuck is that? Who is she?

I finish telling all of this to the Uber driver. He asks me if I'm okay.

● ● ●

Hi there,

It's been a while! I've been doing some exhibition prep - but I have some experimental stuff you might be interested in. I've been

playing with effect makeup, very pretty guy,
some fake glass in his face. Shot on iPhone,
for the gritty realistic effect. Interested
at all? I've attached one, could send the
whole set if you like it. On the house!
Best,
Irina.

My Darling,
How wonderful it is to hear from you.
Please do send the whole set, as a student
of classical beauty, this man's physique and
face are highly pleasing to me.
Only, I don't see any glass? Perhaps this
is later on in the set?
I do enjoy a little 'gore' as the kids say,
and I'd be very interested to see it.
Faithfully,
B

He's right. I scroll through every photograph I took of
'John' yesterday, and there's no glass. Certainly not in his
face, and nowhere to be seen in the general vicinity. I zoom,
and fiddle with the contrast, the lighting – none. No glass,
no blood, just dewy, plump skin.

Hey!
You're right! I sent you a test shot without
the makeup by mistake. The set is showing up
on my phone, but won't transfer to my laptop,
attach to emails, or even upload to dropbox

:(Looks like it might be corrupted. I've attached what I have, unfortunately all test shots. Sorry to get your hopes up there. Serves me right for fannying on with my phone instead of just using a proper camera.

Best,

Irina

Irina,

Not to worry. The test shots are very lovely.

I have sent 100 GBP via your paypal as a tip! Buy yourself something nice.

Faithfully,

B

● ● ●

Hey stranger.

Been a while.

Come over.

Tracked down a download of In a Glass Cage with the right subs.

You'll hate it.

● ● ●

It's Saturday. I wake up with an overwhelming feeling of dread, then remember I won't be going to work this evening. Thank God It's Sabbatical.

I get up, I drink a litre of water, I do my press-ups, my sit-ups, and a Pilates video. Then I shower and do my skincare stuff. Double cleanse, scrub, toner, sheet mask, eye cream, moisturiser, and a primer with an SPF even though I'm not sure I'll go out today.

I lounge on the sofa and make my way through a cafetière while I watch a repeat of *The Jeremy Kyle Show*. A guilty-looking teen mother says she's very confident the father of her two-month-old is her boyfriend, but it also might be his cousin.

It's neither of them. With a shrug, she guesses there are three, maybe four, additional potential fathers. Insisting that she is simply very popular with the lads.

'That Kelis song – do you know it?' she asks Jeremy. He does not. 'The Milkshake one. That's me, that is.'

'Same,' I say.

I stick on the second *August Underground* film when Jeremy Kyle is finished, just for background noise, and start properly going through the photos of Eddie from Tesco. I woke up at, like, two today, and it's gone five now. I'm getting to the point where I think I need to reset my sleeping pattern. I'll sit up for a full twenty-four hours, then sleep for a full twenty-four hours, and wake up at seven a.m., and be a day-time person again. My empty stomach churns, but I ignore it, driving my forearm into my belly to stop the gurgling.

I check my phone. A string of texts from an unknown number, and I panic that I may have left the plastic surgeon my number, even though I know I didn't. There's nothing from Flo. There's a text from Ryan asking if I can drop in for a shift, and a text from my mam asking me if I'm alive. Mam says she saw some of the photos from my night out last week and has some concerns about the outfit I'm wearing. She calls me *mutton dressed as lamb*.

Im 28.

Yeah 29 in nov and b4 you know it

Ur 30

And then u cant just go out wearing lace and plastic mini skirts

And you might think u look fine but ppl who know your age will look @ u and think mutton

I appreciate your concern.

More texts come through: I'm also too skinny, and I look like I'm going to snap in the middle and I should think about packing on a few pounds because being so thin is very aging around the face. And Flo looks fat; do I only keep Flo around so I look skinnier? Remember when Flo used to be a skinny little thing? Mam says skinny girls like that never learn to watch their weight, when their metabolism changes as they age, they pile it on.

I reply to her various updates with a mixture of thumbs up and clapping emojis. She keeps complaining about her friend with cancer. She's recently been diagnosed terminal, and apparently will not stop posting about it on Facebook. Mam says she's always been an attention-seeker.

Wow jealous I am longing for death's sweet release r/n, I type. And then I delete it and replace it with that fucking crying-laughing face that old people use when they're being racist on social media.

The messages from the unknown number are, mercifully, not from the plastic surgeon.

Hey its Eddie, frm Tesco/the other day?

Your business card has your mobile number on it sorry if this is weird

Any way how are you? How are my photographs? Hope i didnt waste your time the other day.

I know its shit for you not to shoot my face.

You mentioned you were into j-horror and pink films and stuff?

Have you seen All Night Long? A friend recced it to me and loaned me a copy.we could watch it together? Maybe tonight if you're not busy. Im working till 7.

I ignore these. I replied quickly to his first couple of emails, and I want to keep him on his toes.

I look at his photo on my laptop screen, still clothed in the one I have open in Photoshop. It's a candid shot of him contemplating the rabbit head. My stomach gurgles again.

I close my laptop and get up to check my face in the mirror, making sure I'm free of lines, and pimples, and slap on a BB cream for a little coverage. Tinted eyebrows, good skin and dyed, extended eyelashes cover the rest. I brush my hair. I put on a cute T-shirt, and the only pair of jeans I own. I look comfy. I don't feel comfy. I took them in at the waist when I bought them because they're a twelve and I had about four inches of bagging on my stomach. But I went a little too far and (hearing my mother's voice ringing in my ear) I'm pushing it with them – the button will leave a deep, red mark on my belly. I stick on my only pair of trainers, too, and walk to Tesco, and feign surprise when I see him. He goes red. I half-wave, and ignore him, and grab a bag of spinach, a cucumber and some peppers. I spend an inordinate amount of time bending down near the checkouts to look at the magazines. I grab *Vogue*, and I go over to the till, where he smiles, and says 'Hi!' slightly too loudly.

'Oh, hang on,' I say, and I grab two bottles of red, while he scans my other purchases.

'Do you have any ID there, young lady?' he says, then chuckles. I make a face at him. 'Sorry.' It takes a moment for the wine to scan. 'Stocking up?'

'Sort of. Some guy I met the other night might be coming over, I don't know. Better to have it and not need it, eh?'

'Oh,' he says. 'Hey… Feel free to tell me I'm crossing a line, here, but…' He clears his throat. 'Ah, never mind.'

'Come on. What's up?'

'Just… It's funny you came in, because… Have you checked your phone?'

I raise my eyebrows and pull my phone from my pocket. I tell him I didn't see his texts, that I've been busy all day.

'If you already have, like… a date, though… I was just… You know. You mentioned you liked, like, Pink movies and J-horror and I just picked up—'

'*All Night Long*. Just read it.' I shrug. 'I've seen one through three already.'

'That's fine. I understand you're too busy.'

'Have you seen *In a Glass Cage*? It's Spanish,' I say. 'It's pretty hardcore – we could watch that instead.' It just comes out. He looks so wounded, and he's trying so hard not to, and then he lights up. I see that gap between his teeth, and his dimples, and I melt.

It'll be fine, just this once. What's the worst that could happen, you know?

'Oh. No. I mean... I'm not really into... I just like Japanese stuff, I guess. But um...' He brightens. 'So, you want to come over?'

'Yeah, sure. What time do you finish?'

He finishes at seven. I say that's fine and tell him to come get me once he's finished his shift. I tell him I have a laptop full of shit, and I'll just bring that. That way he can look at his photos, too. When I leave, I regret not asking for a second shopping bag, as the wine bottles clank together dangerously and tug at the flimsy plastic handles of this so-called bag for life. 10p, fucking liberty.

I have an hour and a half to get ready by the time I get back. I eat half the cucumber, and half a tin of tuna, and one of the peppers like it's an apple. I brush my teeth till my gums bleed. I shower again and shave my bikini line. I am too cavalier with the razor and almost bite through my tongue when I nick the left lip of my cunt.

I drop the razor. I gather myself, take a deep breath and watch a trickle of blood run down the inside of my leg and down the plughole, before I pick the razor up again. I finish my bikini line and give my legs and armpits a once over before climbing out of the shower to attending to my cut, pressing a lump of toilet tissue to it, and watching it slowly soak through with blood. I swear to myself. I smack the sink with my palm and grit my teeth.

I top up my face with BB cream, and put on a little mascara, not wanting to look like I've made an effort, and pack an overnight bag. I put on matching underwear: pink and frilly, because he seems like the kind of boy who probably likes women in pink, frilly things. I put my jeans back on and replace the T-shirt with a crop-top, also pink, with shiny buttons, and little puffy sleeves, cut in a way that shows off my cleavage and my neck, but not in an obvious way.

I look soft. I can look hard, if I'm not careful. Hard and cold and intimidating. I put my hand on my neck, and squeeze it, looking at myself in the mirror as I do. I play with my hair, putting it up, taking it down, brushing it, tossing it around.

I get stuck there, for a while.

The doorbell rings. I make him wait as I pack my laptop and my charger into my backpack. Unable to tolerate the thought of flat shoes, I slip on a pair of baby pink stilettos, answering the door as I put them on.

'Hey,' I say. 'Jesus Christ, mate, is that your car?'

He looks over his shoulder at a battered, baby blue Micra.

'I'm saving for a new one,' he says.

'It looks like a toddler's shoe,' I say.

'It's my mum's old car.' A little snappy, but then he pads it with a laugh, an admission that it's awful.

'I used to have my dad's old BMW,' I tell him, as I clop towards his stupid little car. 'But I sold it. Living so close to town and stuff,' I say.

'Yeah, insurance is a killer. I only keep this because my parents live all the way up in Amble and they'd go crackers if I didn't visit. It's good to have the quick escape, you know?'

I hum, and get in the passenger's side, my knees knocking against the glovebox. He joins me in the car, and puts the seat back for me.

We drive to his, which is in Walker. The journey takes five minutes longer than it should because he drives down the Coast Road instead of going down past the Biscuit Factory. I tell him as much, and he shrugs, and says he doesn't know Jesmond very well. But he works here. Does he drive up the Coast Road every day? How much petrol has he wasted on that five extra minutes?

We arrive at his. A big detached house which, he explains, has been split into two flats. He lives on the top floor, above an elderly woman who bangs her ceiling with a broom if he watches telly past nine p.m.

'It's not as nice as your house, but, you know, it does me,' he says, turning around on the stairs to smile at me. He lets me in his front door, and I am met by the smell of bachelorhood. Unhoovered carpets, unaired rooms and unbleached surfaces. Immediately, I open a window.

'You should get some scented candles in here,' I say. The air is clammy and stale. 'Do you have a fan?'

'In my bedroom. I'll get it in a second,' he says. He seems to notice my nose wrinkling as I run my eyes over his dusty telly and PlayStation. 'Sorry. I guess... I mean, especially compared to yours, it's a bit minging in here.' He chews his lip. 'Do you want me to hoover?' Before I can answer: 'I'll hoover, and I'll get the fan, just, hang on. Have a look round, if you like.'

He hoovers. I look in his bedroom. It is juvenile, but neat. If you told me this was the recently tidied bedroom of a thirteen-year-old, I'd believe you.

The walls are lined with bookshelves that seem to exclusively contain manga, graphic novels and comic books. There are figurines on his windowsill, and he has that *Akira* poster that everyone has, as well as a Bruce Lee poster, and a bunch of pictures of some idol girl group. There are stickers on the headboard of his bed. I imagine grabbing the headboard and feeling stickers under my palms.

I look closely at the manga. He's filed all his porn onto the bottom shelf, as if he hoped no one would bother to bend down and look there.

He catches me with my nose in a comic where, I gather, the protagonist is this boy who has been purchased by a MILF who dresses him as a maid and keeps him trapped in her house. I flip through and stop at a double-page spread of the MILF sitting on the boy-maid's face. The proportions are bad, but the perspective is worse. Everyone's hands are huge, and the MILF character's back is twisted in a bizarre shape, so you can see her breasts and her backside at the same time. I snort.

'What are you doing?' asks Eddie from Tesco. I turn the comic round and show him.

'Being nosy,' I say. 'The art in this one is shockingly shit.'

'Did you look at anything else?'

'No. Why, do you have anything worse?' He does. I can tell by the look on his face. I stick the manga back on the shelf, and my knees click when I get up. I talk before he answers. 'Thanks for hoovering.'

'It's fine,' he says. He looks at me for a while, either waiting for me to apologise, or too mortified to speak. 'Are you hungry?'

'Not really. I'll have a drink, though.'

'I picked up some wine? Red, because… you bought red before. I don't really drink but I got myself a couple of beers.'

'What? And you're going to watch me drink a bottle of wine alone?' I roll my eyes, grab his fan, and brush past him as I head into a freshly hoovered living room, and plop onto the sofa. 'You're trying to get me drunk.'

'No! No, I just…'

'Well, have a glass of wine, then. Make it fair.'

He doesn't own wine glasses (I don't know what I expected) so I drink out of a small plastic tumbler, and watch him do the same, wrinkling his nose with every sip. He chatters. He doesn't really like wine, he doesn't really drink, he feels like a *proper grown-up* with this red. I make him have another before he switches to beer.

'Can I ask you something?' His eyes are big, and brown, like a cow's.

'No.' He looks stricken. 'I'm joking. Ask.'

'When we met at the coffee shop, you asked me why I wanted to do this. But… Why me?' he asks. 'I mean, like… Why are you interested in me? For photographs, for anything?'

I knock back the rest of my wine and mull it over. There are a few possible answers: I like curly hair; I like weak men; you're well behaved.

'You're really cute,' I say. He doesn't believe me. 'You are! Honestly, I can't believe you're single.' I smile. I'm half telling the truth – he seems like the kind of man whose girlfriends are perpetually younger than him. Like he dates fourteen-year-olds when he's seventeen, eighteen-year-olds when he's twenty-five – never enough that it's illegal but enough that it's weird. I can also see him with some bossy, frumpy pony-club type or an adult-emo with a dated haircut and a lot of Joker merch. He smiles, just a small smile, but then it drops, and he starts chewing his fingers.

'Okay,' he says. 'If you say so.'

I ask him to show me his camera. He gets it for me, apologising as he does, because it's *just a hobby*, and it's his *brother's old camera*, and it's *not very good*, and neither is he. It's a digital Nikon, maybe five years old. I'm a Canon girl, myself, and I tell him, prompting another apology. I flip it on, and immediately go to his photographs. A lot of squirrels, in black and white, and macro shots of leaves. There's a shot of the Serpentine Sackler Gallery, so he must have taken these on a trip to London. They're all a bit too dark. Like he's tried to do something with the settings, but he's just cocked-up the exposure instead.

'This is Hyde Park,' I say. He nods. 'I used to live in London,' I say.

'I know. Your website says you went to Central Saint Martins and the Royal College? Amir – my brother – did London College of Communication. That's like, the same uni group thing as Saint Martins. Isn't it?'

'Yeah. The LCC photography course always read as really commercial. Your brother does, like, photos of food and stuff, doesn't he?' And the checkout boy nods. 'Mmm. I couldn't do that. I mean, obviously I've done my share of freelance commercial stuff, but usually it's fashion photography, so you get a lot more artistic freedom.'

'Yeah, well.' He shrugs. 'It pays the bills for him, I s'pose.'

'My work pays my bills,' I say. 'Not having a go, I'm just saying, like, I couldn't do that. And, like, fine art photography can be very lucrative. So, you *can* make money and have some integrity at the same time.'

'He hasn't… *sold out* or anything it's just… his job.'

It's more than just a job, I think. But I realise I'm being hostile. He's frowning at me, so I relax my face, smile, shrug.

Hey, if he wants to take photos of M&S roast chickens, and he's good with that, then whatever.

'Do food photographers really microwave tampons to make the food look like it's steaming? Like, does your brother do that?' I ask. Eddie from Tesco colours at the mention of tampons.

'Erm… If he has, he's never mentioned it.'

'Ask him for me.'

'Okay.'

There's a photo of the back half of a dead rat on his camera. Still in Hyde Park, I think, next to a clump of dandelions. Just its foot, its tail, with a clump of flies bunched at the edges of its flesh. It's good. Well composed, and there's the rat, the flies, the dandelions: all pests, all living and dying together. It's also a bit A-level, but it's like… edgy A-level, like you see that sketchbook and you think, *aye I'd give this a B, that'd be fair.*

'This one isn't bad,' I say. I turn the camera to him. 'It's the first one where the exposure's right.'

'Ah. Amir took that one. He fixed the settings on it for me. He said I'd messed up the aperture, or something.' He looks embarrassed, again. 'It's… stupid. I wanted it to be high contrast, so I… fiddled around with it, and I didn't really know what I was doing. I'm a bit frightened to touch it now, to be honest.'

The rest of the photos are fine. A few more in the park, then a portrait of a man who looks like Eddie from Tesco, but a little older and quite a lot bigger. Bigger nose, bigger shoulders and, overall, not quite as good looking; he's missing the cleft chin, the dimples, the freckles. Just a normal alright-looking bloke – he wouldn't turn my head. Amir has a better haircut than his brother, though, it must be said.

'Is this your brother?' I ask. 'Is he quite tall? He looks big.'

'Yeah, he's over six foot, actually.' Eddie from Tesco clears his throat, shoulders hunching up to his ears. I watch his hands clench and unclench. He's thinking giving me the camera was a mistake – that I prefer his brother now. I've seen Flo look like this before. She'll introduce me to someone, then I'll watch her get stiff and sad out of the corner of my eye, because now she's the Ugly Friend.

'Genetics are a funny thing, aren't they?' I say. 'My mam's only about five foot tall.'

'Yeah… Our mum is tiny, too. I always used to say, when I was a kid, I used to say that Amir shouldn't pick on me, because I'd be bigger than him one day and like… it just never happened,' he says, forcing a laugh. 'He still picks me up in front of people.' He cringes. 'I don't know why I told you that.'

I smile. I go to tell him it's okay, *it's cute*, even.

Then he says: 'Do you think you could pick me up?' His voice cracks. 'Not in a *weird* way, just…' I make a face at him. 'That was stupid. A stupid joke.'

I smile at him, and I think I do it wrong, because he shrinks like I'm glaring, or staring, and there is a long, heavy silence. I forget to keep smiling, because I'm watching him watch me. His eyes dart around, and he stammers, like he wants to speak but can't. He mustn't like being looked at, but he stares at me all the time. I like looking at him.

'We'll look at your pictures,' I say. He balks.

'Oh. No thank you.'

'You should look at them. They're good.' I open my laptop and pull up his photos, cycling through them. He flinches, now avoiding both my eye and the laptop, eyes up to the ceiling.

'I'm sure they're great! I'm sure they're really great. You took them, after all; they must be really good. They're just embarrassing. It's embarrassing to see photos of yourself. Photos like… that.' He apologises. He tells me he's shy. He's not used to it. He hates looking at photos of himself. I don't get it. I tell him I don't get it, that he's talking shite.

'Come on, look.' I put the MacBook on his lap.

He looks. When he looks away, I tap the screen with my nails. I tell him I've barely deleted any; I like them so much that I can't choose favourites.

'On your website, I noticed you're in some of the photos. Your hands, and your shoes and stuff…' He says. 'Could we take some like that? Next time? I think I'd like that.'

'You're into that shit, are you?'

'Oh. No. Just for the art. I think those are your most dynamic photographs.'

'Right.' I snort. 'So, what was that comic all about?'

'It's actually part of a series? Um… The plot is a whole commentary on exploitative labour and sexual harassment, and the way that society devalues service workers, actually…' When he sees that I'm smirking, he raises his voice a bit. 'It's not a sex thing. I can have some… *explicit manga*, it doesn't have to be a sex thing. Like… I mean, your photos. You can't want to… every single model you shoot, can you? You'll just pick some because they're best for the idea you have, or whatever, you know?'

'Are you asking me if I want to fuck every model I use?' I shrug. 'Well, sort of. Why else would I want to take their photos?'

Eddie from Tesco looks horrified. Like the possibility was so absurd, he hadn't even considered it. He asks, '*All of them?!*' like I've actually fucked them, or something, like my artistic practice is this non-stop, record-breaking, Annabel-Chong-style gangbang. The checkout boy wrinkles his nose. I try to work out what that means: if he's disgusted, or if his ego is a little bruised.

'Do you actually think I sleep with them? *All of them?!*' I ask, mocking his intonation from before. He screws up his mouth, and shakes his head, shoulders hunching up as he tries to edge away from me, to take me out of his personal bubble.

I roll my eyes, and I explain to him that I generally don't shit where I eat. Sexuality is obviously important in my work, and there needs to be chemistry, but that doesn't mean I'm opening my legs as soon as I pop off my lens cap.

'I'm sorry,' says Eddie from Tesco. 'I made an assumption. Stupid. Really stupid.' He wriggles on the sofa, going red again. I don't think I've ever seen anyone blush this much, and then I remember when my mother went through menopause. I remember her hot flushes, her face turning beet red at the drop of a hat; ripping off her coat on the high street in January and rubbing ice on her chest in restaurants.

'Stop blushing,' I say. He can't help it, he whimpers, like a kicked dog. I'm irritated. I'm so annoyed I can feel it in the pit of my gut. My cunt clenches like a fist. I snap my laptop shut and place it on his grubby coffee table. 'What assumption did you make?'

'I thought… I suppose I thought you liked me. I didn't realise that was part of it with everyone.' He thought he was special. His lip trembles. Is he going to cry?

He's wringing his hands, and even though he's looking down at the floor I can tell he's grimacing. He glances at me, his eye line slipping into its comfortable rhythm, darting between my cleavage, my face and the floor while he waits for me to say something else – to confirm or deny that I *like* him. I let the words hang between us, like a body.

'Maybe I do,' I say. He looks at me, properly. Not in the eye, but in the face, at least. He leans in, lips puckered, eyes closed, and I lean back. When he doesn't find my lips, he opens his eyes. 'Not on the mouth,' I tell him. I get off the couch, and nod for him to follow. 'Bring the camera.' I hear him scrambling behind me. I poke my head into his bedroom: the figurines, the idol posters. 'Actually, I can't do it with all those skinny Japanese girls looking at me. We'll stay here.' I march back into the living room, finally kicking off my shoes.

'They're Korean.'

'Same thing,' I say. 'I'm allergic to latex, FYI.' I direct him to my purse in my backpack, where he finds the latex-free condoms, in a variety of sizes.

'How did you find that out?' he asks. 'That you're allergic.'

'The hard way.'

He looks a little offended by the 'trim' packet, and I tell him not to take it personally, that I always carry them, that you never know. 'Trim' is placed to one side, and 'King' and 'King XL' are considered. I always wonder why they don't do condoms like cup sizes – A, B, C – rather than letting people guess what size they are based on what euphemism they feel most appropriately describes their dick. *I know I'm not Trim — but am I King-sized? Could I even be King XL if the next one after Trim is King? What if this is a big brand? Maybe I am Trim after all?*

'Erm,' he says. 'Which one is just… the normal one?'

'Left hand,' I say.

'Cool,' he says. *'Cool, cool, cool.'*

I pick up his camera while he juggles johnnies. I take his picture. The flash is off, so he doesn't even notice. He stops looking at the condom and starts looking at me. Staring. 'What?'

'You're so pretty,' he says.

'I know.'

'I mean you're like… You're properly beautiful, aren't you?'

'I know,' I say. I run a hand through my hair and take another photo of him. He asks if he can have a go, if he can take my picture. I tell him to take off his clothes. I tell him not to kiss me on the mouth. I tell him not to pull my hair. I tell him I hate spit, that he shouldn't lick me; that I only like to be on top and I don't like talking. He nods, tripping out of his jeans.

'Anything you want.'

I don't think I'm drunk enough for this. Watching him stretch out on his grotty couch with his underwear still on and poorly disguised panic on his face, I'm wondering if this was a bad idea. I know it's a bad idea. It's a cheeseburger, and me sticking my fingers down my throat in an hour.

I unbutton my jeans, and it takes me a while to pull them off. I take off my shirt, and I stand in the middle of the living room, and stare into space while I think for a moment. I hear a bell. I twist my neck.

'What's wrong?' He asks. I tell him nothing. I tell him to lie down on the floor, because we won't both fit on the couch. He lies down next to his coffee table, and I stand over him. He stares up at me with big, grateful eyes. 'It's been a while,' he says. *No shit.*

I take off my underwear, he shuffles out of his briefs, and I perch on the sofa and watch him fiddle about with the condom for longer than he should. I don't help, I just watch, and when he's done, I straddle him. He tries to put it in me and misses, mashing the blunt head of his dick into my thighs before I smack his hand away and guide it in myself. I tell him not to move, though I doubt he could, with my weight on his hips. He's breathing heavily, his eyes shut tight. I run my hand up his chest, through the hair, and settle my palm on his neck. I squeeze it. I squeeze it hard, with both hands, and I let go when he turns purple.

'Um,' he says.

'Just try it,' I say. Then I shush him. I shush him, and I squeeze his neck again, moving my hips, because I feel him going soft inside of me. He squeaks, and he gurgles, and I let go when he bats at my wrists. He takes great gulps of air, and splutters, and doesn't fight when I start choking him again. I can feel him twitching; I can feel the sharp knot of his Adam's apple wriggling against my palm.

He's small, purple, stiff, and silent. There's a moment when I think I might have knocked him out, but his eyes flutter back open as soon as I let go. He starts coughing, and I keep riding him. I slap his cheek.

'Hey. You good?' I ask. He nods, still coughing. 'Gimme a thumbs up.' I get a thumbs up. I've been moving hard and fast enough that we've travelled across the living room. The checkout boy's head is now up by his radiator, and my knees are stinging. His eyes are streaming. The shaky, sudden breath he takes could be a cough, or a sob. When I go to grab his neck again, he grabs my wrists, and pushes them away, and slaps my hands. I smack his face. He could be lifting his hips to meet mine, or he could be trying to throw me off. He's still hard. He's crying and coughing.

'Please get off,' he says. He wipes his eyes on the back of his wrists, and shoves me. I lose my balance. We both hiss when he slips out of me, and I bang my tailbone on the floor.

'Ow!' I snap. 'You said you were good. You... The thumbs up, and everything!'

'I'm sorry,' he snivels. He hugs his knees to his chest. 'I'm sorry. I thought I was fine, but I wasn't. I'm sorry. Don't... Please don't hate me.' I'm getting up to grab my underwear, and he asks me to come back, catching my leg with his little hand. 'Please? I'm sorry. Come back.' So, I come back, and I sit next to him on the floor. 'I'm sorry.' He grabs my breast with one hand, and moves around, so he can slip his fingers between the lips of my cunt. 'I'm sorry.' I try to remember his face while it was purple and tune out the sound of his snotty nose by my ear. 'I just want you to feel good,' he says. 'Is this good?' The angle is awkward, and I'm embarrassed for him, but I nod. Despite myself, I nod. 'You're beautiful,' he says.

He pets my hair when I finish. I hate it. I pull back, clearing my throat, and making a successful grab for my underwear this time.

While I'm dressing, he's all like, *so do you want to get pizza, do you want another drink,* he stands in the kitchen and wipes off his dick with a tea towel, and dumps a filled condom in the bin. I didn't notice him come.

'You must be hungry. I'm starving,' he says.

'Nah.' I clear my throat again. 'I might go?'

'Oh. Okay,' he says. He's washing his hands. 'I could drive you home?'

'I'm good,' I say.

●●●

The Uber driver agrees that I've had a weird evening, and while I'm drafting a post-mortem to send to Flo, I get a few texts from Eddie from Tesco.

Hey!

Hope you're okay.

Sorry it got weird.

The more you apologise the weirder it gets.

Okay.

I don't know what to say because I feel like I should be apologising.

Thank you?

FRANK

I've been putting off going back to the archive because I know which bit is next. I get an email from Jamie with a soft deadline when I tell her I've been too busy to go through my archives in full. *As long as you've got some bits to us by September, it's fine!*

I can see myself putting it off – dragging it out to the last minute, so I get myself halfway down a bottle of red, then crack on. The box for most of second and third year of uni is next, which means I have to go through Frank's box. I give up on my glass and drink straight from the bottle.

An email. I pull my hand from the box lid, and lunge for my phone.

```
Dear Ms Sturges,
My name is Dennis. You gave me your card
on the bus around three weeks ago. I have
looked at your portfolio and I am interested
in being involved with your work. Due to
your prolificacy, and the fact you mentioned
you scout lots of men a week in your bio - I
have attached an image of myself to jog your
memory.
Kind regards,
Dennis
```

'Ms Sturges' is oddly formal. And PC. I use Miss, personally, because Ms always has a 'divorced thirty-five-year-old boho-chic cat-lady' smell to it.

To my surprise, the attached photo is not a dick pic.

It is a charming image of an older man – a *suit* – smiling shyly and standing against a plain white wall. The photo is slightly out of focus and taken with a low-spec front-facing smartphone camera. He has stubble, greying hair and what I assume is a Dad Bod hiding under that shirt. He has one dimple and kind of a domesticated, northern Jon Hamm look to him. I have no memory of him. I've always taken a scattergun approach to scouting, and it's rare for me to remember them, unless they contact me immediately.

I'm almost disappointed by how brief the email is. It doesn't require a long response, so I just send a boilerplate email.

```
Good Evening Dennis,
Of course I remember you. Attached is
```

my address, as well as parking and public
transport information. Are evenings and
weekends best for you? If so - I am free all
week.

    Irina

I think he'll chicken out. Suits always do.

I've lost steam. The bottle is empty, and a new one is
uncorked before I break into the boxes.

At first glance, the pictures of Frank actually don't stick
out at all, except for being a tad more conservative than my
output at the time.

You know how every uni has one of *those* lecturers. Like,
they step in front of a PowerPoint presentation and open
their mouth, and you can hear knickers dropping all over
the lecture theatre.

That was Frank. *Frank Steel*. Not her real name, obviously.
Christened Francesca Leigh, she dropped her much-loathed
parents' surname in favour of something she just *liked the
sound of*, paired with her preferred masculine moniker.

She was from Manchester – a guest lecturer they wheeled
in once or twice a term to tell us about feminist photography
and Judith Butler and queer theory and shit. I have a distinct
memory of her 'Introduction to Michel Foucault' lecture,
writing 'I'd let her *Discipline and Punish* me' in my notebook.
She'd occasionally come in for a few days to deliver one-to-
one tutorials. You had to sign up for them – spots always
went in a flash. I'd wanted one since first year but didn't
get one till January of second. I bragged, really rubbed it in
to whoever would listen. Weird for me. Even me at twenty-
one, and I was weird at twenty-one.

Frank had that effect, though. She was shorter than me but not short, she was slim and flat-chested, with solid, boyish shoulders. Very butch — not *Stone Butch Blues* butch, but getting there. She looked a bit like James Dean, and she leant into it hard. Always in Levi's and biker boots and a leather jacket. I always thought she was too pretty to properly pull it off, though. She had these huge eyes, big and blue, with eyelashes so long they looked fake, like a doll. I'd try and get her to wear makeup, sometimes, but she'd always get annoyed with me. Frank is the only woman I regularly photographed.

She started it.

I went in for this tutorial. I remember it being first thing on a Tuesday morning, and I'd gotten up at seven a.m. to do my hair and makeup. She looked me up and down and said, 'Christ, you're tarted up for this, aren't you?'

I was wearing this baby-blue summer dress, and a beehive, with my hair loose and curled. I had on that heavy sixties eye makeup I was obsessed with at the time. I was mortified – men don't usually clock this shit, do they? But she did.

I told her I had a date that afternoon, and she told me I looked like Priscilla Presley on her wedding day, if she was ginger. I think I'd been aiming for more of a Brigitte Bardot thing, but I told her I'd take that.

She sort of negged me. She looked at *What would you do to be my boyfriend?* and told me it was an incredibly cruel piece of work. She said my other photographs had a pervy feel, and she was almost impressed that such a young woman would come out with something this nasty. She said, based on both the work and my writing around it, I had a contemptuous attitude towards my models. I clearly saw them as interchangeable, disposable objects. She asked me if I hated men, or if I liked men and hated that I liked them so much.

'At the end of the day, Irene,' she'd said, 'and stop me if this is too personal… you're not making art here; you're making porn. And you know what? I think it's interesting to see this kind of work from a young woman. But you could be so much better than this. Fresher. The world doesn't need more nasty, voyeuristic photography, does it?' And she went off on one for a bit about empathy – had I looked at Arbus or Mapplethorpe? Or any other photographers who looked at sexuality and strangers with a sensitive lens. Did I exclusively consume the photography of heterosexual men? Because that's what it looked like to Frank.

'Have you ever modelled, Irene?' And then she snorted at herself. 'I mean, look at you. Of course you have.'

I told her I hadn't. She looked genuinely surprised. To this day, I have no idea if she was pulling my dick or not. I told her I'd done it casually, for friends, but no agencies would take me, that I was too big to be a normal model, but too skinny for plus size. There was probably glamour and fetish stuff I could do, but…

She waved her hand to stop me, apologising if she'd touched a nerve. I felt stupid.

'I think it'd really help you empathise with your subjects if you did some more modelling yourself. In fact…'

I have her business card glued into my sketchbook. She took one out of her wallet and handed it to me. She told me about her latest project – photographing LGBT northerners transplanted to London. She needed more femmes. She assumed I was straight, from my photos, but told me with a wink, 'What the gays don't know won't hurt them.'

I stuttered; I'd been with women, I just didn't make a big deal about it. Frank cut me off and told me not to pull a muscle.

So, I turn up at her studio in Hackney about a week later, after bragging about it to anyone who'd listen. She told me to bring makeup but arrive barefaced. Bring a couple of my favourite outfits, but come in something basic. So, I did. I wore the only pair of jeans I owned at the time and a plain T-shirt. I felt like an absolute fucking clip, and rode the Overground with my head down. I didn't turn heads, or get cat-called at all, and that put me in a foul mood. It's annoying when it happens, but when you get used to it and it doesn't happen – that feels worse.

When you're that age, it takes a lot to make you feel young – or to realise how young you are – and I spent the whole journey, the whole walk to her studio, feeling silly, trying to impress my fucking teacher. My nails and thumbs were bitten bloody by the time I actually got to Frank's studio, and I had a face like a smacked arse. That's what Frank said, when she let me in. She asked me if I was okay, and I snapped something about how I *hate* being dressed down, and I *hate* going out without makeup on.

She laughed at me, and said I looked fine.

The first set of pictures in this box are pictures Frank took of me. I made her give me copies, and I bought this scrapbook with black pages to glue them into. First picture, I'm just standing in the jeans, the T-shirt, no makeup. My hands are by my sides, and I'm staring down the lens, trying to look anything but uncomfortable. I think I was aiming for defiant, but I landed on stiff and weird. Jesus. That face. I trace the line of my skull with a long, acrylic fingernail. I still have puppy fat on my cheeks. I hadn't quite filled out around the hips, either, so I'm all limbs, all legs and arms and ribs with these disproportionately large tits that look like someone stuck them on with an ice cream scoop.

Frank had me get changed, and watched me while I dressed, and told me I looked like something a little boy drew in the back of his notebook.

I finally flip the page. The next shot I'm wearing this dress I used to love. This horrible nylon, A-line mini dress. Vintage, bright pink – it clashed with my hair and squashed my chest. I'm all legs in it, with these nasty white platform boots, plasticky and skintight. Frank asked me, 'Do you only wear this retro shit?' so I'm sneering at her in the next picture. Frank was dry. I've never had much of a sense of humour. I took the dress off. I shrugged at her, and asked her if she was happy, like a child snapping at her mother.

'I was just joking, Irene,' she said. And then she fired off a self-deprecating quip about how she goes to Topman with a photo of Marlon Brando for reference, her big white teeth flashing like her camera. On the next page I'm pouting in my conspicuously matching underwear, arms folded over my chest, my mouth half open because I was in the middle of telling her my name was *Irina*, not Irene.

The next picture ended up in a gallery when she showed. Underwear and boots, hair almost hanging down to my waist, brows raised, hands on hips, left foot in front of right, eyes rolled back, lips twisted. I'm sucking my stomach in hard, so you can see my whole ribcage. *Breathe, sis*, is what little cunts on Instagram drop on each other's pictures now

— breathe, sis, when you've spotted someone sucking their stomach in like that.

I take a picture of Frank's picture on my phone and upload it to Instagram. I caption it: *RARE FACE PIC. This is me by Frank Steel, circa 2011? In b4 'Breathe Sis' because I'm literally 21 here. Still have the waistline, still have the bra, lost the pants and the boots moving, gained about 5 inches on the hips.*

I have over fifty thousand followers on Instagram. I don't really use it that much, as I can barely post any of my shit on there on account of 'community guidelines'.

Frank told me she was sorry for getting my name wrong, and she *was* just kidding, honestly, and *put your fucking dress back on, come on.* So, I took off my bra. I remember her sighing, her finger hovering on the shutter release. I remember her pinching the bridge of her nose and looking down at her shoes, and telling me to put my dress back on again. I told her to take a picture, because it would last longer. The next photograph's framing is off, because she took it without looking at me. But she took it. There I am, smirking, tits out, left arm cut off, pushing my hair off my face. I run my nail along the line of my round breasts, my concave stomach, my hipbones.

And that's the last one. She murmured something about *students*, and *straight girls*. Then *I don't do this, but...* I smiled, always happy to be the exception to a rule.

I peel the previous photo out of the book, the one I put on Instagram. Not one of mine, but maybe it'll be good for the book. They'll have to drop Frank a line – I'd get a kick out of that.

I grab a glass, some ice and a generous splash of vodka, before I open the next book. Intimate photos, a mix of mine and ones Frank took, mostly Polaroids and disposables. Lo-fi, pretentious. Frank grimacing in red lipstick I drew on her with her pinned down and struggling; me wearing one of her jackets and nothing else; Frank wrapped up in my Ikea bedsheets; me sitting on her kitchen bench in pyjamas, eating cereal from the box. I look very young in all of these.

She only sat for me properly once and told me she'd probably never work at the uni again if I showed them. I took the photos in her studio, with her camera and her lights. I made her wear this shirt, the same shade of blue as a Tiffany box, *Open Me* blue. Her body was flat, shapeless and bony. Her breasts were too small to grab (in what she'd call my *big snatchy spider hands*) so I'd always end up scratching her chest, looking for something to hold. She has one of my scratches in these photos – you can just make it out, on her sternum once I'd gotten her to pop a few buttons.

They're not much like any other photos I've taken. I guess because I did have a *thing* with Frank. An okay thing, too. You compare these to the *What would you do to be my boyfriend?* photos, the pictures of boys in nightgowns, the stuff I do now – it's like a different person took them. These photos feel warm. She's smiling in them, having fun. There's no weird power dynamic, just… Frank. Her grinning with her hand on her stomach; her slipping her shirt off her shoulder, unbuckling her belt, laughing. There's one where half her head is cut off because she's coming towards me, because I whined about the white balance being off, *come fix it for me*, but I just wanted to kiss her. Her lips were always chapped.

She ruined it, in the end. Six months we'd been fucking around, and then my mam visited and Frank wanted to meet her. I laughed in her face. Then she takes me to the PV for her LGBT northerners in London project, and I'm angry she put my photo in it without asking me (she just assumed I'd be fine with it) so we have this huge champagne-fuelled argument outside the gallery. She told me to get over myself and *come out* (*be bi, be a lesbian, be Frank-sexual, be* something *other than a fucking closet case!*) so I told her to fuck off. I shoved her against a wall and stomped off by myself.

The last straw was this dinner party she made me go to, where she introduced me as her girlfriend, and her friend asked her which cradle she stole me from. I was horrible all evening, and we screamed at each other in the taxi.

'Since when am I your girlfriend?' I snarled. And she asked me if I was fucking joking. I ended up on the receiving end of this monologue – 'I spent ten miserable fucking years in the closet; wearing lipstick, and having these insecure, transient relationships, where we never said I love you, and we never did normal shit, and it was all behind closed doors... And you know what? No, Irina. I'm not fucking doing it. I'm not going back. Not for you, and not for anyone.'

And I was just like... *Whatever*. And she went off on one at me about my nasty streak. I'm *rough*, and I'm *judgemental*, and I'm *self-involved* and *cruel*. And I ask her if I'm so awful, why's she still fucking me, then?

She didn't say anything. She got the cab to drop me off at mine, booted me out, and I never spoke to her again. She came to my final show at BA, and I blanked her. I haven't seen her since.

Stuck into the back of the book of those Frank photos, there's one of Flo. When Frank and I split, Flo cut all her hair off. Then it was all blue jeans, white shirts, cigarettes, sports bras that kept her chest flat. It was creepy. In the photograph, she's even standing with her thumbs hooked through the belt loops of her jeans, like Frank used to, fag dangling out the corner of her mouth.

I let her do it. I mean, when she came home the first day with short hair (a *week* after I stopped seeing Frank) I was like, *are you fucking joking, Flo,* and she was just like *what?*

Flo was my hair of the dog – a shot to get you over the worst of the hangover. And when Flo just fucking stood there, looking cute and butch, with her fucking mouth shut, it was absolutely fine. It was a warm bed.

It got weird. It was already weird, but I think the amount of cocaine we were doing, and the drinking, exacerbated the weirdness of the situation.

Flo kept over-sharing the way people do when they're fucked up. And I'd shout at her, for making it weird, and she'd cry and start telling me she thought we could *work*, and I'd shout at her more. Then we'd wake up the next day, and act like it never happened. Rinse repeat, for a whole summer.

I go to text Flo: *do you remember when we used to get coked up and have bad sex where neither of us finished and we'd argue because you wanted to be my girlfriend and you'd cry and i'd scream at you and stuff. Lol.*

But I don't send it. I don't think I do. I delete our message history, because if I don't remember doing it, and I destroy the evidence, it never happened. I laugh to myself. The sound echoes around the garage.

I pull out a couple of the Frank photos, the one of her in the lipstick, and a couple of the blue shirt ones. I pick my phone up again and type her name into Facebook. I see someone who could be her, and then I wipe the search, and close the app, and pour another vodka.

The next box is what I call *The Forbidden Selfies*. It's scrawled on the side. I laugh again.

This is my only set of self-portraits; I went off having my photo taken properly after this. The photos I take of other people – men I never have to see again – they are perfect little imprints, like those photos of my boy. They go away, and I have the photo, and that's all that matters.

I don't go away after I've had my photo taken. I have to look at myself every day, so a collection of selfies, for me, is less of an exercise in narcissism, more a record of my own gradual decay.

I check my phone before I open the box. My Instagram is going *off*. Over a thousand likes, a bunch of new followers and a lot of comments.

Lol do you still look like this now tho??? I delete that one.

We stan a queen who misplaces her underwear. I recognise the username, a young girl who comments on all my photos and covered me in her A-level art class.

post smth more recent – also deleted, along with, *do u have kik.* I don't even know what 'kik' is.

slides into you DMs – a photography bro who has actually slid into my DMs, who I am going to ignore, and a few more like that. Generic *Wows!* and emojis and shit from other brotographers. I get a lot of backhanded BS from them — a lot of *came for that one selfie from three months ago, stayed because your photos are actually good?* Like they're in any position to judge who's good and who isn't.

You look hot AF, remember to crit my photos bitch x – Finch. Ugh. I reply.

For someone who's supoosed to be a commubnist you're really big on free work bb x

He replies very quickly. *Haha. Supoosed. Will buy you a coffee. Crit me x*

I'll do it tomorrow. Nothing else jumping out from the comments, apart from one dude, in all caps. *JUST NUTTED.* I reply telling him I have a PayPal and a Ko-fi account so he can tip me if he liked it so much.

I have, like, five or six new DMs. Good hit rate. There's a dude offering to pay for my nudes, and not offering anywhere near enough money for me to consider it. Like, selling your headless nudes for a couple of hundred quid is fine when you're a student, but I'm about to have a comeback, and I have all these followers, and it's just like… Not unless you offered me Mr B levels of scratch.

Nah m8, I reply.

I put my phone down and crack open the box.

I came back to third year with no work, but photos of Frank. I handed those in because she asked me not to, and my new tutor, this generic posh art man, takes them and he's like: *Hmm. Is this Frank Steel. Hmm. I don't know if you should be showing me these. Hmm. These seem very personal. Hmm.*

I tell him, this is what I do. I violate people's privacy. It's kind of my thing. And he's like, *Hmm. Interesting.*

The word *cruel* is used again. He's all like, *I'm very aware of your work*, and he tells me that if I want to progress, I need to look at making some more personal stuff. If I'm into revealing things about other people, I need to level the playing field.

We had a show at the start of third year where you're encouraged to do something completely different. He *told* me to take photos of myself, to do work about myself.

At that point, I probably wasn't doing so good. I was day drinking and taking drugs during the week, escalating the amount I was taking, what I was taking. During this period, I got chemical burns inside my mouth after swallowing GHB that wasn't diluted; I broke one of my fingers after mixing acid and cocaine (which was probably *mostly* speed, upon reflection) and punching a shiny kettle because I didn't want to look at my face, distorted on its surface. I got bored. I got very bored, very quickly.

I tried casual sex with women I didn't know, a couple of times, in the hope that'd give me a bit of a thrill. But after Frank the novelty of being with women had properly worn off, and the girls I went with were all too nice: older butch women, artsy bisexuals, breakfast in the morning, conversations about mutual friends we didn't realise we had, non-threatening offers of phone numbers and second dates. Low risk. Even with drugs thrown in, it was always low risk.

So, I went back to men. I remember going home with a strange man, whose name I didn't know, not telling anyone where I was going, not being totally sure what was going to happen when I got back to his. Even though it was fine, I remember the way my heart was pounding. I remember the lurch in my stomach when he grabbed my wrist a little harder than I expected.

It got better when I got someone rough – when it felt like I really might get hurt, when I did get hurt.

But that just turned into Tuesdays, you know? You do anything enough, and you can get sick of it – particularly when you're doing stuff to self-destruct, not because you actually like it. It took me a while to work out what I liked.

It is during this period of my life that I'm advised to level the playing field. And I think I did level it. I got the idea to build a self-portrait out of a bunch of self-portraits. Like a snapshot of Irina, at this moment in time, warts and all.

It didn't go down well with the tutors. My work got pulled from the show, and I got referred to the uni's counselling services.

First picture from this set, I have a bruised cheek, a bruised neck and a burnt mouth. It's a portrait from the shoulders up. I'm not wearing a shirt, my hair is pulled back, and I'm wearing no makeup. No makeup, but some no-makeup tricks: the telltale glisten of Vaseline on my lips, eyelids and cheekbones, my lashes artificially tinted and extended and my eyebrows tinted. My skin is milk-white, the bruises on my neck are purple, the one on my cheek is yellowing. The burns are red and angry.

The next, a photograph of my hip, moments before cutting it; after a moment; then a while: with the blood messy, claggy on my thigh. My fingers are strapped up in these, and my knuckles are black.

I'd set up my camera on a tripod next to my toilet, go for a night out, drink myself sick, and get Flo to take pictures of me instead of holding my hair back like she usually did. And she just did it, too, no questions asked. There are a few of me in the same position, different outfits, throwing up – in one picture I'm throwing up blue, and I honestly have no idea what I'd been drinking. There's one of me pissing in the street, looking wistfully into the distance (I assume Flo took this); a photo of me in my underwear digging an ingrown hair out of the inside of my thigh (fingers still strapped up, it's a close-up crotch shot); a photo of a man I don't remember feeding me a shot (angle's awkward, I must have taken this without a tripod). There's one of me taking what I assume is cocaine off a very big man's chest, and then a photo of him choking me.

Honestly, I reckon if I'd dumped the cutting photo, I wouldn't have had any faff. It's a bit OTT, on reflection, a bit self-consciously edgy.

I only half-remember my presentation – when you do a crit, you have to explain your work to your group – because I was on this massive comedown, and I was just shaking, sweating, explaining each photo, and I snapped at the tutor, 'You wanted me to level the fucking playing field, so here you go: it's level!'

David French was the first person to say anything. *Are you okay, Irina?* And then I think someone said it was brave for me to be so candid about my *mental health issues*, and then the tutor sent everyone to get a cuppa, and held me back, telling me he had to *inform someone.*

Like nipples and swastikas are chill, but a bit of GHB and self-harm and it's all *ooo, u ok hun?*

I pull out the one where I'm pissing, the blue vomit, the cut thigh and the bruisey-GHB face for the book.

I find a photo that doesn't fit with the others. One I was fairly certain I'd burned. It's me, somewhere green. Me by a dead old tree with a great hollow mouth. My arms are folded, and my hair is bobbed to my chin, face blank. Bobbed hair means it's MA. And the tree means I should have burned this. I rip the photo in half, and into quarters, then eighths. I throw all the scraps in the bin, but eat the chunk with my face on it.

I do a sicky burp, so I call it a night.

● ● ●

Another nightmare. A boy is sitting on my chest, and I can't move. He is a dead weight, and I can barely breathe. I think, for a moment, I'm dreaming about Eddie from Tesco. But I'm not. The boy's face is too thin, he's too long. His neck seems to crumple beneath an invisible hand. He coughs. He picks a piece of glass from his skull, and brings it to my eye.

I sink into my bed, and I am in the ground. My head is in the ground, in a hole. The boy – my boy – fills the hole with dirt.

I wake up.

therabbitheartedgirl:

I've been thinking a lot about irina lately. she keeps trying to get me to come round or texting me about the lad from tesco i told her to scout like rubbing it in??? and other weird shit she probably sent me while she was drunk or smth. I'm ignoring her textxs but im still really worried about her. the last time i tried to cut her out like this, she got reallly messy. Ive done it a couple of times before. Tbf the first time i did it she was with her gf (her only relationship ever fyi) during second year of uni, i literally did it bc i freaked out n got super jealous and i just couldnt stand to be round them when they were together. but when irina was with her gf it was just 'gf gf gf' all the time, she was so fucking obsessed she didnt even notice her best friend (and FLATMATE at the time) completely ignoring her lmao.

but yeah she noticed next time. it was when rini was still in LDN bc she got into the RCA and i was having a go at graphic design/illustration stuff before i did teacher training, and i was doing this internship in manchester. and i just wanted a fresh start because this was less than a year after her breakup and she'd... u kno... used me for sex for like 3 months because she was sad.

I left my cat with her which was dumb. i took in this stray when we were living together and she named it Fritz and I didn't want to take him to manc with me, so she used him as an excuse to just kept texting me like 'fritz wants you to come back' or 'come pick up the cat plz i cant rlly afford to feed it' and I just ignored it. She also kept sending me pics of her and her new MA friends having

fun, especially this one girl who was all tall and skinny like
rini (Serotonin shes like a proper artist now, HATED HER
tbh) and she'd text me all the time about fritz. But yeah i
managed to ignore her/give her the cold shoulder for ages
and then she rang me one night at 3am having this full
blown meltdown like not actively being like 'i'm going to kill
myself' but she has a history of self harm (which got BAD
after she broke up with the gf her hips are just shredded
like she'd cut out chunks of her skin with nail scissors it
was so grim) so when she rang me like that iw as literally
just like 'fuck' and got in the car.

ive never seen her cry sober so by the time i got to
ldn i found her in a puddle of red wine and tears and TO
THIS DAY i do not know WHAT THE FUCK happened to
make her like that. She SAID that she lost fritz and she was
sorry and I was *ShOoKetH* because ive NEVER heard an
apology from her EVER. Fritz was actually lost, we never
found him, but i just sincerely doubt she was actually
upset about the cat.

Any way by the time we were both back in NCL, when i
first got w michael actually and she was really shitty about
it — i tried again and the same thing basically happened.
idk tbf she has rung me blackout drunk and crying when
I havent been not speaking to her but she's also rlly
calculated sometimes and not super??? stable???? (which
i know sounds like an oxymoron but she kind of is an
oxymoron of a human being)

but yeah so the tl;dr version of this is rini doesnt do
well when shes left alone for long periods of time and idk
if its attention seeking of if she's actually just going a bit
crackers on her own. Who the fuck knows!!!! either way

DENNIS

I arrange to meet with that suit – the bloke from the bus. We spend an afternoon emailing back and forth, and we settle on the evening after next for a shoot. I am, as the kids say, 'shook' that it's gotten this far. Honestly, his is the worst demographic for not turning up, for panicking last minute. The last time I scouted a bloke his age, I got a text from his wife the day of, all like *stay away from me husband slut*. I have a boilerplate response along the lines of *it's not my fault your husband is a cheat, you thick bitch*. I usually get a response along the lines of *sorry, you're right* and an occasional screed about how he treats her badly and how he never does the washing up.

As much as I love a Hot Dad, I try not to go for this age bracket. Maximum faff, and a big risk they won't even turn up for the pics.

I am still highly sceptical when I put the shoot into my diary, and I spend the entirety of my yoga class feeling weirdly pissed off. Granted, this could have been triggered by the skinny bint with white-girl dreads leading the class. Not our usual teacher, she smells of dirty hair, and keeps talking about how Mercury is in retrograde and chakras and other shit. She tries to correct my form while I'm in a perfectly acceptable bow pose, and I 'accidentally' let go of my ankle and boot her in the stomach. Mercury is blamed, and I am left to my own devices for the rest of the class.

I've barely closed my front door when the bell rings. Eddie from Tesco is distorted in the peephole, clutching a bouquet. I open the door; the flowers aren't even from Tesco. He tells me straight away that they've been teasing him all day at work for having flowers, saying they were probably for his mam. I ask him what he thinks he's doing. He says that he can't stop thinking about me. He doesn't understand why I'd sleep with him but he's really grateful that I have. He wanted to give me the flowers as a thank you.

'For... fucking you?'

'Yeah,' he says. 'It sounds weird when you put it like that.'

'It is weird,' I tell him.

'Can I come in?'

'What for?' He just wants to see me. Chat. Maybe watch a film. 'We didn't watch a film last time though, did we?'

'No,' he says. 'But... we could?'

I let him in. We don't watch a film. I haven't even had a chance to change out of my 'active wear', so I tell him I'm taking a shower, and leave a trail of Lycra behind me as I ascend the stairs. I shower with the bathroom door open, assuming he'll take a hint and get in with me, but he doesn't. He stands in the doorway, and watches.

'How are you real?' he asks.

'Dunno.' I look over to him, wiping water from my eyes. He is smiling at me. His neck is rimmed with bruises, a print of my hands wrought on his light brown skin in purples, reds and blues. 'Your neck looks fucked up,' I say.

'Yeah. I've been telling people I got into a bar fight.' He snorts. '*You should see the other bloke!* And stuff. I told my best friend? So he could vouch for me. Like, *yeah this mental charva grabbed him at 'Spoons.'*

'Are you embarrassed of me, or something?'

'No,' he says. 'I don't really want people to know I've… like… been doing, um…' He clears his throat. '*Kinky stuff.* Plus, I just don't think anyone would believe me if I, like, told them, and they looked you up on Facebook, or Insta or something. The friend I told called me a liar when I showed him you – he said you were probably catfishing me, and I'd done the bruises myself in a wanking accident.' He laughs, awkwardly. 'I followed you on Instagram by the way – hope that's okay.'

'Fifty thousand other people do,' I say. I shampoo my hair. 'I don't give a shit.'

'Cool…' He clears his throat. 'Cool, cool, cool. Do you have anything to drink? Not wine? If that's okay?'

'I have a little fridge in the garage. There's some old Moretti in there. Bring me a bottle, if you're going.'

He comes back with two very old bottles of beer, which I lean around the shower curtain to grab. He sits on the toilet and drinks his beer.

'Who's Frank Steel?' he asks.

'Who?'

'F… Frank Steel? You posted a picture the other day from ages ago. It's you in your underwear and the caption said Frank Steel took it? And I just… I saw a box in your garage labelled *Frank*, which made me remember. He's a photographer, then?'

'Oh. Frank. Yeah. Frank was like a guest academic at CSM. I modelled for them once or twice, no big deal. Sort of an ex. We had a brief thing. Don't worry about it.'

'Okay… *Pronoun dodge…*' he says, with a knowing smirk. I purse my lips. When I'm done finger-combing in my leave-in conditioner, I poke my head out of the shower, and scowl at him.

'I didn't *pronoun dodge,*' I snap. He's still smirking. 'Fuck off.' I see him pull his phone from his pocket. 'Don't you fucking dare google it.'

'Too late,' he says. I catch a palm full of water, and fling it at him, like a chimp flinging shit. '*Irina!* So she's a woman, who cares? It's fine. It's cool, I'm not like… I'm not… homophobic. Biphobic. Whatever. Like, if anything, I think this is great.' I'm still scowling. I sit down in the bath and start shaving my legs, waiting for my conditioner to sink in. Eddie from Tesco rambles, and rambles. 'Oh God, not in a gross way, I mean. I really don't care like… I'm not one of these men who's really into lesbian porn stuff? I'm like… I mean I've done *stuff* with men before, it's just *so* not a big deal.' I perk up at that, give him an expectant *oh aye?* from the floor of the bath. He colours and chugs half his bottle of beer. 'Yeah. I mean. Whatever, you know?' He snorts, makes a show of shrugging even though he's about as red as I've ever seen him. '*What-ever.*'

'Tell me about it, then, if it's not a big deal, all these blokes you've—'

'*All these...*' He forces a laugh. 'It wasn't... I'm. It was one other boy, I was... young.'

'If you're going to google my sort-of-ex, I want details.' I'm smirking now – imagining him skinnier, during uni, with his curls ironed out and fringe dragged across his forehead. I imagine someone taller, paler, in an empty room at a party, awkward hands lifting hoodies – lips that are too rough, sloppy tongues. I'm *there*.

'Mmm.' He clears his throat. 'One of Amir's football friends used to like... I was like fourteen at the time, so. I mean, it was fine, but upon reflection, it wasn't really... cool. Because he was eighteen. And... well, bigger than me, like. The power dynamic was kind of... I mean, as someone who is about to go into teacher training, it's like... *aaah! Safeguarding issue!*' He looks over to me, expecting a reprieve. I expect a story. 'So, my parents would make Amir take me to football, and to hang out with his friends at parties and stuff, and they'd give me beer and... um, obviously I don't take drugs ever anymore, like *ever*, but they'd give me... weed, sometimes.'

'Hardcore.' I snort.

'But yeah so his friend B-Ben. Would follow me to the bathroom all the time, and... at first he would just kiss me, and stuff, and I'd just kind of... take it? But.' He stops. I tell him to keep talking, and he does, but only after a moment. 'He started getting me to touch him.' He clears his throat again. 'This isn't like a *fun* story, really I mean. At the time I was kind of into it, I guess? Like, now I've had some, uh, therapy, and I've done loads of work with kids, and I've learned a lot about um... grooming? And stuff? It's...'

'Bit rapey, innit?' I stick my head under the spray and rinse out the conditioner. My mental image has changed, but I'm still there. Less furtive, cheeky experimentation, more... big, frightened eyes, and heavy hands, knotted into dark curls. Was Ben rough? So rough that Little Eddie knew things wouldn't end well if he were to protest. Did Ben's hands ever snake around Little Eddie's neck? Did Ben back Little Eddie up against the door of a pub toilet cubicle, pick him up by the waist, cram his tongue into Little Eddie's mouth, and probe at him with unpractised, unlubricated fingers?

'Yeah. I just... I shouldn't have brought it up... I just didn't want you feel like... I was. That I thought you... having a thing with another woman was... an issue? I mean. I'm sorry. What happened with me and him wasn't a... I know it's *fucked* to think like this.' He says the word *fucked* very quietly, as if he's worried an adult will hear. 'But I've always thought of it as being like... my first relationship?' he says. 'I haven't really told anyone... ever? Outside of counselling? Amir was best man at his wedding. His *straight* wedding. I figure he was more of an opportunistic offender than a preferential... Well, I say that; he did wink at me when we were all in the pub, last Christmas?' Eddie from Tesco finishes his beer.

'Did he ever fuck you?' I ask. My eyes are closed, but I figure he's giving me a look. Hurt, confused, whatever. I throw him a bone. ''Cause, you know, I had a thing with my art teacher when I was sixteen,' I say. '*Mister Hamilton*. He was... forty-odd? I think? He'd take me to dinner and then we'd sit in his car a street away from my house, and he'd get me to suck his dick, and stuff. Now *that's* a fucking safeguarding issue. We could never go to his house because of his literal wife and children, so we'd only ever do it in his car, or public bathrooms. Lost my virginity in the disabled toilets at an Odeon cinema.' I think for a moment. 'We were seeing *Notes on a Scandal*. Even at the time I was like… *mate*.'

'*Jesus*,' says Eddie from Tesco. 'I'm so sorry, Irina.'

'It was fine. I quite liked it,' I say. 'Your thing sounds way more traumatic.'

'It's not a competition,' he says. 'But no, he never. There was no penetration… With regard to… Uum. The particular orifice I assume you're referring to.'

There's a lull. He looks like he's thinking.

'I mean, it just happens, doesn't it? Practically a rite of passage.'

'I don't know about that, Irina,' he says. He looks at me in a way he never has done before: right in the eye, with his brow crinkled. His big cow eyes are shiny, and his lips are pulled into his mouth, pressed to a tight line. 'I'm really sorry that happened to you,' he says, after a moment.

I am suddenly very aware I'm naked. I go *pfft*, and I wave my hands. I sneer. I roll my eyes.

'Honestly, it's *fine*. He got caught, he got fired.' I shut off the shower. 'End of story. It has literally never been a big deal for me. It only lasted six or seven months. I've had longer relationships with toothbrushes.'

I get Eddie from Tesco to wrap up the Ben story. It is depressing, and nowhere near as pornographic as I'd hoped.

Little Eddie and Ben's relationship fizzled out unceremoniously when Ben went to university. At the leaving celebrations – the last *hurrah* when Amir and his group of friends got their A-level results – Little Eddie followed Ben to the toilet at a house party. And Ben told Little Eddie he wasn't in the mood, because he'd gotten two Bs and a C, and hadn't made it into Newcastle Uni, *or* Northumbria (his second choice), and had only just gotten into Edinburgh Napier through clearing. Ben had cried on Little Eddie's shoulder, instead of molesting him, which made Little Eddie feel strange. No longer was he going through the motions of a sexual relationship with this older boy, he was providing support. Like a real boyfriend, or something.

Then Ben moved to Scotland and very quickly got a girlfriend, which Little Eddie tragically discovered via Facebook. Facebook's presence in this story suggests that Eddie from Tesco is younger than I had initially assumed. Little Eddie decided, however, that their dubiously consensual fumbling would continue over the Christmas break.

Little Eddie was allowed to tag along with Amir to the pub at that first post-freshers Christmas reunion. As usual, Little Eddie bought a Diet Coke, and Amir bought vodka shots, which he would pour into Little Eddie's drink when the bar staff had their backs turned. Amir, in high spirits, lost track of the amount of shots added to his little brother's drink and, thus, Little Eddie became very drunk, very quickly.

Little Eddie stared at Ben from across the table all evening, and Ben would not meet his eye. The older boys traded stories about sex, and booze and soft drugs, and Little Eddie stared, even stretching his stubby legs to rub Ben's calf under the table. Little Eddie announced, with a slurred, pointed voice, that he was going to the toilet – knocking into Ben on the way. Ben did not even acknowledge the shove, and Little Eddie found himself in the toilets, completely alone. He burst into tears. He sobbed alone for ten minutes, wondering *what is wrong with me?* Why had Ben lost interest, and why was Little Eddie trying to rekindle something that had made him so uncomfortable and confused?

Intellectually, I know this is a sad story. But as I imagine him – fifteen, drunk, half hard, humiliated, sobbing – my skin prickles. My nipples grow tight against the fabric of the towel I've wrapped around my chest, and I lick my lips. I imagine his tears on my tongue.

'Sorry. Jesus, sorry that story is so pathetic, like… *TMI, Eddie!* Not that this whole conversation isn't TMI, but…' He laughs, and buries his face in his hands, talking to me through his fingers. 'Hey, at least there's no danger of us having sex tonight,' he says, with a sniff. 'I'm definitely up for a film, though. A nice film.'

● ● ●

I drop him onto my bed. The towel around my hair unravels. I frantically suck the bruises on his neck. I drop the towel around my body, and he notices the scars on my hips for the first time. He runs his fingers over them and seems not to believe me when I say *stretch marks* into the crook of his shoulder. He catches my cheek in his hand.

'I feel so close to you,' he says.

● ● ●

I go downstairs for a glass of water, and by the time I get back to my room, Eddie from Tesco has cleaned up, tucked himself into my bed and fallen asleep. I sigh. It's only ten p.m. Like, four hours before my usual bedtime. I fucking hate sharing my bed, too.

I think about booting him out, but I just end up leaving him.

I sit downstairs with a glass of wine, and watch *Snowtown*, because checkout boy's story made me think of it. I watch the rape scene near the start a couple of times. I once told Flo I thought it was hot as fuck, and she was like, *hmm, deleting that info, thanks.* Like she hasn't been creaming herself over *Call Me by Your Name* since it came out. She was all like, *oh well that's totally different Irina*, and I don't really see how, to be honest? She'd be shitting herself about a straight film with that age gap.

I drop her a text, briefly considering what would wind her up the most before sending her anything.

> Hey, guess youre still freezing me out.
>
> Sorry you can't just be happy for me when i finally find someone i like.
>
> Lame.

Three dots. She's typing. I grin.

> **This has fuck all to do with the fucking tesco guy lmfao Irina????**
>
> SURE.
>
> But yeah blanking me is super mature!!!
>
> Not fucked up and upsetting at all
>
> From my perspective you basically accuse me of lying about getting raped, you vanish out of my life it's bizarre and wont even talk to me when i start dating someone I actually like and im trying to get your opinions and stuff like.
>
> All this stuff is happening to me and you just ditch me.

Then you're acting like the victim here like.

Honestly youre always acting like im this monster

How do yio think this makes me feel?

If it's not about eddie (the guy from tesco fyi) I don't get it?? Whatd id i do???

If you have a problem with me, if ive done somethig just tell me??

But the silence is cruel flo. It's fucking cruel.

I throw in a few typos, like I'm cry-typing. I put my phone down and go back to *Snowtown*. I finish my glass of wine before I pick it up again. I have an essay to read. The first text:

Youre right.

I cackle.

Im so sorry

Michael just like hw ereally doesnt tryst you he thinkis you make stuff up to manipulate me and make me feel bad and I KNOW YOU DONT

i know you dont do it on purpose but sometime you do like you do say stuff and its upsetting anmd manipulative but michael just always assumes the worst of people and its so exhausting to have like.

Maybe you hurt my feelings and i tell michael and he convinces me you did it on purplseand it s hard not to getworn down n convinces by it and i jsut felt really confused I didnt mean it i felt like i needed some time on my own and honestly

Mauybe i was jealous of the guy from tesco and yourem texting me anbout him all the time i know aftr what i said 2 you I desrv to feel like shti its really stupid im just used to having you to myself and i felt confusedx and territorial and angry and michael was being werid and i s2g he does it from a place of concern

Being caught between the two of you all the time is so tiringj imn so sorry

It's okay.

You know, I actually think that's really shitty of Michael.

He's always been threatened by you.

Mmm. Just don't let him like grima wormtongue you

You know i'm not a bad person.

I know I'm not always nice

but i'm not like evil??? Or anything???

I don't know flo

i have a lot of baggage and im trying my best.

I know.

I'm so sorry.

Can i come over tomorrow? About 10-ish?

It's my day off?

Okay.

I smile. I finish the bottle of wine, and fall asleep on the couch.

● ● ●

Eddie from Tesco wakes me up in the morning, about nine. Nine *a.m.* I tell him to fuck off.

'I made breakfast,' he says.

'I don't eat breakfast.'

'I was wondering why you didn't even have eggs or bread? That's wild. I went to the Waitrose and got some stuff, I, like… I mean, I figured you weren't vegetarian because you had some tuna in your cupboard? I've only ever seen you buy salady stuff and wine. So, I got some smoked salmon and avocados and made you eggs? I can make toast, if you want.'

'Waitrose?' I say. 'Bougie. I don't do carbs, though.'

'I figured,' he says. 'Toast is optional.' He drops a plate on the coffee table in front of me. As promised, smoked salmon, avocado, and he *poached* the fucking eggs. 'Why didn't you come to bed? I missed you this morning.'

'Don't you have… work?' I say. I shuffle up on the couch, my laptop still on my stomach. He sits on the floor with his legs crossed, on the other side of the coffee table, eating poached eggs and toast. *Poached.*

'Not till twelve,' he says. 'Uh… Sorry if this is a bit much, I was just… hungry?' He clears his throat. 'I'm sorry.'

'That's my T-shirt.' It's big on him, and I only own like three T-shirts. It's white, with a print of one of my photographs on it. Flo got it for me – a birthday present.

'I didn't want to put my work shirt back on, sorry. Is this one of your photos?'

'Yep.' I move my laptop onto the floor, and replace it with breakfast, which I eat slowly and carefully. He's squeezed lime onto the salmon and the avocado for me.

'So, um, when do you want me to come round for the video?'

'Eh?'

'For the show. Hackney Space? You said you wanted to try me out for your film?'

'*Oh.* Yeah just... When are you off next week?' He grins. He's off on Friday. 'Then. Just come over whenever. Not before one, though. And text me first.'

'Cool,' he says. 'Cool, cool, cool.'

He does the washing up when we're finished eating. I eat the avocado and the fish, but I leave the eggs. I poke them, and watch the yolk dribble out and soak the plate. He brings me a coffee when I tell him to. He says he needs to leave soon, to pick up a clean shirt for work. There's a love bite on his neck now, just above the bruises. Who the fuck over the age of seventeen gives someone a hickey? I remember climbing all over him, picking him up, grabbing at him.

'Are you gunna go, then?' I call.

'Yeah, as soon as I'm done washing up.'

'Just. My friend is coming over soon,' I say. 'So... You know. Get a wiggle on.'

'Sure, just gimme five, I'll be out of your hair.' The doorbell rings. I swear under my breath. It rings again. 'Do you want me to get it?'

'Nope.' I pull my robe closed, realising I've been lying here with one tit hanging out, and jog to the door. There's Flo, brow crinkled. Her lip wobbles as soon as she sees me. I cut off her apology, and tell her I have company. Before I can send her upstairs, Eddie from Tesco wanders out of my kitchen, drying a pot and smiling.

'Hey, I'm Eddie,' he says.

'I got you that shirt,' says Flo. She looks at me like I've slapped her.

'This is Flo,' I say. I watch her, watching him. I see her clock the bruises on his neck. She side-eyes me.

'Hi. It's a cool shirt,' says Eddie from Tesco, cheerfully. 'Really neat.' Flo hums, and he smiles, turning on his heel and going back to the kitchen. Flo points at her neck, and mouths *what the fuck* at me. I mouth *fuck off* at her, then *bitch*. She raises her eyebrows, and sits on my sofa.

Is he washing up? she mouths, making a scrubbing motion with her hands. I shrug. *Oh my God*, then she mimes a whip. I scowl. *Sorry*.

Don't be a cunt, I mouth, and stomp into the kitchen. The checkout boy is in there, putting pots away. I tell him I can put them back, not to worry about it, to go. He asks me if everything is okay, and I say it's fine. Honest. Me and Flo just had a bit of a falling out, and we're trying to patch things up. He apologises – is it okay if he keeps my T-shirt for the moment? He'll wash it and bring it back on Friday. He asks me if I want to go for lunch first.

'Sure, whatever.'

Satisfied, he rushes ahead of me, puts on his trainers, and picks up his backpack.

'It was nice to meet you, Flo!' he says.

'No, it wasn't,' I say. 'See you next week, then.'

'Maybe before then?' I shrug. I'm slouching, so he stretches to kiss me. He aims for my lips, and lands on my jaw because I jerk my face away. He laughs, and tries again, and I sidestep over to the front door and open it.

'I put the flowers in some water for you.'

'Cool. Bye.'

'Okay. Um. Bye bye!' He steps outside, opening his mouth to say something, but the door's already shut before he can get it out.

'I'm not interested in your opinion,' I say, immediately. 'I don't want to hear it.'

'He seems nice. I'm glad you're happy together,' says Flo. 'I'm getting *choked up* just thinking about it.'

'Fuck off,' I snarl. 'Like you get to blank me for weeks then come in here and get judgey. Seriously, fuck off. I'm like… I'm actually foaming with you. Actually foaming.'

Then she cries.

I shout at her, she cries, she pleads, then we kiss and make up. Not literally. We both agree Flo has been very unfair, and Michael is due a bollocking. Maybe a dumping. She just wants the two of us to get along. I'm trying – and she *knows* I try. She knows, but he's so jealous.

'He seems super controlling.'

'Um… Like… It's… It is genuinely coming from a place of concern,' she says, her nose stuffy. 'He knows I'm here. He's not happy about it, but he isn't like *you can't see her*, or anything. It's difficult. I don't like being stuck between the two of you.'

'I'm not doing anything,' I say. 'It's him.'

'I know,' says Flo. 'I don't want to talk about him anymore. I just want you to know…' Her voice breaks. 'I love you, and I'm sorry.' She sniffs. 'Can I have a hug?'

So I hug her. I'm feeling very generous today. She wipes her eyes, and then tells me to dish about my *weird choke sex*.

I hate it when Flo talks about sex. Basic feminist internet discourse has made her think she's *sex positive*, comfortable discussing the minutiae of her sex life and other people's sex lives. She isn't. I know she isn't, because I've fucked her, so I don't know why she even pretends with me.

There was a time when I was still with Frank – Flo had invited herself along to drinks in Soho with us. I told her I needed to nip into a sex shop to pick up a new vibrator, because the motor had gone on mine the previous evening. She flinched when I said vibrator, and I told her she could wait outside, or go, but she insisted on coming along. 'Maybe I want to get something,' she'd said, with the same forced, casual tone she'd used to say *weird choke sex* a moment ago.

We walked into the first one we saw, and she kept looking at us and going, *well this is just fine, isn't it?* And going as far as to inform me that she was *in her element here, really* and that sex shops were feminist spaces, in a lot of ways. I remember pointing to the wall of pornographic DVDs behind her, flanked by a mannequin with enormous plastic breasts and a cheap wig, modelling a strap-on and a neon pink bra with nipple cut-outs – *what about that stuff, Flo; is that feminist?*

She thought for a moment, and concluded that the strap-on was feminist but the mannequin and a vast swathe of the pornographic DVDs probably weren't. If some of the porn had been made by a woman it would be feminist, but the majority of it probably hadn't been. *However*, if we were to *buy* some porn, it would be a queer and feminist act of disruption.

I'd never seen Frank look so unimpressed. I couldn't even laugh at Flo, I was so embarrassed.

She looks up at me, with the same eyes – crinkled at the corners now, but still desperately seeking my approval.

'Yeah. Well.' I shrug. 'It's just… Like. It was his idea. And I'm… cool, with that, if he wants to do that sort of stuff. And we have… things in common. I mean, he *really* understands my work, and he's a great model. We'll see, I suppose. It's… nice, so far.' She's crying again. 'What?'

'I'm just so happy for you,' she sobs.

● ● ●

Eddie from Tesco asks if he can come over after his shift the same night Dennis is due round. I get a bit of a cheap thrill telling him I've got a model coming round. I can almost feel the jolt in his stomach through the screen. I can see his cheeks going red. I imagine him sat behind his till, tears prickling the back of his eyes, blaming phantom allergies when a customer asks him if he's alright.

Have fun! he says, and I ignore it. I watch an episode of *Toddlers & Tiaras* and a documentary about the Wests while I wait for Dennis. He rings my doorbell just as the police are digging up the patio. I let him into the house, leaving the documentary on. I offer him a coffee, and he says yes, so I make him one. A little begrudgingly, but I always try to be a bit more normal with new models, you know? If you're nice, it loosens them up a bit.

Coffee in hand, he starts telling me about himself. I keep one ear on the telly while he talks about his middle management job. He has a good jawline, which is softening a little with age. He hasn't shaved, and he's still wearing his shirt and tie from work. He's handsome, but his nose has been broken, maybe twice, and he has a chunk of scar tissue splitting his left eyebrow in half. One of his teeth is a little chipped, and his earlobe is ripped too, forked like a tongue. I interrupt him.

'How'd you rip your ear?' I ask.

'Fighting,' he says. 'Had an earring, some Mackem cunt yanked it out on a derby day.' His accent thickens when he says *Mackem cunt*. He's rougher than I'd originally assumed. He shuffles on the sofa, and the white fabric of his shirt pulls tight around his arms – I can see a web of black tattoos through the cotton.

I don't know how the fuck he gets onto his wife and kids from that, but he does. While I pick up my camera and twiddle idly with the settings, he delivers a snarling monologue about his ex, how she took the kids down to her mam's in Plymouth to make it as hard as possible for him to see them. There's a faded N-U-F-C across the knuckles on his left hand, and a tan-line where his wedding ring used to be.

'Sounds shite,' I say.

I switch lenses and I take his photo while he talks (and talks). I turn the flash on, and he just keeps talking. Honestly, if I'd known he was going to be this much hard work, I'd have had a bump or something.

He asks if he's boring me.

'I'm on a tight schedule today.' I'm not. 'But it's great to get some background on you. Shall we head to the studio?' I beckon, he follows.

He asks again – is he boring me?

I give him a mint. Coffee breath ruins the vibe.

He wants to know if he's *fucking boring me*, spitting around the mint, which he still took, despite now looking as if he'd like to skin me.

I sneer. He goes off.

Blah blah blah, *jumped up bitch*, something about how I think I'm better than him even though he pulls in x-amount of money a year, like I'm supposed to be impressed by his bank balance, which I imagine is exaggerated because I *did* meet him on a bus. That's what I tell him. He doesn't like that.

He slams me against the wall. I feel my head hit the brick. He is so angry that he drools.

'This is such a massive overreaction,' I say. My camera is slung around my neck, the lens pressing into his belly. I tell him to chill out.

'Fucking *chill out*,' he hisses. I duck out of his grasp; I lunge. I bash him over the head with my camera.

If we were playing rock, paper, scissors, but it's camera, toxic masculinity, skull – camera wins. Not a dent in the equipment, but a significant dent in Dennis, who crumples and lies gurgling in a rapidly growing puddle of his own blood. I snap a photo. I snap a few. He glitters like glass.

Glass. Glass in his cheek, glass in his eye. I must have broken the lens. I click a new one on. I sit on his stomach. I take more photos, and with each flash, his skin seems to get smoother, darker. His hair a little longer.

When I pull the shard of glass from his eye, it shifts from a cold blue to a warm brown, and stays that way when I put the glass back. I can't feel him breathing anymore, and I… I don't know. I feel sick. I jump, because I hear a bell, but I don't know where it came from.

It's fine. It's fine, because I've done this before. I go onto automatic pilot. I dump my camera, and climb off him, rushing to the kitchen for the cleaver (because you can't quite get through bone with a knife) and rubber gloves, and bin bags.

But when I get back, he's sat up, and there's no glass, and his eyes are blue again.

'I'm sorry,' he says. 'Don't call the police. No ambulance, no 999.'

I tell him to hang on, doing a bit of juggling with the cleaver, the bin bags, chucking them in the cupboard under my stairs while he says something about his kids and his wife's lawyer, and a police caution for domestic battery.

Christ, I need to start running fucking background checks.

'I won't tell if you won't,' I say. And he goes *what?* He rubs his head, his eyes are unfocused, and his speech is slurred. I crouch down next to him. No glass. 'You need to go to A&E. I'll get you an Uber,' I say.

'No,' he says. 'No, no Uber, no one... What if he rings the police? They've all got fuckin' CCTV.'

And I tell him an Uber driver's not going to ring the fucking police, but he's not having any of it. He says he'll just get the bus home, but I don't think he realises how hurt he is. When he touches his head, his fingers come back bloody. He looks at the blood, and his droopy, unfocused eyes roll back in his head. He flops to the ground again. I slap his face (no glass) and try pulling his ankles. I can move him – he's heavy as fuck, but I can just about move him. My shoulder makes a popping sound, like a plastic bottle being twisted. I hiss.

Now he's unconscious, I agree with him: it looks too shady for Uber and a lot of them do have those little dash-cams, but I'm not ringing an ambulance. Fuck that.

Who do I know who has a car?

Flo doesn't have one anymore. Eddie from Tesco is at work, and I honestly wouldn't be caught dead driving that thing. Mam and Dad would ask questions, and they live too far away.

I order an Uber, just for me. I text Will.

> Coming over its an emergency.

Okay?

It's a four-minute journey, and I spend the whole time jiggling my leg, chewing my lip. I stand on Will's doorstep ringing the bell. His car is there, a deep scratch still decorating the door.

He answers. He cut his hair off.

'I need to borrow your car,' I say.

'What the fuck,' he says. 'What the actual fuck? Why?' And then. 'Don't you have a driving ban?'

'My nana is ill, she lives in…' I shrug. 'Berwick? And I need to get up there *right now.*'

'No,' he says. 'You can't just… I swear to *God* I remember you telling me you got caught drunk driving. I remember, 'cause you had that fucking BMW, and your dad made you give it back!'

'Will,' I say. I put my hands on his shoulders, my fingernails biting into his skin. 'My nana is *ill.* And do you know how she got ill? Some cunt gave her *loads* of ketamine, and tried to rape her. And now she's at death's door. From what my mam has told me, this scumbag couldn't get it up. But he still tried to rape her. And just because she was on ket doesn't mean she can't remember that someone tried to stick his flaccid little cock into her, okay? And wouldn't it be an absolute fucking shitter for him if she posted his picture to her Instagram page, with a warning to women everywhere to avoid this attempted rapist. I'd be shitting myself if I was him, because my nana has *a lot* of followers on Instagram.' My breath is ragged. His face is red. 'So just... give me your fucking keys.'

He gives me his fucking keys. I jingle them in his face and tell him I'll be back. He slams the door in my face. I drive back to mine. Will's car smells of weed and sweat. His gym bag is on the back seat.

Dennis is still breathing, still on my garage floor. His eyes are flickering open and shut. I open the garage door, and drag him out, my shoulder popping again when I do. He leaves a patchy trail of blood behind him, like a huge, wounded slug. When the sunlight hits him, he stirs again. I ask if he can move on his own, and he sits up. Unable to stand, he crawls to the car, and we manage to get him into the passenger's seat. I buckle him up.

It's quick, getting him to A&E. We get caught by a couple of red lights, and I keep asking him to grunt if he's alive. He does, and I keep seeing *glass* in the corner of my eye.

'You're my dad,' I tell him, 'and you fell off a ladder changing a light bulb in my house, okay?'

'Dad,' he says. 'Ladder. Light bulb. No police.'

'No. No police.'

He thanks me.

And while there's a temptation to just push him out of the car and fuck off when we get to A&E, I go in with him properly. I tell the people at the front desk the story – Dad, ladder, light bulb – and tell them I need to go, like *now*, to pick up my baby from the childminder. They don't seem suspicious, and bundle Dennis into a wheelchair, and I fucking leg it. I get in the car, and I just drive. I drive till I can't see the city anymore.

I switch on the car stereo, which is this old, shitty thing. It has a CD player, and no aux cord, so I listen to what I assume is a *Best of Johnny Cash*, and try to level out my breathing. I try to laugh, pass it off to myself like it's a joke. Like this is just *classic Irina*. But I can't. It's not funny. I remember the plastic surgeon – how there was no glass in his face either. And Will, how much of that I imagined, dreamt. I could take the fact he lent me his car as proof, you know? That it did happen, that I wasn't just filling in the gaps.

Jesus, I don't know.

I keep coming back to the glass. I keep coming back to my boy with glass in his face – in his eye – lying on my kitchen floor. His thin face, his wet, black hair, his cloudy, dark eyes. Bloody and bruised, the colour drained from his olive skin. He looked green.

I keep driving. I drive somewhere I fucking swear I've driven before. Somewhere green, somewhere with a little gravel car park, and no CCTV. I get out of the car, and I walk into the green, the sea of trees. I walk for a long time, till I find a dead old tree, with a hollow like a huge, yawning mouth. And I dig. I dig with my fingers.

I should find a skull – and I do. A little cat skull. And a cat skeleton, and a tattered collar with a bell, and tag that says 'Fritz' on one side, and a London address on the other, the address of the place I shared with Flo.

I bury the skeleton again, pocket the collar, get back in the car and scream. I smash my hands against the dashboard until my filthy knuckles split.

Either I buried it somewhere else, or there was nothing to bury in the first place. But if there was nothing to bury, then why do I remember it? Why do I remember having pictures?

I burned the bad ones, but I think I saved one of the good ones. Just one of his face. And if I can find it, and…

It's getting dark. I switch the stereo back on and drive back to Newcastle. It takes me a couple of hours. I go back to mine first. I wash my hands, and change my clothes, and fix my makeup, because I look as pale as a corpse, and I have eyeliner and lipstick all over my face. My hair is wild. I remember looking like this after a night out, once, and Flo telling me I looked like a sexy clown. I snort, and then I laugh, and then I cackle, and smack my head against the mirror. The glass is cold on my forehead, solid. When I pull back, I am still there. I take my makeup off, and I feel cleansed. Calm.

I have a quick few mouthfuls of vodka before I get back in the car.

Henson answers when I ring the bell. He smiles at me, and Will shouts after him, 'Is that her?'

'Aye,' he calls back. I throw the keys over Henson's shoulder, and they land, with a clatter, in the hallway.

'Thanks,' I shout. Will says nothing. Henson steps out of the house and closes the door behind him. He asks if my nana is okay. I blink. 'She's dead.' What a strange question, I think. And Henson looks very upset, and I remember how I got Will's car in the first place. 'Oh. I made that up, today. She died, like, ages ago. I just needed a car,' I say. 'It's a really long story, and I just… It's like private, but it was an emergency, and… You know what he's like.' I shrug, and smile at him, trying to be casual, flirty.

Henson crinkles his eyebrows, then raises them, and finally settles on looking confused and annoyed.

'Why would you lie about that?' he asks. Fuck's sake. I try to make myself cry.

'I really don't want to talk about it,' I say. My eyes are dry, but it's dark and the voice is good.

'Oh. Christ, I'm sorry. I didn't mean to pry,' he says. I turn around.

'No, it's fine. It was a weird lie, I know. I shouldn't have, I just… It really is private. I'm so sorry,' I say.

'Don't worry about it… Let me walk you home, at least.'

I let him. He apologises again, for prying. I say it's fine. I apologise for being weird. I can hear this little bell jingling behind us. I turn around, expecting to see a cat, but there's nothing.

'Can you hear that?'

'Hear what?' he asks. I tell him it's nothing.

He confesses, shyly, that he's been trying to ask me out for a drink, but he keeps chickening out. And he gets if he's missed his window, but it'd be nice if we could go out. I take him into a narrow alleyway, and he asks if this is a shortcut. I kiss him. I grab his face, and his hair, and crush him against the wall.

'Woah,' he says. 'I'm, um, not that kind of girl?' He chuckles, and pushes me away, firmly, but gently. I try to unfasten his belt, my bony wrists awkward against his big stomach. He protests: *rats in the alleys*, and *I know you must be feeling vulnerable right now*, and finally, *no. No*, when I get my hands into his underwear, and *stop it*, when I grab his dick, which is completely soft. He pushes me hard.

'What?' I snap. 'What the fuck?' He's fastening his belt, shaking his head.

'I don't… I told you, I'm not like that.'

'So, what am I then?' I snarl. 'What am I like?'

'You're not *like* anything! It's fine if you… I just… I don't do stuff like this.'

'Why not?' I ask. He tries to leave the alley. I yank him back, try to fold him into my arms. I feel the fabric of his T-shirt against my palms, his soft buttocks against my crotch. I kiss his neck. 'Why not?'

He wriggles free.

'It's just not for me, okay? It's… seedy,' he says.

'What the fuck ever,' I say. And then, 'Okay, fine, we'll do it at mine.'

'We're not going to *do it*, Irina,' he says. 'Just let me walk you home, and we'll… we'll just forget it.'

'I can take myself home, you fucking… *girl*.' I stomp off, muttering. 'I'll make a note you can't get it up without a *candlelit fucking dinner*!' He doesn't come after me. I turn around, and he's still there, standing on the pavement, by the alley. 'Can I just double-check that that happened?'

'What?' he shouts back.

'In the alley, did that happen?'

'Yeah?'

'Okay. Fine.'

'Are you alright? Are you… Are you sure you're okay?' he shouts. His voice echoes in the street.

I give him a thumbs up, and keep walking.

I can still hearing that fucking bell.

345 BUS STOP

I go straight to the garage when I get in. I get on my hands and knees, with a bucket of bleach and hot water and a sponge. I scrub the floor till the blood is gone. The water is grey and tinted pink by the time I'm finished. I dump the bucket into the bath, then I bleach the bath as well, and mop the bathroom floor. Then I mop all the floors, and tip bleach in all the plugholes. I shower. I make the water as hot as I can stand – I scrub at myself with the soap. Everything stings. I lose track of time. I don't get out till the water runs cold.

I check on the photos of Dennis from earlier. I feel like I took them a week ago. I don't even feel like I took them. There's a Susan Sontag book called *Regarding the Pain of Others*, which Frank made me read — there's a bit where

Sontag talks about how when people see terrible things happen, they used to say it felt like a dream, but now they say it feels like a movie. Movies have supplanted dreams in the popular consciousness, and have become our benchmark for the unreal, and the almost real. Today has been a movie, playing on an old, warped videotape.

Dennis is bloody in the photos, but not as bloody as I'd thought he was. There is no glass. My camera is fine, but the bottom is sticky where it connected with his skull. I wipe it off before diving into the boxes where the photo (photos?) I want might be.

I try the other box from third year. Everyone tends to 'go big or go home' with their BA show, and do some elaborate installation, which is sort of what I did. I set up this big fancy backdrop, and brought a bunch of costumes, and during the private view I ran around, grabbing boys and men and making them dress up, taking their photos. I'd print them out and pin them to the backdrop. It cost me a fucking fortune in glossy paper and ink, but it got me into the Royal College.

Honestly, I thought I was hot shit. I was one of two people in my year who got in (me and David French, who follows me around like a bad fucking smell) – both of us on the MA photography programme. I remember ringing my mam to tell her I'd gotten into the Royal College of Art, and she didn't get why that was good. I listed off some alumni – Tracey Emin, Mam? (*The dirty bed woman? Shite.*) David Hockney, Mam? (*Who?*) James Dyson, the hoover bloke? (Finally, she was impressed.) She wasn't particularly arsed that I wouldn't be coming home, but my dad was upset. He said he missed me. Mam said he just didn't like paying London rent.

I went to the RCA expecting solo shows and a Turner Prize nom within the next five years. I got into another show, a little corner in a big exhibition at Whitechapel Gallery, right at the start of the year – at my first tutorial, my tutor called me *the one to watch*. About a month later, I had that *Vice* write-up, the one that still pops up when you google me, and I was interviewed by a bunch of small journals. I felt like a minor celebrity. I kind of *was*. I got invited to every party, and all the rich, skinny, fashionable girls wanted to be my friend. I picked Serotonin, still Sera Pattison at the time, to replace Flo because she was the tallest, blondest girl who showed an interest in me. And she always had coke.

Flo said she needed a change of scene, but she just didn't get into any MA programmes, so she went to Leeds for an internship. I ended up moving in on my own. Professionally, things were going really well, but personally I was still a little… whacky. Whacky; with mounting pressure, and long evenings with no one to worry about me, or keep a proper eye on me.

Flo shouldn't have left me. I shouldn't have let her.

After a week of living by myself, I took a series of photos I titled *Inconsolable Naked Man*. I rip through the set looking for the photos I thought I burnt, but there is nothing hidden there. All of the photos are of a grown man crying on my kitchen floor. We were fucking on the floor, and he asked me to slap him. It was the first time a man ever told me to hit *him*. So, I did. I hit him, and I hit him, and I hit him, until his lip burst. I hit him until I came. He started to cry, even though he hadn't asked me to stop. He went soft inside of me. He said he was sorry, and then he sat on my floor and wept like a child. I handed him pieces of kitchen roll to wipe his nose, and watched him cry. I grabbed my camera, and periodically took photos. I didn't know what to say to make him stop, nor did I ask why he'd started. I just watched. I watched his shoulders shake, and his eyes swell, and blood dribble down his chin. He looked up at me, like I was supposed to do something.

The transition from being hurt to hurting was natural. Even though I didn't really know why he'd started crying – it felt like something I did. It felt like being a great big black widow and realising that all the male spiders were tiny and *weak* and covered in soft vulnerable bits, whereas I had this hard, shiny thorax and great big teeth.

When I took the photos to college, I was surprised by the extent to which everyone was on my dick about them. I couldn't tell if I was actually good, or if everyone was just *telling* me I was good because I was hot property. It was infuriating.

Sera said I should have filmed the shoot. The main feedback I got from my final BA show is that I should have filmed that on top of taking the photos live, because watching me shoot was more interesting than the individual photographs I'd produced. And I can listen to criticism, even though everyone says I can't. The next lot of photos I took (with street-cast models), I filmed the shoot.

When I put the films online, everybody liked them. More cover in artsy magazines, more momentum. I booked a little solo show, which was very well received. The first box from my MA is mostly DVDs, and some prints of the photos I actually took. The DVDs are mostly the same thing – street-cast men, with me barking orders at them. Occasionally I'll go into the frame, and fit them into place, or put a mask or silly accessory on them. All the DVDs are labelled in Sharpie with a vague description of the model: *ponytail & goatee; fat boy; acne; adult braces & lazy eye.*

I don't watch them, the way I might have another night. I'm not looking for DVDs. I dump the box out, pore through the prints. I pull the DVDs from their cheap plastic cases and shake them, to see if anything falls out. Something does. A Polaroid. A Polaroid not anywhere near as battered or faded as it should be.

There he is.

Pretty, dead-behind-the-eyes, forcing a smile under a fluffy towel, and sitting on my bed. His skin is still lively and flushed here. His eyes are flat, but they aren't cloudy. Not the one I thought I'd kept, which makes me worry I may have kept them all.

I get my rubber gloves from under the stairs, just in case I end up handling something I shouldn't. I go over the Frank box, again. I pick through my foundation stuff, my A-level stuff. *Nothing.* I find a shoebox buried deep in the garage, full of clippings, articles about myself I've printed out, and it's not there either. I try under the sofa cushions in the living room. I don't know what the fuck I'm expecting to find there, but I do get 73p.

I spot my DVD case behind the TV, one of those big, black things where you can file like four discs into a sheet of plastic wallets, to save space. It's thick with dust – probably the only dusty thing in the house – and I unzip it.

On a gut feeling (or, remembering) I flip to the Bs, to *Boy Meets Girl*, the film from '94, not the BBC sitcom from 2015. Predictably, there is something folded up behind the disc, tucked into the wallet. I extract it from its home, like a rotten tooth.

'I burned you,' I tell it. The Polaroid shows a young man, a very young man, with sallow skin, and black, curly hair which is plastered to his forehead and sticky with blood. His left eye is brown, his right eye is ruined, with a piece of glass splitting it in two. I put the chain on the front door and shut the curtains. I figure that all the photos must be stuffed behind films that were rejected by the BBFC when I find the next one folded up behind my imported copy of *The Bunny Game*. I find more photos behind *Caged Women*, *The Devils*, *Freaks*, *Grotesque*, *Hate Crime*, *Love Camp 7*, *Murder-Set-Pieces*, *The New York Ripper*, and finally *Sweet Movie*. I have a few more banned films, after S, but *The Texas Chainsaw Massacre* and *Visions of Ecstasy* reveal no additional photographs. Sticking one behind *The Devils* is a fuck-up, on my part, because it was never actually rejected – just controversial and cut heavily. I sigh. *Stupid bitch*. I could have easily missed that one, couldn't I?

I go over the DVDs again, just in case. No more.

The Polaroids lay around me, like a circle of salt. I grab one – the boy is intact, in my kitchen, no glass. Skinny, greasy, eating a piece of bread, not even bothering to butter or toast it. I hate Polaroids now – they're so cliché – but they'd just gotten trendy again. I must have just had this to hand.

I found him at a bus stop. I'd been drinking in Clapham, that night, like a fucking estate agent or something. Two a.m., just me and him at this bus stop. I asked him if he was waiting for the 345 – he shrugged and didn't meet my eye. I took him for a rough sleeper. I asked him if he wanted a shower, a sofa for the night, and when I scooted closer to him, he flinched away. I said *suit yourself*, and he asked me what happened to my neck, because I was sporting a noose of bruises.

Bad boyfriend, I told him. Then, twisting my lips, *I could really use the company, you know.*

He got on the bus with me. I paid his fare. We went through Clapham Common, Lavender Hill, to Battersea, where my flat was. I explained, *I'm a photographer* and then, as if it hadn't occurred to me before, *hey can I take your picture? It could be, like, pay for the food and the shower.*

He shrugged. There was a distant look in his eye – unfocused, dislocated – one I recognised, one I identified with, I guess.

I remember him flinching away from the flash, like something feral. I'd asked him how old he was; he said eighteen. I didn't fucking believe him, but I was just like... sure, whatever. Looking at the picture, I'd put him at sixteen. Maybe.

I put the photo of him in the towel next to it; the next in the sequence. I'd popped one on his head, for his hair, and one across his shoulders, and told him to give me a little smile. That's what I've got here, his little smile. I put his clothes in the wash while he was showering, telling him they'd be done in an hour, and I had lots of stuff he could wear. I offered him a nightgown, and he laughed, because he thought I was joking. I wasn't joking. Drunkenly, I told him, *I don't have a good sense of humour, babe,* and I threw the nightgown at him, telling him it was that, or nothing. He chose nothing.

Another bad one next. Another one I did burn, I swear to fucking God, I burned it. The landlady lived above me, and I remember her bollocking me for burning stuff in the garden. Clear as fucking day, I remember her stomping up

to me, fag hanging out of her mouth, complaining. I told
her they were pictures of my ex, and she took a look at my
fucked-up face, and my neck, and my bandaged-up hand,
and said *oh, sweetheart…* and left me to it. God knows what
I burned instead.

In this one, the boy from the bus stop is in the kitchen,
and he is naked and betrayed. He has a panicked look in his
good eye, and a hand over the bad one.

I tried to get him to let me hit him. I barely touched him.
He went from zero to sixty like *that*, and knocked me to
the floor. He went into animal-panic mode, all adrenaline
and wiry strength. He hit me – not with an open palm, but
a closed fist, again and again and again, till he was out of
breath and I could barely see. I grabbed an empty wine
bottle, from by the bin, broke it on his face because he
wouldn't *stop*. He could have killed me. He was going to
kill me. He scrambled away, felt the glass in his eye and
immediately started squealing, freaking out, making noise
that my landlady would hear. I took his photo. I tripped
him, and he landed on his face, with all that glass. He
stopped squealing.

The next photo is before the bottle. He's in the shower,
with his head tipped back and his mouth open. His back
was covered in cigarette burns, old ones. He didn't notice
me take the photo, but he noticed when I got in the shower
with him. He noticed me when I touched him. He noticed
me when he came, and he slipped, and I caught him. He
could have cracked his head open and died there.

That's the last photograph of him whole.

I thought he died when he fell, but he didn't. I turned him
onto his back, and he was still breathing. I poked his legs and

arms hard, and he didn't respond; there was no reflex at all – like the glass had gone into his brain and severed something. I don't know. I didn't know then. I decided he must be dying. I decided, if he was dying, if he was going to die, there'd be no point in taking him to a hospital – no point in getting myself in trouble, you know? Lose everything for some fucking kid no one cared about, who was going to die anyway.

I put him out of his misery. I carried him to the bath and did it there.

What shocked me most weren't the sounds he made, the bulging of his eyes, the colour he went – not even the shit. It was just easy. I'd always heard manually strangling people was really hard – like, serial killers who strangle will try to do it once, fuck it up, and graduate to a tool – stockings, a belt, piano wire. But his breathing was so faint, and his neck was so thin, it just… He just *died*.

I squeezed his neck. I remember his Adam's apple pressing against my palm. I can still feel it. The photo in my hand is another close-up, a close-up of his poor face, full of glass, his head now separated from the shoulders it had once been attached to. I have a photo of each leg, each arm, and his torso: all these boy parts, which I can arrange on my living room floor like a jigsaw.

I fucked it up, at first, because I tried to use a knife. You can't get through bone with a fucking kitchen knife, can you? Stupid. I got blood on my shower curtain, hacking away at him, sawing away with a knife so dull it would barely cut through a broccoli stem.

I ended up having to nip out to the twenty-four-hour Asda in Lavender Hill to buy a cleaver. I had to shower around the body, and sit on the 345 again, like nothing had happened.

When I came back in, fucking Fritz had gotten into the blood in the kitchen and trekked it through the whole flat. I'm just lucky I didn't have carpets. So, Fritz had to go. He always liked Flo more, but he did trust me. He didn't scratch or bite when I picked him up, and when I snapped his neck, he didn't make a sound.

I hacked the boy up. I took more Polaroids, and got the camera so bloody I ended up having to rinse it off, then bin it. I put the cat in the bin bag with the head, the cleaver in with the left leg, and everything else separate. Bin bags, in bin bags, in bin bags, and I remember being very pleased with myself for bulk-buying bin bags the week before, because I forgot to buy more at Asda and fuck me if I didn't need them.

I was panicking about what to do with the bin bags, though. Panicking, because all I could think about were serial killer fuck-ups. That they caught Dennis Nilsen when he started flushing bits down the toilet, and how all the concrete in the world couldn't hide Fred West's skeletons. Dahmer's fridge full of heads and penises, the Acid Bath murderer and his poorly-disposed-of drums of human soup.

Then I remembered the Moors murderers – how there were bodies scattered all over the countryside, so vast and green that no one would ever find them. And those were whole bodies, not just bits.

I packed up my boy and Fritz into two suitcases, wheelie suitcases, and I stuffed them into my boot. I mopped the flat. Mop water down the toilet. Suspiciously pink mop head, my dress and heels from the night before and the rubber gloves were shoved into another bin bag, under the sink, to be burned upon my return.

My hands were red with a rash, from fingertips to wrist. This is how I discovered I'd developed an allergy to latex.

I kept my car in London, even though I barely used it. I just drove for a few days. I drove to green, leafy places, dug, dumped and took photos with my proper camera, so I'd know where the bits were.

But I only saved the photo of me by the site of the skull.

But there was no skull, was there? Just Fritz.

And if the police had found it, they'd have taken Fritz, surely?

Maybe kids dug it up, took it. Maybe, maybe (even as the evidence sits in front of me) there was no boy. No boy at all. I touch the photos, like they're a trick, like they'll crumble beneath my fingers. I wouldn't be dumb enough to photograph something like this, surely?

I remember looking for my boy on the news, on the internet – any call for missing persons, a boy in his mid-teens, 5'9", very slim build, black hair, brown eyes.

No one was looking for him.

It's like, if a tree falls in the forest, and there's no one there to hear it, did I even chop it down?

I stuff the pictures in an envelope.

Hey B,
Been a while! Sorted that glass effect out
– sent some polaroids to the PO box.
Just some experimental stuff, hope you
like it!
Irina

It's three a.m., and I power walk to the nearest postbox with a hoodie pulled tight around my face, even though there are no cameras around here, and it's hot as fuck.

They're gone. I tear my house to bits looking for more, but they're all gone. No more. None in the DVD case, none. Gone. Done. I click and drag this whole incident to the recycle bin icon in my mind, and I empty that bin, and I take a magnet to my hard drive in the form of a bottle of vodka and two Xanax, which have me out for the count for a full twenty-four hours.

● ● ●

I wake up to an email from Dennis letting me know he's okay, and nothing else. I'm grateful. If he contacts me again, I'll ring the fucking police.

I feel extremely dopey. I keep dribbling, despite how dehydrated I am, and I cough so hard I gag. I down a few glasses of water too quickly and spew a little back into my mouth.

I'm about to worry about the fact I've had no email from Mr B, and I've barely gotten my kettle boiled, when the doorbell rings, and there's courier holding a huge stuffed bear, with a fat stuffed heart. I panic for a moment, thinking Eddie from Tesco sent it, before realising it's well out of his price range. The courier calls me a lucky girl when I sign for it, and with a lascivious look at the gap in my robe, he says whoever sent it must be lucky too. I smile and take the bear. It has a little card with it, with a letter opener taped inside:

Break my Heart,
B

I take the letter opener and split the stuffed heart open. It's Velcro'd to the bear's hands, and shockingly heavy.

It's heavy because there's about 30k vacuum-packed into a plastic bag inside it. I count. Thirty rolls – every roll a grand in fifties.

I ring Ryan and quit the bar. I laugh down the phone at him, and before he can start to argue with me, I'm literally like, '*Bye bitch!*'

No more sticky bar shoes, no more tiny humiliations. No more. There'll be more like this after Hackney, more money, more recognition. The recognition I deserve. The recognition I *earned*.

Then I go to my emails, I type a very excited thank you note – but it bounces back. And again. And again. I go to reply to the last email he sent me, but it's gone. Every message is wiped from my inbox, like blood from a wooden floor.

```
Hey Finch,
Finally getting around to critiquing
your work! I know it's been ages since
you asked, but I've been VERY busy. As you
suspected, the heavy praise you received
for these photographs was likely motivated
by performative allyship. While technically
competent, you rely too heavily on your trans
schtick and yeah top surgery is brutal, but
I feel like it's very obvious for you. I
don't know if you've heard of Frank Steel
but I used to do a little work with her
when she was still lecturing at CSM, and
you should look at her career trajectory as
a warning. Vanished from academia and now
```

everyone thinks she was like a 2000s flash
in the pan, and she could have been really
important if she'd moved away from the LGBT
stuff, don't you think? Hacky! Boring! All of
Gen Z is queer now so it's a little… whatever
if you're aiming for your work to be gnarly
and transgressive. Am I saying the photos are
bad? No, they're just meh. Identity politics
is always a hard sell any way, and you should
try something else.

I'm a big fan of a bit more detachment in
work, I think it shows a little maturity -
instead of it being like 'me, me, me' you know?
Hard not to be me me me with ID Pol work, and
ID Pol is hard to separate from immaturity,
like I see these pics, and they're fine but
it's hard not to see the genetic connection
between these and teen girls taking pics
of their period knickers and dyed-unshaved
armpit hair. Yawn! So I'd say detach yourself
from your work - dump photography for a while
and try something else, even.

See you in the pub,
Irina.

EDDIE FROM TESCO, II

I keep the money in a plastic bag under the sink, deciding I'll deposit one or two rolls a month. I buy some dumb shit – I used to buy dumb shit all the time, and then my parents took my credit cards. No credit needed now, I guess.

I come home with a bunch of shopping bags, and none of the lights will turn on in my house. I hide the shopping in my spare room, then ring my dad and tell him to come fix it. He's over in half an hour. When I open the door for him, he hugs me, and kisses my cheek. His hair is still red, even though he's almost sixty. He's an ugly man, but I see the sketch of myself in him. We're the same height and colouring. He has a sharp nose that points upwards, and high cheekbones. Mam and I don't even look related.

'Daddy,' I coo. 'I can't work out what I've done!'

'I'll sort it, love, don't worry.'

He sorts it. The bulb in the living room has blown and tripped the fuse. He sorts the fuse, then changes the light bulb for me. I follow him around the house and tell him about how well things are going. I tell him I'm seeing someone, and prep for the show is going really well, and I'm getting so many private sales that I was able to quit the bar.

'Well, you can tell your mam yourself. I'm not telling her.'

'I never said I wanted you to tell her,' I snap. He climbs down from a wooden chair, a new light bulb in place. His knees click when he gets down.

'Is there anything else you need doing, love?' he asks. 'While I'm here? How's the pipes? Your sink still leaking?'

'No,' I say.

I direct him to the drawer of my bedside table, the one that won't close properly. I make him wait outside with the door closed while I move all of my bedside-table shit into the wardrobe. I perch on the bed and watch him work. He smacks aimlessly at the drawer with a hammer.

'Thank you, Daddy,' I say. He smiles at me, and the corners of his eyes crinkle up.

'I do worry about you, love. Quitting your job like it's nowt. I know you've been on the sick,' he says. 'I popped into your work, and that lad told me. The muscly one.'

'Why did you *pop in* to my work?'

'I'm sorry. I haven't seen you; your mam hasn't seen you. I just wanted to say hello,' he says. 'I worry, it's my job. And you're just full of secrets, aren't you? Always have been.'

'Maybe it's because you're so fucking weird about everything I tell you – did Mam tell you what she said when

I told her I had the exhibition? She just started going on about how she hasn't heard of the gallery, and how she's not homophobic because she thinks my photos are shit, or something. It's literally like... why would I bother?' I say. 'Seriously, Dad, I'm asking. Why should I bother if you're both just going to give me gyp whenever I sneeze?'

'I'm sorry,' he says. 'I'm not giving you gyp, love, I'm just—'

'Worried. You said.'

Dad convinces me to come home for dinner, even though I'm meeting Flo for drinks in a few hours. He waits while I put my makeup on. I only go because I'm hungry, and I only have a bag of spinach in the fridge and I'm not in the mood to deal with Eddie from Tesco today.

Dad has this awful, racing-green vintage sports car, and he always looks so fucking pleased with it. I keyed it once, when I was seventeen, because he dobbed me in to Mam for smoking after she found an open pack of tabs in *his* jacket pocket. He said they were mine and I'd worn his jacket out.

Mam complains that she didn't know I was coming over.

'I'll fuck off then,' I say. Rather begrudgingly, Mam lets me into the house, and continues to complain that they'll have to rethink dinner. Dad will go and pick up fish and chips. I complain about carbs.

'Just eat the fish,' snaps Mam. 'This has really thrown my evening off, Irina. It really has.' She was going to catch up on *Corrie* tonight.

While Dad is out hunter-gathering, Mam sits me down at the dinner table and interrogates me. She says her curtain-twitching friend, Susan, (who lives on my street) saw me getting into an old car with a short foreign-looking man, and worried, because she'd been reading all about these Asian grooming gangs.

'I was so embarrassed when she rang me, Irina,' she says. 'What on earth were you doing?'

'I'm seeing someone,' I say. But she snaps that I should be more careful about who I'm *seen with*. 'Are you telling me not to go out with men who look like they might be Asian? Or are you asking me if I'm being trafficked or something?'

'Oh, so I'm a racist now,' Mam snaps. She tells me the issue was the height difference and the dodgy car, not the 'racial thing'. She was embarrassed because Susan had said *your Irina got in a battered Micra with some little foreign-looking fella*, and then brought up the grooming gang stuff, because she thought it was strange that I was with such a little bloke. Mam says Susan wouldn't have brought up grooming gangs or pimping had we not looked so strange together.

'Susan looks like she's been hit in the face with a shovel,' I say. 'And she dresses like it's 1997. Why would I care what Susan thinks?'

'You know she had that stroke, Irina. So, who was he, then? I had a look through your tagged Facebook photos again, and I didn't see anyone matching Susan's description.'

'*Oh my God*,' I say, under my breath. I need to delete Facebook. 'I just... It was just the once. He works in the Tesco near mine.'

'You said you were seeing him a second ago. Susan didn't make him sound very attractive,' Mam says. 'Not my type – working in a Tesco. Honestly. At *your* age.'

'Well I might see him again. I don't know.' I look down at the table. I can't look at her face. She's smirking. I feel sick. I tell her he's in teacher training. I don't comment on the age thing. I think he might be twenty-four. At the most. I couldn't find his Facebook page, because I don't know his last name. 'Anyway, I'm not going to pick dates based on who I think my mam will find attractive. Sorry he's not conventionally handsome, or whatever. I'm a broad church.' I think she's about to drop it; she falls silent for a moment. Her fat upper lip is curled, and her over-plucked eyebrows are raised to her tight hairline.

'I know you are,' she says. I ask her what she means by that. She clicks her tongue. 'Not everything's a dig, Irina,' she says. 'But it must be if I've said it, because I'm the worst mother in the *whole world*, aren't I? Just the horrible bitch who nursed you, and bathed you, and who pays your rent.'

'*Half* my rent. And I never asked you to pay it,' I say. 'You did it to make me move out, remember? And it's Dad's money, anyway.'

'You are *so* ungrateful. It's like you were *born* ungrateful.' She snarls it at me. Like I was born just to spite her. And she goes on to talk about the expensive Barbie whose hair I coloured red, the wrong-coloured bike I screamed about on Christmas day when I was ten, and the time I told her to fuck off in Tammy Girl when I was twelve, because she was trying to make me get a thong to wear with these jeans I allegedly had a 'VPL' in when I put them on. She tells me that I'd always pour salt in the wound by crying to Dad, and that I was an angel for him. Which isn't true. I used to bite him, like, all the time. He just forgave me, and she never did.

I get up from the table while she stews.

'Where are you going?'

'I'm getting you a glass of wine,' I say. And I go to the fridge. Suddenly relaxed, she tells me to make sure I get the

Riesling and not the Chardonnay, because the Chardonnay they've got is bloody awful.

'I want red,' I say.

'We don't have any.'

I pour us both a glass of the Chardonnay. She makes a face, and I tell her it's best to get rid of it – she slides her glass over to me with her eyes narrowed. 'You drink it,' she says. 'I know you like a drink.'

She gets herself a glass of the Riesling, and there's something petty in how little wine she pours for herself. She puts her glass beside mine to compare it, telling me that she only likes a splash of wine on a weeknight.

I ask her about her cancer friend – the annoying one, on Facebook.

'She's gone into hospital now, not long left,' says Mam. 'And you think she'd be spending a bit less time on Facebook, wouldn't you? But *no*.'

That keeps her busy, till Dad gets back. He drops the bag of fish and chips on the dining table and begins dishing it out. He runs back and forth with cutlery, and condiments, and kitchen roll, while Mam and I sit and watch him. Mam points out there's three portions of chips.

'I got Rini a portion of chips as well,' he says. I whine. 'You don't have to eat them, love; they're just there if you want a treat.' He smiles at me. 'A few chips won't kill you, you little skinny-mini.' He kisses the top of my head.

'Thank you, Daddy,' I say. He lovingly moves a large cod from its sweaty box to my plate.

'*Thank you, Daddy*,' repeats Mam, in a high-pitched voice. Her splash of wine disappeared rather quickly. 'Are you going to cut that up for her, as well, Nigel?' she asks. He cut up a steak for me when we went out for his birthday one year, and she's never let it drop. 'What did you do on your date, Irina? Did you have that short lad cut your food up for you?'

'Oh.' Dad smiles at me. 'Is this the bloke you're seeing? The one you told me about?'

'*Of course* you told *him*,' snarls Mam. 'I had to hear it from Susan.'

'Oh, you're seeing the little feller?' Dad says. 'I didn't think he was in a grooming gang, love. I said he was probably just your friend.'

'He is sort of just my friend,' I say, shrugging, beginning to extract the cod from its batter. 'Just.' I shrug again. 'It's like a pity thing, basically. I feel bad for him.'

'Ah, well,' he says. 'You always used to say you only went out with me 'cause you felt sorry for me, didn't you, Yvonne?' says Dad. Mam grunts. 'I remember asking her out at the disco. Have we told you this story, love?'

'No,' I say, as Mam says *she's heard it a thousand times*. I have; it just winds her up. I think it's the equivalent of someone who had a terrible car accident being told the story of how they nearly turned left, but turned right instead, and drove straight into a truck.

'Well, I saw her across the dance floor, sitting, face like a smacked arse – beautiful smacked arse, mind you. And I went over, and asked her if she wanted to dance, and you know what she said?' Dad purses his lips like Mam does. '*Erm… I'm minding my friends' coats.*' He laughs, I laugh. Mam forces a smile. ''Course, she did dance with me, in the end – didn't you, Yvonne? 'Cause you felt sorry for me. That's what you say.'

'Mmhmm,' she says. 'Well you kept asking, didn't you?'

Dad's a plumber, and at some point, plumbing started

to go very well for him, and he started buying nice cars, and looking at big houses. And that's when skinny, angry Yvonne from the disco developed a proper interest in him. There's this photo of the two of them, when they first moved in together in the mid-1980s, and Dad's wearing this awful big suit where he looks like an uglier, ginger David Byrne. Mam is tucked under his arm, with her big blond perm, and she's got this skintight, metallic-gold dress on – it's framed, and it sits in the living room, and Dad always points it out to guests. *Me and Yvonne, back when she was just my trophy girlfriend!* And Mam will usually say that she stopped wearing that dress so Dad would stop making that joke.

Aside from their wedding photo, all the other pictures hanging in this house are of me. Me as a baby, me at nursery, all my school photos. There's a gap between the ages of twelve and sixteen (when I did not photograph well), then the photos start again, in earnest. Dad even had me print out a couple of my selfies for him to hang. I stare at myself on the wall as I pick at my fish. A little girl with freckles and orange pigtails. She is missing her front teeth. I run my tongue over my veneers.

Mam sulks over dinner and has a go at Dad for telling the same stories over and over again. She really lays into him and doesn't stop till she runs out of breath.

'Irina has some news about her job,' says Dad. He blurts it out while Mam is between sentences, then curls down into his chair, avoiding my eye.

'Oh?' she says.

'I quit.' And then it's my turn. She doesn't believe I'm making enough money from photography to pay my half of my rent, that if I want to do stupid things, like quitting my job, she'll cut me off, completely. That was the condition: I work part-time, at least, or she cuts me off. I pay my half, or she cuts me off. 'It's Dad's money, though!' I shout. And when Dad doesn't argue with me, or back her up, Mam stomps out of the kitchen in tears. Dad follows her.

I eat my entire portion of chips. I eat them with my hands.

I hear my mam screaming and crying upstairs. I can't hear my dad. When he comes back, I tell him I need to go because I need to meet Flo.

He drives me to the pub. He says Mam is having a hard time at the moment. She rings and rings and rings the both of us, as soon as she realises we're gone.

Flo is there when I get to the pub. Flo is there, and so is Michael. I could kill her. She sees my face drop, and grabs my arm, leading me to the toilets where we bicker. She just wants me and Michael to get along. She wants us to be normal with each other. She hopes that a little alcohol and quality time will lubricate things between us. She goes back to the bar, and I piss, and scowl, and check my phone.

Eddie from Tesco has been blowing my texts up – I've been a bit cold on replying this week, and he doesn't seem to be coping well. I tell him we're still fine for Friday, for the third time. I even finally tell him I'll be fine to go to lunch with him beforehand – he's been pushing that all week. Still, I'm distinctly aware of a buzzing in my pocket for minutes after I get back from the toilets. Flo sips her pint, and Michael glares at me above his. Flo ordered me a red wine; it waits for me on the table.

'What?' I ask.

'Your phone is going off loads,' he says. 'The vibration is *so* loud.' I shrug. Flo laughs.

'Popular! She's a popular girl! *Woman*. Irina has a boyfriend now, you know?' says Flo. *No I don't*, it sits on my tongue, like he's here, like he'll hear. Michael looks sceptical.

'Does she?'

'It's great! Works in a Tesco. I pointed him out to her.'

'He's starts teaching soon. We've seen each other, like, twice, it's not—' I shrug. 'It's fine. I'm out with him on Friday.'

I think Flo is trying to bait me. She knows how I feel about *boyfriends, girlfriends*. She's seen me seize up, sever ties, snarl and snap, time and time again over those words. I've called her bluff. She purses her lips.

'I'm just… Toilet,' she says. 'I'll just be a second.'

'You just went,' says Michael. She ignores him. Michael sighs. I look at my texts.

Eddie from Tesco is intermittently trying to hammer out details for Friday, while apologising for bothering me and asking if everything is okay. I'm about to reply with something irritating and non-committal when Michael pipes up. The two of us have an unspoken rule – if Flo isn't in the room, and we don't have to, we just don't speak to each other. More his rule than mine, I think. He might hate me, but I'm completely indifferent to him. I sip my wine and fold an arm under my cleavage.

'Boyfriend,' he says. 'Does that mean you're finally going to leave her the fuck alone?'

'What do you mean?' I say. He takes a deep breath.

'You know what I mean.'

'Don't think I do.'

'You're like a cold that won't go away, you know that?' He says. 'She gets better for a bit, and she's normal, and

then she'll start spending time with *you* again, and she...'
He trails off, staring at me, staring at my chest.

'Are you looking at my tits?'

'Yes, yes I am, because they are *always* out, aren't they?' he
snaps. 'Fuck off, *am I looking at your tits* – like you put that top
on by accident. Fuck off.' I lean over and stick my fingers in his
pint, I flick beer in his face. 'You're fucking pathetic,' he says.
'You know why she's like this with you?' He's hissing now,
spitting on me. 'She feels sorry for you. She knows she's all you
have. And that's why she can't... untangle herself from you,
because she's not a horrible person. She's not like you.'

'If I told her to leave you and move in with me, we both
know she'd drop you like a bag of hot sick. So.' I shrug.
'Whatever helps you sleep at night.'

Flo comes back. She's bought me another wine even
though I've barely touched the one I have. As she's putting it
down, she slops some of it into Michael's lap. She apologises
to me, not him.

●●●

I pick my outfit for lunch with Eddie from Tesco quite quickly.
I put on a dress – I have four of the same one in different
colours, this body-con thing from American Apparel, which
fits like a glove. I put on half a stone, once, about a year
ago, and the dresses went from understated-sexy to sausage
casing. That was a lesson learned: gluten truly is the devil.

I have it in red, black, white and blue. Red seems a bit
much for lunch, and I don't know why I bought the blue in
the first place because it clashes with my hair. I just go for
the black and stick a denim jacket and a pair of flat-forms on

with it. I take one step out of the house and realise the jacket
was a fuck-up, and it ends up jammed in my backpack. I
cover myself head to toe in sun cream on the bus; I can feel
my skin cooking, wrinkles erupting, cancer cells multiplying.
I should have worn a sunhat.

I get a frantic stream of texts from Flo. Something about
a huge argument with Michael, and the logistics of leaving
him if he owns the house. I let her dangle, still annoyed that
she sprung him on me the other night.

I find Eddie from Tesco sitting at Grey's Monument,
bouncing his leg, fiddling with his phone, headphones on.
His clothes look strange. Like, they're new, and they fit
him. Just plain jeans, and a grey T-shirt, but definitely *new*. I
announce my arrival by coming up behind him and pulling
his headphones off the top of his head. He shits himself,
which I laugh at, and then fumbles his words.

'New outfit?' I ask.

'Oh? This? No,' he says. I tell him his label is hanging
out, and he tucks it back into his collar. *All Saints*. So he's
getting bougie with his Tesco money, apparently. 'Okay, it is
new. I mean. Just. All my clothes are shit, I just… I dunno, I
don't want you to feel like you're out with a fifteen-year-old
boy.' I tell him that's a very specific concern, and he explains
that upon asking his brother (the most fashionable man he
knows) for advice, he was informed he dresses like an incel.
His brother told him to just buy something *plain*, that *fits*,
because there was nothing worse than some dorky, short-
arse bloke trying to be fashionable for the first time in his life
and ending up looking like he'd fallen on the Topman sale
rack. 'Er… Is it okay?' He squirms. 'I mean, you look lovely,
like… really nice. Like. What are you doing with me?'

'You look… fine,' I say. He does. Absolutely fine. 'Bit basic, maybe.' I shrug. 'You'd probably have looked a bit of a twat if you turned up in a leopard-print shirt or something, so…'

'I totally agree,' he says. 'The table is booked for half past, so we should probably get a shuffle on,' he says. He stands, and I'm still looming over him.

'Booked? Shit,' I say. 'I thought we'd just be like… going to a cafe or something. I don't know.'

'Err…' He looks sheepish all of a sudden. 'I mean, I've not booked us into a posh one or anything, just… semi-posh?'

'*Semi*-posh.'

'Yeah.'

I tell him it had better not be too far away. 'It's fine for you being out in this heat; you tan. You're always tan. You look like you've just been on holiday or something,' I say. He laughs.

'Are you joking?'

'What?'

'I'm mixed race, Irina? Had you not twigged? My last name is Arabic, it's proper obviously foreign?'

It's cute that he thinks I care what his last name is.

We walk to the semi-posh restaurant – a nice French place down by the train station, where the waiter is extremely enthusiastic and explains how French-style tapas works, and offers us the wine list. Eddie from Tesco asks the waiter to bring his recommended bottle of red, in what would have been a baller move if he hadn't been sweating and stuttering the whole time.

There's a lot of dairy on the menu, a lot of carbs, but Eddie from Tesco has anticipated this, pointing out the large selection of fish, and salads, and fishy salads for me to peruse. The wine the waiter brings is very nice. I'm struggling to find something to complain about.

'This is a bit much,' I say.

'I know.' He smiles and reaches over the table to take my hand. 'I just think that… that you deserve nice things.' I pull my hand away and tuck my hair behind my ears. 'I worry that you don't… Maybe you don't see that. But it's okay, because. I get it. I do the same thing.'

'We're nothing alike.' I snort. He's still smiling. He's being patient with me, and he just drops it; he ignores me being a dick.

'Do you want a starter?'

'I *really* don't think we're anything alike,' I say.

'Okay. Sorry. Stupid thing to say. Do you want a starter?'

I don't. I watch him eat bread for twenty minutes and make my way through the bottle of wine before the smiley waiter comes and takes the order for our main meal.

'Camembert,' I say. It falls out of my mouth, along with an order for potatoes dauphinoise, and a charcuterie-thing. Eddie from Tesco blinks at me. He smiles.

'Wow,' he says. 'Go big or go home, then.' He gets a steak. I think he orders a steak, and some other meat stuff, because he wants to look like one of those big, masculine men, whose personality revolves around craft beer and red meat consumption.

While we wait for the main, I eat his leftover bread, which is slathered with garlic butter. My eyes roll back in my head. They bring us another bottle of wine, and Eddie from Tesco gets a beer. I am too busy drinking the wine to make him drink any.

'So, do you like Nan Goldin?' asks Eddie from Tesco.

I do like Nan Goldin. And we play art bingo for a bit where he asks me if I like different photographers and I say yes or no. When it's a *no* to Helmut Newton, he seems really taken aback.

'I like him,' he says. 'I think there are loads of similarities between your works.'

'Fuck off,' I say. 'Like, literally, fuck off.'

'What's wrong with Helmut Newton?'

'Are you joking?' I say. 'I thought you were like… a *woke bae*.'

'I am! I just…' He shrugs. 'I mean, I don't have an art degree – an MA, even – do I?'

'It's not my job to educate you on…' I take a big mouthful of wine, '*misogynist* photographers, and why they're *misogynist*. It should be obvious.'

'Oh. I'm sorry.'

'I'm just shitting you,' I say. 'I get why you'd say that. I just don't like him much. Bit… bland-white-male-titty photographer, isn't he?'

'Um. Yeah, guess.'

'And I mean, I *do* take like… So all the women he photographs are like boilerplate sexy ladies, aren't they? And I mean, I'm taking *your* photo, aren't I? Not exactly *Vogue* material, are you?'

'True,' he says, nodding. It's a bit sad that this is his default setting. My mam always used to tell me that you catch more flies with honey than with vinegar. And Eddie from Tesco is a fly, but he's got a taste for vinegar. It's like vinegar is all he's ever had from people, and now he doesn't even know what honey tastes like.

They bring the main. It's sublime. This is the first time I've eaten cheese in about two years. I struggle not to drool while I eat. I keep the napkin clutched in my hand, dabbing at the corners of my mouth every time I eat a glob of Camembert, a little piece of smoked meat, a gooey potato. I ignore the sound of my waist expanding, and the intrusive images I have of my stomach in this dress once we're done.

'Hungry?' he asks.

'No,' I say. I eat everything. Eddie from Tesco watches me, with his chin rested on his hand. Placid, and interested, like he's at an aquarium. 'What?'

'Nothing,' he says. 'You're just pretty. And you have cheese in your hair.'

I do have cheese in my hair.

By the time we're finished eating, I'm too full to even think about dessert – but I order an affogato, with a shot of amaretto, anyway. I feel ill. I feel like throwing up, sticking a feather down my throat, like a decadent Roman empress.

There's a dispute over the bill, which is quite hefty. Eddie from Tesco briefly tries to *insist* on paying. *I told the waiter to bring that wine, I booked us in here,* and I just drop a couple of fifties on the table and shrug, telling him rather a large invoice came in for me the other day.

'Are you sure?' he says. 'Like, honestly, I was expecting it to be—' I shush him.

'Cover the tip, if you want.' So, he drops a twenty on the table, and we leave. I am *very* wobbly, like my centre of balance has been thrown by the amount of food in my stomach. While Eddie from Tesco is trying to suggest another drink, I tell him the Uber's on its way, and we'll just go back to mine.

I get him to do shots with me when we get in. I try to offer him coke, and he looks horrified. I shrug, have a bump – more for me, I guess. He's wittering on (*minimum sentence for Class As; becomes toxic in your bloodstream when mixed with alcohol; deviated septum*). I usher him into the garage. The studio.

I have the video camera set up opposite the sofa, on a tripod, in my studio. I want it simple – gritty, I guess, but not handheld. Handheld feels a little too Gonzo porn for my liking. I just want it static, a cold Pasolini vibe. It's been a while since I filmed anything. I have half a bottle of red in the garage, which I polish off while Eddie from Tesco gets undressed, affixes the bunny head and the tail.

I sling my camera around my neck. I have another bump, and another. Things get a little blurry from there.

● ● ●

He's a controlling piece of shit

I didn't want to shit stir but when you went to the toilet at the pub the other night he said you're only friends with me because you feel bad for me

He said i was pathetic and he started talking about my tits it was SOOO WEIRD.

Ask him about it.

If you break up with him, i'm here for you and so is my sofa

<3

I've watched the video through eight, maybe nine times now. The first thing you see, the first shot, is him. Standing by the couch, in front of the bare, brick wall. I went without a backdrop.

I'm off camera. I ask him if having his picture taken gets him off, and he laughs.

'Maybe. Yeah, I suppose?' His voice sounds weird; it's all muffled, with the bunny head. I do have an external mic, so you can make it out, at least. I zoom in on his crotch – at the time I thought he was getting hard, but you can't really tell so much in the video. You hear me asking him to *gimme a twirl* and shake his bunny tail.

'I think I like you more than… *modelling,*' he says. I ask him if he's a sub. Another shy laugh. 'I mean, a little,' he says. 'I just… I don't do this for everyone.'

I tell him to grab the couch and bend over, and I walk into the shot. I look great – same outfit from the date. I look *skinny*, despite the carbs and the dairy. My camera is dangling round my neck, the lens protruding from my belly. If I'd thought ahead, I'd have strung it lower – phallic symbology and shit.

I'm like a foot taller than him in the shoes I'm wearing, and I take a minute to stand over him. I take a picture of his back. The way his spine curves, his bones beneath his skin, freckles, shoulder blades, dimples either side of his coccyx.

I drop the camera. My hand lifts, stops over his waist, like I want to touch him, like one of those awkward pictures of fat high school boys hover-handing a hot girl. I'll edit that out.

I spank him, really hard, and he goes, 'Ouch! Irina!' I do it again, and I laugh on the video.

He goes, '*Um.*'

I remember doing it, but not laughing. I remember his skin.

I had a dream once, where I sat up in bed and left my body behind. And I rolled next to her – to my body. I touched her skin. I kissed her lips, and they were soft, and mine, but cold and rubbery.

Watching the video is like that dream; I know that's me. I know that's my body. But she isn't cold and rigid, she's pink in the face, and frantic, snapping photos, pinching and grabbing flesh like a greedy child.

She gets to be there forever. Skinny and gorgeous and young, and I'm stuck out here. I'm stuck watching the video over and over again, rotting.

I pull down his underwear and brandish the wine bottle I'd been drinking from. He squeals when it goes in. And he flinches. His elbows give way and he flops over the arm of the couch like a flaccid dick.

I step back, take a bunch of photos. I lie down on the floor to get a better angle. I stumble on my heels, which I'll edit out as well because it looks so stupid.

I didn't notice it at the time, but you can see him trembling. You can see the shallow, sharp rise and fall of his shoulders. He was hard the whole time, I'm sure, but on film it reads less like poorly contained arousal, more like a prey animal, pinned, helpless.

'You good?' I ask him. 'Hey – you good?' And he splutters, in the bunny head; you hear him splutter.

I stomp over to the tripod and stop the film. He picked himself up from the couch, his chest making a wet, peeling sound as it parted from the leather, took off the bunny head. He'd been *crying* – probably the entire time. Not like crying like an emotional release; it was just genuine distressed *crying*.

I probably would have stopped if he'd said something.

I told him, *if you were uncomfortable, you should have told* me. *Don't put this on me. You're a Big Boy, Eddie from Tesco*. He shrugged. His arse was bright red, and he winced when he pulled on his jeans. He stared at the floor instead of my face or my tits.

'I'm fine. It's fine,' he said. But I didn't believe him.

He left. He gave me a shifty goodbye and left. He walked home, I think. I don't know.

That was a week ago. I've been feeling strange about it. Bad, but then annoyed that he's made me feel bad. Like, don't make it my fault, you know? Say something? I watch the video again and again. I watch it until the sun goes down.

Then he turns up at my door, paralytic drunk and sobbing. He knocks – hammers – saying he's sorry for freaking out, and being weird and *yes*, he should have said something, and can he *please* come in. I don't open the door. I pretend I'm not in, but I don't think it works.

'*Why is my life always like this?*' he asks. He starts punching the door, and screams for about twenty minutes before wandering back off into the night. I feel creeped out. Actually frightened, in a way I know I have no right to be, given the things I might have done.

There's a story about Ted Bundy – that during his trial lots of women turned up dressed like his victims. They would wear hoop earrings, dye their hair brown and part it in the centre. And there was one girl who would sit in the courtroom, dressed like that, and mouth *I love you*, over and over again to Bundy, *I love you*. And Bundy asked his girlfriend to stop this weird groupie from coming to court because she was creeping him out so much. Like, I'm Ted, and I'm about to ring Flo to see she if she'll come round and wait with me, in case he comes back. Fucking Susan comes over to ask if I'm alright, and I don't even have to pretend to be shaken up. I tell her that I'm going to call the police. I beg her not to tell my mam, then I threaten her.

'I swear to God,' I say, 'if you tell my mam, if you *fucking dare* tell my mother about this…' I don't finish it. She leaves.

Like putting on my American Apparel dress after a few weeks of errant bread consumption, this is a lesson in self-control. It's a lesson in fucking sad little men.

The video is cool, though. Very effective. A nice souvenir.

At least I know he's leaving Tesco in September – I can't go to Waitrose every day. I'm not made of money.

Irina,

This is a hard email to write. I assume you think I'm thick because I work at the Tesco and I'm training for primary and because of the way you speak to me in general, but I do actually have an English literature degree, from Leeds and everything, so I can write well if I want to. I am drunk.

I'm not even sure if I'm going to send this, and if I do send it, it'll probably be because I've gotten even drunker, and it's 3am, and I've decided that I'd rather just send you my heart on a platter than let all of this fester inside of me with what's left of my dignity. I don't know how to feel about what we did together, and I don't know how to feel about you. When I'm with you, I feel like the only person in the whole world, and no one at all at the same time. No one has ever made me feel so wanted (which is a weird thing for me to say, because I don't think I've ever ever ever felt sexually desirable before) but so awful at the same time. It's weird. I don't know if you realise how you speak to people sometimes, the way you feed people table scraps. I know that's what I get from you, table scraps, but because it's scraps from your table, it's better than a 3 course meal with someone else. And you've given me glimpses into your life, your real life, and I wonder if it's your fault. I wonder if you've got anything but scraps to give.

Everyone is always telling me I'm too sensitive. And I think I am. Every little knock with relationships leaves me in pieces. I always manage to pull myself back together again, but I think there's only so many times you can break and glue your bits back together before you start to lose pieces of yourself. I always looked at these times where my heart gets smashed as the climax to a relationship. The smashing is Ben ignoring me in the pub, or the girl i was in love with for 2 years in high school telling me 'you must be at least this tall to ride' and holding her hand a foot above my head. It's realising you're being catfished after nine months. Long, drawn out things.

I've only been with you a handful of times, and I feel like I get smashed up and put back together on the hour - every time you open your mouth, or put your hands on me, or send me a text, I don't know if I'm about to fall to bits or feel brand new.

I don't think this is healthy. But I've never been good at healthy.

I don't know what I'm trying to say. I don't know if I'm trying to tell you it's for the best if I stay away from you, or if I'm begging you to stay with me forever. Do I want to keep these shitty pieces of myself together, or do I just want to give them all to you.

I think about you all the time. I hear your voice in my head, I rehearse conversations with you, I talk to myself, and imagine I'm talking to you. And I wish you felt like this about me, but I know you don't and I don't think you ever will. I think you're happy giving people your scraps. I think that's easy for you, and I don't blame you, because I hate being like this, and I wish I was more like you.

I don't know, Irina. I don't think you'll reply to this. I don't know why I thought someone who looked like you would ever be remotely interested in me, and I almost wonder if this is a slap in the face from my own entitlement, that part of me ever ever thought that YOU could be really, truly interested in ME. It's a joke really, an absolute fucking joke. I'm a joke.

I'm stopping now. If you're reading this I'm sorry I sent it.

THE FALLOW YEARS

Jamie is pressuring me to send her stuff for the photobook. I tell her I'm most of the way through my archive, and I'll have something for her soon. I ignore her response and click through to my website.

I look for my own favourites, then bestsellers. Then I wonder if I even have favourites, if there are any prints that stand out as bestsellers or if they're all much of a muchness. In the years since I finished my MA, and came back home, there has been an indistinct parade of flesh through my house, slabs of which between it is difficult to distinguish. These years, my *wilderness years*, have been very productive, but for what? Samey photos, for prints. Waiting to get another gallery show, getting nothing. Radio silence, and print sales. Instagram followers, and reasonable cashflow, but no prestige, no recognition.

After the thing that didn't happen happened, I felt strange on my own. I felt strange about my photography. And I stopped. I stopped taking photos of boys – I stopped fucking and I stopped leaving the flat, other than to go to college, where I'd sit in the studio and stare at the wall.

I did some fashion-y stuff, made more of a thing of photographing women wearing clothes, rather than boys without them. I collaborated with some people I knew from the CSM fashion course (which didn't go *super* well because, apparently, I'm 'aggressive' and 'a control freak'). My tutors hated it – I hated it, to be fair – they said it was commercial, boring, very much 'not what they had signed up for' when they gave me a place on this course. It felt like a regression, a 'castration', of my work.

I didn't care. Everyone else stopped caring. I stopped turning up to uni. I didn't go to graduation. I did some freelance fashion stuff for a couple of months, and then I couldn't bring myself to apply for the work, to schmooze with the designers and the editors. I thought… fuck this. After about a month lying in bed, doing nothing, my parents twigged I wasn't working, and they made me come home.

I lived with them for a bit, got a job in the bar. I felt like a zombie, for months. I'd work, get trashed on my shift, I'd come home and sleep it off, I'd go back to work again. Rinse, repeat. I scroll and scroll and scroll through my website, till I reach the oldest image from my newest work, my post-London work.

I remember him. At first glance he is just a man with an unfortunate birthmark. It is huge, the colour of wine, and splashed across his face, his neck and his chest. However, a discerning viewer of men will notice that he is actually very good-looking, underneath the unfortunate birthmark. He has a sharp jaw, a Roman nose, high cheekbones, and dark eyes. But this birthmark is so jarring, so ugly – you would only see an angry blur of purples and reds, were you not a worshipper at my Broad Church of Boys.

I served him at the bar. I stared. He told me to take a picture, because it would last longer.

Can I? Can I actually?

I wasn't even carrying business cards at the time. I wrote my phone number on the back of a receipt and Ryan huffed and whined, because I'd give *him* (*the fucking elephant man over there*) my number but I wouldn't let Ryan take me out for a drink (back when I was a potential conquest for him, rather than a massive pain in his arse).

I worked the whole shift feeling jittery, lost in my own head as I imagined hypothetic ways to light him, pose him. I imagined he must feel so angry about the birthmark. Because he must know he's like a solid 8/10 underneath that awful, ugly skin.

I thought about myself. I thought about when I was a teenager and standing in front of the mirror feeling furious because I knew I was pretty. I knew that under the freckles, the extra weight, the big ears and the nose I hadn't grown into, I knew I was beautiful. I could see it; I've always had an eye for aesthetics, and I could tell I was pretty, the same way I only had to look at the birthmark guy for a few moments, and I knew.

He agreed to the photoshoot, reluctantly, and turned up at my house, and looked at me like I was a steak and he hadn't eaten in weeks. That was enough.

I took my photos, and I kept my distance, and nobody touched me, and nothing bad happened.

I've been getting handsy again, lately. That's why everything went sour with Eddie from Tesco. I got handsy. Will, I got handsy; the fucking teenager whose mam hit me, I got handsy. It's hard just to look, isn't it? It's hard to look, and not touch, not squeeze, or prod, or squash all that soft, private skin they show me.

I didn't touch Birthmark. And the photos are fine. All the photos, of all the men, they're all *fine*. Whatever I've dressed them up in, or sat them against, they're just… fine.

largely of Flo's friends, apart from Finch, of whom Flo and I share joint custody. I took cocaine and complained that the majority of my friends lived in London, unable to attend on such short notice. Neither Finch nor Flo pulled me on this. Finch just kept buying me drinks.

My memories of the evening are faint, from pub onwards. I bragged about the exhibition, and split half a pill with Flo, and bragged more, and danced. I recollect going off on one, pure party chat, about how you don't have to be in London, and people *do* know my work, and I'm not just an Instagram photographer or whatever, and I'll be everywhere after this exhibition.

I personally made my way through a gram of coke over the course of twelve hours, my memory coming back into sharp focus at around nine a.m. the following morning, with Flo shaking and sweating on my sofa, arguing with a stranger because he was trying to open my curtains. I drank a large glass of water and threw up in the sink – which Finch, smoking out my back door, declared to be the end to the evening. He threw everyone but Flo out, and dropped a Xanax in my hand. Flo said she'd stay up and keep an eye on me, in case I was sick in my mouth and choked while I slept.

I took the Xanax, and lay on my bed, while Flo took my makeup off for me with a cotton pad. I remember being sure that this was how I was going to die – choking on my own vomit, with Flo's sweaty face being the last thing I saw. I wouldn't have to worry about turning twenty-nine on Wednesday, or thirty next year. I wouldn't have to worry about boys, or Frank, or photographs to burn. I wouldn't have to get old and ugly. I'd missed the twenty-seven club, but I could still get a cult following, a posthumous retrospective of my work at the Baltic, Tate Modern, then MoMA. Maybe they'd even find out about the boy. Then my work would be worth a fortune – like how John Wayne Gacy's snidey clown paintings go for thousands. But I woke up, disappointed, with the sun down, and Flo's arm slung across my belly.

● ● ●

Happy bday love x

Sorry about your mam x

Will ddrop off your presents when ur back from London & have sent you some £££ for a treat when your down their

Don't get 2 drunk tonight remember you have a train!!! Lol xxx

Dad has sent me £££, and Mam hasn't even texted, unwilling to speak to me since I binned off the bar.

I wait on the sofa for Flo, who is lighting candles in the kitchen, and Finch balances a party hat on top of my hair, kicking through the balloons he's spent the evening blowing up.

Flo has set up her little makeshift nest on my smaller sofa, and her bags of clothes are stuffed into the cupboard under the stairs. It's my turn to have her tonight. She's been at Finch's since Sunday, driving him up the wall, I think. Complaining about his smoking and the fog of white spirit following him since he took up painting. He helped her make the cake – I could hear them bickering in the kitchen like an old married couple. I watched telly with my eyes out of focus, the comedown hitting me harder than it normally does.

'Cheer up, duck,' Finch says.

'I'm fine.'

'London tomorrow,' he says. 'That'll be good.'

'Yeah.'

He turns off the television, and Flo comes in with the cake. They sing 'Happy Birthday', Finch's voice breaking like a pubescent boy's, Flo's high and shrill.

It's a vegan chocolate cake. Dark, with ginger. Flo is a decent baker. I blow out the candles with a sigh, and the party hat falls off my head. Flo pours me a glass of red, and hands me a piece of cake. I take a tiny, tiny bite.

'I *told you* she'd eat some,' she says to Finch. I'd spit it out if I hadn't already swallowed. It's good. My favourite, actually, this specific recipe. 'It's her favourite,' Flo adds, smug.

'Meh,' I say, shrugging. But I eat the cake. The first time I've eaten something this sugary since... well, that affogato with Eddie from Tesco. Flo smiles, doting. She hasn't gotten me anything, knowing I'm never in a good mood on my birthday. It's better to get something for me next week, when I'll feel better.

'Is she always like this?' Finch asks.

'On her birthday? Yeah,' Flo says. I grunt. 'Since she turned twenty-four. Every year.'

'Shut up,' I say. 'Don't talk about me like I'm not in the room, like my fucking parents or something.' They talk, and drink wine, and I remain uncharacteristically restrained. Finch jokes: eating cake, not drinking wine, should he ring 999?

He leaves to smoke a cigarette, and a tipsy Flo shuffles over to me on her knees. She tucks my hair behind my ear and kisses me on the lips. I let her.

I think, *this is fine, isn't it?* She could live in my house, and clean it, and eat me out on scheduled days of the week. I don't have to tell my parents we're together, because she sort of lives with me anyway, and they wouldn't notice much of a difference. It'd be convenient, and it'd probably stay my inclination to start fucking choking my models. Because I know she'd be there, and I couldn't hide it.

She'll have to lose weight and cut her hair, of course, and I can always dump her if someone better comes along.

I wait to feel a twinge, a twinge of anything, something anatomical, or even one of familiarity. But I feel nothing. She's so soft, now.

I shove her, harder than I'd meant to.

'Don't.'

'Why not?' she asks. 'You need it.' I grunt at her. She lurches towards me, but I push her again. I'm surprised this hasn't happened sooner, really. I wipe my mouth with my sleeve. 'I… You told me to leave him. You stopped seeing the Tesco boy, and you *told me*—'

'Michael was a bellend. The Tesco thing was just like… It didn't work out. It happens,' I say. 'What did you think I was going to do here?'

'I don't know,' she says. I expect her to cry, but she doesn't. She shuffles back to the other side of the room, and sighs, hugging her knees to her chest. 'Never mind,' she says.

All these years, and I've never really questioned *why* she loves me. Or why she thinks she does. With men, it's always projection – a cliché, I know, but they fall for *the idea* of me. But Flo has known me for such a long time. She's watched me putrefy, and twist, and get thinner and meaner, and stranger. But here she is.

'What do you want from me, Flo?' I ask. 'Like, what do you think I can give you?'

'What do you mean? I just want you to be happy,' she says. She's quiet for a moment, thinking, frowning. 'I'm sorry I'm not *it*.'

'It?'

Finch comes back before she can explain what she means. And I'll never know, because fuck me if I'm bringing this up again.

'Which one of your horrible fucking films do you want us to stick on, then, Irina?' Finch asks.

We watch *Haute Tension*. It's a pointed choice.

●●●

Do you want me to come to the station with you???

I could meet you on my lunch break????

Nah.

Are you excited????

Meh.

Okey dokey.

Do you want me to do your bedding

Or anything else while youre away?

Whatever you want.

Dont go in my bedside table

Lol :P

Gunna lick all your stuff while you're gone!!!!!! :P

Flo sends a kissy face emoji. Part of me wants to tell her to make sure she doesn't top herself while I'm away. I put my phone in my coat pocket. It's the first time I've worn a coat since April. Over the knee boots, hold-ups, a black PVC trench coat, and I haven't ended up soaked in sweat in five seconds. You just can't *dress* during summer. It's been so hot I haven't even been able to get away with a waist trainer under my clothes, but I have one on today. It's tight across my belly, like a hug.

My hair flops into my eyes as I drag my suitcase into the Starbucks opposite the train station – I am growing out my fringe, from a Bardot Bang to something I can part on the side. But it's not long enough, yet, and is persistently in my eyes.

I grab a black coffee, and sip, and wrinkle my nose. It's shit, but it'll do. I listen to Sutcliffe Jügend, and window shop. I see a boy in a university hoodie, and shorts. He is carrying a gym bag, and his calves are thick and shapely. I see a tall, thin man, with a beaky nose which is wet, red and sore. I see a dark-skinned man with a shaved head and glasses, carrying a satchel, and talking on the phone. He seems pissed off. He's wearing a tweed suit, with a pocket square, and I watch him for a while, because he stops outside the window to talk more, growing more and more irritated the longer the conversation goes on. He catches me looking at him, and I smile. He smiles back, though it's awkward, and he walks away when we break eye contact. I'm in an aquarium – if you tap on the glass the fish swim away.

I buy another coffee before heading into the station, where I procure a salad from M&S. I board the train comfortably before it pulls out from the station. I've ended up on the shit one; there's one that takes two hours and fifty minutes, which just stops at York, then goes straight to London, but I'm on the one that takes over three hours and goes to every shitey little town on the East Coast. I start getting a bit pissed off by the time we get to Northallerton, because who the fuck lives in Northallerton. Like, Durham and Darlo I can forgive, but Northallerton feels like it specifically exists to wind up people on this train. I eat my salad, and try to sleep, but two coffees has me buzzy and jittery.

I drop Serotonin an email. I haven't really spoken to her since I left London, even though we were quite close for a while. There's a couple of good photos of us together on Facebook. Two from Halloween weekend, 2014. There's the Friday night where I'm Jessica Rabbit and she's Holli Would, then the Saturday night where I'm Ginger Spice and she's Baby. She was almost my replacement Flo – my pet skinny blonde – but she just didn't have the temperament for it, in the end.

She got a bit pretentious. She started working for Damien Hirst, and changed her name, and suddenly it was all *I don't want to go there! I hate that restaurant! I'll pick my own outfits, thanks!*

I email her, anyway.

```
Hey Sera,
I get into LDN in a couple of hours. Drinks/
dinner tonight, Y/Y?
Irina
```

Her response comes through when we go through Doncaster.

```
IRINA STURGES AS I LIVE AND BREATHE.
Sounds amaze. Got in from NYC last night
(dont know how much you've been keeping
up with me but i'm living in brooklyn now
#gentrification) and I would suck like 50
dicks for a brick lane curry. Shoreditch HS
station for 5??
I missed you u fucking BITCH.
Sera xx
```

I'm glad she's still quantifying how much she wants to do stuff by how many dicks she'd suck to do it. I have a very clear memory of her grabbing my face in Heaven and complaining about the fact we were in a gay club with no 'viable targets'. *I'd suck twenty dicks to suck a dick right now, Irina.*

I remember pointing out a guy on a night out and telling her I'd cut off one of my toes to fuck him, and she was like, *eww.* Like her sucking a hundred dicks isn't a more visceral image than me cutting off a toe. Just the one.

I agree to meet her for five. My train gets in at two, so it should be fine. I panic for a second that I don't have my business cards. I got new ones made – I've brought a box of about two hundred, just in case. I wobble down to the luggage rack and dig through my suitcase till I find them.

The rest of the journey passes uneventfully. I get texts from Flo, which I ignore, and an email from Jamie at the gallery letting me know all of my prints have arrived.

The hotel is in Islington, so I'm near an Overground, and the tube journey from King's Cross is painless. The hotel is nice – really nice, in fact. Big room, nice furniture, king-sized bed and a mini bar. The bathroom has heated floors, a good selfie mirror and a fancy bath.

I don't change. I'm already overdressed for London; the capital's casual dress code is something I never really adjusted to. People go out clubbing in trainers and jeans, and it's fine. If you go out in heels and a dress you look provincial, like, *oh bless her, it's her first time out in the big city.*

I still fucking hate the Overground. After growing up with the Tyne and Wear Metro, the fact that people complained about the tube used to boggle my mind, but the Overground *really* is a pile of shit. Like, trash-tier public transport – I'd genuinely rather get a bus. But the buses in London have a threatening aura that I'm not really in the mood for. So, Overground it is, with an eleven-minute wait for the next one, by the time I get there. I remember telling Finch once that he shouldn't even consider London for his MA, and that living there just makes you aggro as fuck. And he said he thought it was funny I thought like that, because I'm pretty aggro on the best of days. I told him to fuck off.

Sera is late. She tells me she walked, and double-kisses me on the cheeks before I have the chance to dodge it.

She nips her hands around my waist.

'Sturges, you skinny *cunt*,' she says. She never lost that public-schoolgirl habit of calling people by their surnames. Sera has put on weight. Her stomach bigger than her breasts now. It's not exactly a big belly, but it's a belly on a body with a tiny pair of tits. She's not wearing makeup – bar a little mascara. Her hair is back to its natural mousy brown, and her complexion is red, rough and wind-chafed. There are little lines around her mouth, and the skin is beginning to sag around her cheekbones. She's got that proper posh girl look to her — a turned up nose, and a long philtrum so she always looks like she's just smelt something that stinks.

'I hate you,' she says. Her accent is different – an American twang, now. 'You haven't aged a day. Honestly, what the fuck.' There it is again. It's *fuck* with a U through the nose, instead of one that curls, long and soft from the back of her throat. 'You're making me want Botox.'

'I haven't had Botox.'

'I fucking know you haven't. And I used to laugh at your fucking five-billion-step skincare routine,' she says. It's just a ten-step routine – one she would have benefitted from. She looks like she could be ten years older than me, even though there are just a few years between us. She's tall as well, and we used to tell men we were models, and that we lived together in a house with six other models, and maybe if they bought us some more drinks, we could take them back to the afterparty at ours. She'd never get away with that now. She takes my hand. 'It's wonderful to see you.'

She drags me to her favourite curry house, hoping it's still good. The curries in NYC aren't the same; she doesn't know if it's because they're more authentic, or less. Every curry house has a banner declaring it the definitive *Best*, or at least the provider of the best curry, in 2018, or 2017, or 'ten years running'. Sera is jabbering about moving back.

'I mean, I know it's all gone hashtag Pete Tong with Brexit over here, but Trump's America.' She looks at me and rolls her eyes. 'Of course, we all *hate* Trump in New York, but there's just *such* a bad vibe there right now, like, honestly. I went to speak at a uni in one of the flyover states – real Trump country, and it was literally like… *ugh*, you know?' I don't know. I've never actually been to America. I tell her so. 'Oh *babe*, you *have* to come over? I'll… literally, as soon as I get back to my Airbnb I'll email Carmen? She'll love your stuff.' I don't know who Carmen is. 'She owns this *sick* little gallery in Soho – NYC Soho, not *Soho* Soho. I showed with her, and that's basically how I got into MoMA; it's a great little connection. I mean, she showed *my* work, so she'll show you, I'm sure.'

We get seated immediately in this curry house where we're the only customers. Sera assures me this one really is *the* best.

'How's Newcastle?' she asks. She says Newcastle with a nasal 'a' now, too, and that makes me wrinkle my nose. I tell her it's fine. I take plenty of photos, I make plenty on print sales. 'I'm so glad you agreed to this show,' she says. 'I told Marnie about your work, and she was like, *I've never heard of her*, and once I sent your portfolio over, she was literally like O-M-G, how have I *not* heard of her, you know?' I raise my eyebrows. The papadums come. I order a large Cobra, which I take a huge gulp from as soon as it arrives. 'Marnie *owns* Hackney Space? I went to school with her brother, so we're like… We're not *besties*, but we have brunch together when she's in NYC.'

'Mmm.' I don't eat. 'You… You got me this?'

'No, *you* got you this,' she says, the patronising fucking cunt. I remember why I didn't keep in touch with her. 'I just *suggested* you. It's just always such a shame the way you dropped off the face of the Earth? Like, if I had my money on a Turner Prize for anyone, it would have been you, babe. Not David French. You used to fuck him, didn't you?'

'Mmm…' I drink more beer. 'That Jamie girl said she'd met me before, like it was her idea to have me.'

'Oh, God no. She was an intern till a few months ago. They've literally *just* taken off her training wheels. She's such a little liar, oh my God.' My face heats up. And I think Sera catches it, too. She looks mortified. 'You don't need to feel embarrassed, Sturges. Like, honestly, it confounds me how much working-class talent goes to waste. Like, if me or the David Frenches of this world have *a bit of a breakdown*, it's like… we spring back because Daddy always knows someone. It's just not fair that your career gets completely fucking derailed because of your mental health, you know?'

I am speechless. What I want to say is *I'm not fucking working class*, but we've had this argument before. Just because I'm nouveau riche, doesn't mean I'm not working class. My dad might be successful but, at the end of the day, a plumber with a big house and a dodgy accountant is still just a fucking plumber.

'I didn't have a breakdown,' I snap. 'Where did you hear that?'

'Um… Well, I used to drink with you. And like, I know we were all deep into coke and stuff, but *fuck me*, you were erratic back then. My flatmate used to call you the Party Monster – don't you remember? And you basically vanished halfway through second year. It's not... You don't have to be embarrassed, like, you're an artist; it practically comes with the territory,' she says. 'I just always thought about you, and I always thought about how unfair it was, and like... I've seen people make shitty versions of basically your work for—' I cut her off.

'I didn't have a breakdown... Fuck off, I didn't...' I clear my throat. 'I know you think you're this fucking champion of the working classes, or whatever, but I'm not a... I'm not mental, I'm not like a fucking... *baby* who taps out of her MA because she's *sad*, I was just... *Fuck* London, you know, fuck this scene,' I say. 'I make loads in private sales, just because I'm not in the Tate or MoMA or whatever.'

She smiles. I can see her pitying me.

'I'm really sorry. I shouldn't assume,' she says, with this fucking look on her face like she *knows*. She doesn't know the half of it. 'I'm being a smug cunt,' she says. 'I'm like... I really am trying to be aware of my privilege, so just... I, like, really appreciate you keeping me grounded.' It's very mature of her. I could smack her with this huge beer bottle, but I'm not going to.

'Well, that's what the *little people* are here for, isn't it?'

'Don't,' she says. Her accent slips, the American twang vanishes. 'Don't be like this. I know it's weird accepting help, but—'

'Oh, oh shit, you want me to *grovel*, now?' I laugh. 'Three seconds ago I got the show myself, but now I'm *accepting your help!*' I'm still laughing. 'I mean, really, that's fucking *unreal*, Sera.'

'I knew you'd be like this,' she says. 'I should've kept my mouth shut.' She sighs. 'Tell you what, Sturges, I'm going to go out for a fag. And when I come back, we're going to pretend I didn't say anything. We're going to eat, I'll pay the bill *as an apology*, not because I think you can't afford it; I'm sure you can. Okay?'

I shrug.

I order for both of us while she's smoking, and I stew. My jaw is clenched tight, and so are my fists. I mean, fuck me for thinking I got this on merit, right? Fuck me for thinking this was anything other than a handout.

My eyes feel wet. I poke them with my fingers. The feeling is so foreign – it's like when you bang your head and check to see if you're bleeding. Liquid on my fingertips, nose running, I blink, and I blink hard and I blink fast until it's all gone. I dab my nose with my sleeve, but I can still feel the heat radiating from my cheeks, down to my neck, spreading across my chest.

'Are you okay?' Sera asks. The fake accent is gone again. 'Jesus, Irina, I'm really sorry. I shouldn't have said anything.'

I don't reply, because my voice might crack. I screw my lips up, and I nod. I shrug, and I drink my beer. I wash away the lump in my throat, and let it settle in my belly. It curdles.

'Excuse me,' I say. I go down to the toilets, where I spend five minutes slamming the balls of my palms into my face, and my thighs, screaming with a closed mouth. I hit my head till my ears ring, then sit on the toilet with my skull between my knees, till the ringing stops and my breathing is steady. I smooth down my hair and my clothes and go back to the table. Sera's brow is crinkled, the worry lines on her forehead are deep. 'I'm fine,' I say. It sounds snappy, so I smile at her. 'I'm *fine*.'

●●●

Sera buys us a bottle of champagne at this nice bar in Soho. We're reminiscing, laughing. I can't quite shake the last of that feeling in my stomach, though. It lingers, like flu.

'If you tell anyone about getting me this, or about before, I'll kill you,' I say. I'm laughing through my teeth, and she laughs too. 'I will *literally* kill you.'

'I know you will,' she says. She taps her nose. 'Our little secret.'

●●●

'I like the bunny head, the bunny head's *good*,' says Jamie. We're in her office – the film playing in the background while we talk. I suspect she hasn't watched it the whole way through yet, because she keeps catching it out of the corner of her eye, and then looking away from it very quickly, and staring me right in the eye. She's very vanilla-looking. A bog-standard posh bitch, with long, brown ombre hair and a Zara cardigan. The accent says Sloane Ranger, but the lack of second-hand sportswear tells me she's at peace with that. Sera did say the training wheels have only just come off, and, fuck me, you can tell.

She's pulled me in to tell me my film will be showing in a room with one of Cam Peters's shorts – they're well suited, apparently. His is like a Gilbert & George-esque, cottaging thing. There'll be headphones, which we agree is better for me, so you'll pick up on all the little sounds.

'I hope you're not disappointed. To be sharing the screening room,' she says. I shrug.

'You're the junior curator.'

'Your accent is very charming, you know. You're from Newcastle, aren't you?'

'Born and bred.'

'I went once; there was a thing on at the Baltic. It was actually quite nice there, which I was really surprised about.'

'Mmm.'

'I bet you're so pleased to get this. The opportunities are so... limited up there.' She's looking at me like I clawed my way here out of a fucking coal mine. 'What year did you finish at CSM?'

'2012.'

'I was at the Slade for undergrad about the same time you were at the RCA then! 2014?'

'Good for you.'

I used to laugh at people from the Slade. They're all a bit like this. I used to call it the Suh Lar Day, in a faux posh accent whenever someone told me they went there.

Jamie closes her laptop when the film is done.

'I'm so excited to show this. And I *love* the photos as well.'

'Yeah, I'd better go get on with hanging, actually,' I say.

'Oh, someone will do that *for* you, darling.'

'Yeah,' I say, with a tight smile. 'I know, I meant... to direct it.'

'Oh,' she says. 'Well, I mean... *I'm* curating, obviously. It's not like a uni show, or a solo show. Everything has already been decided. You can watch, though, I mean...' Jamie shuffles in her desk chair. 'I *suppose* you can make some suggestions about the placement of the photos, if you have any.'

'Sounds good. I'll go down now, then, yeah?'

'If you like,' she says.

Sera is downstairs. Her work is on the first floor, but I find her walking the ground, watching a man hang my photographs.

'That one is really grotty,' she calls to me. 'I love it.'

'Thanks.'

'Excited to see the film, too! I thought you'd kind of dropped out of filmmaking.'

'I had but…' I shrug. 'Jamie said they wanted a film to show, so I made one.'

'You're showing a film *and* photographs?' says a little boy. He's dressed like an eastern European crackhead circa 1997, so I'm going to assume he's someone's assistant. 'That's not fair. I wanted to show a film, but Jamie said the only person showing a film was Cam.'

'You're in the show?' Sera says. We exchange a look.

'*Obviously,*' he says. With me. On the same floor. He points to his work, some stuff in the corner I hadn't even noticed. A few cork noticeboards and a piss load of Polaroids pinned to them, of what could be the same skinny naked white girl over and over again, or could be several skinny white girls. Some of them are tied up, so I *guess* that's why it's fetish art? 'I'm *Remy Hart*?' he says, like we're supposed to know. Sera and I look at each other again. They're not good photos. He clearly hasn't kept his film refrigerated – they're already sun damaged, with extra little pinholes where they've been hung elsewhere before. He's hanging them right by the door, too. They'll be bleached to shit by next week.

He walks over to my photos. Only one has been hung, so far. A photo of Eddie from Tesco's bruised backside, with the offending wine bottle wedged between his cheeks. They're all a little over a metre long, all in portrait. The other five are stacked, waiting to be hung. The boy creeps behind me, and hovers. I know he's there, because I can hear his tracksuit.

'*Six?* They're letting you have six?' He snorts. 'Who even are you?'

'Who the fuck are *you*?'

'I didn't even know we could bring work this big,' he says. 'I'm so fucked off. This is so unfair. Like, who is she?' he asks Sera, and points at me, sticking his finger right in my face. I slap his hand.

'I'll go and get Jamie,' Sera says. She's sniggering as she walks away.

'I'm going to call *my uncle*, and there's nothing *Jamie* can do about it!' he shrieks after her.

Cute: he's shy enough about his privilege to cosplay as someone picking up methadone from a pharmacy on Shields Road at twelve-thirty on a Tuesday, but not so shy he won't scream about how big his uncle's dick is in front of professional colleagues.

I get a closer look at him while he furiously stabs at a brand-new iPhone XS and waits for his uncle to pick up. He's white (shock), and we'd have to guess straight, from the skinny lassies in the photographs. He is dripping in retro sportswear, each article of clothing a different brand, and *dreadfully* well spoken. He's wearing round, ultra-trendy glasses, and an ugly toothbrush moustache.

I wonder, what do charvas in London wear now? Now that their whole craic has been gentrified. Full suits? Quirky tweed? Joy Division shirts? Is goth the new chav? I'm genuinely interested.

I look for his exhibition text – he's getting a little card. I'm getting something printed right onto the wall.

Remy Hart. Born 1995, UK, Hertfordshire

Polaroid Collections 1, 2, 3, 2018

Little Home Counties prick. I bet daddy is a banker, and mummy has a column in the local paper. I bet they moved out of the city before he was born, to make sure he grew up safe and sheltered and racist in a constituency where everyone votes Tory but pretends that they don't. I bet everyone shops at Waitrose and has a gilet and wellies and weirdly strong opinions on fracking.

On the phone, he's asking why some woman he's never heard of has space for large-scale work *and* a film. He asks why his work has been placed next to mine – *but it'll distract from my piece, I've been shoved next to the door – she has a whole wall – who even is she?*

I point to where they've got my name and my bio on the wall. I give him a thumbs up.

It's almost as if life isn't fair, Remy. It's almost as if it's not fair that you're in this show at all. His work is very first year of uni, honestly – I wonder where he went? Did his ego deflect any useful crit he got, or did he just… not turn up. He wouldn't have even gotten away with this shit at CSM (home of pictures of skinny white girls and their nipples) while I was there, and I'm surprised boys like this still exist. Still this entitled, still this generic, still this wealth of privilege and connections filling a void where there should be talent. I blame the adjusted uni fees for this shit.

I'm so angry I can feel it in my cunt; muscles twinging, balling up like a fist. My acrylic nails are digging into the meat of my palms. I could slap his phone out of his hand

and stamp on it. I could slap him. I could yank his fucking Umbro cap off and stuff it in his mouth.

I don't need to slap his phone from his hand, because he throws it at my photograph – the one they've hung. He damages the glass on the frame.

'What the *fuck*.'

'This isn't fucking fair,' he squalls. 'Jamie. Where the fuck is Jamie? I want to be moved. I want more space.'

My acrylics are filed to a point – I could drive them into his eyeballs. I could run across the room, and I could drive my fingers into his eyes, or into his neck and pull out his throat.

I just spit in his face instead. He squeaks, and a moment later Jamie and Sera arrive on the ground floor.

'Oh, what the fuck, Remy?' Jamie whines. He storms out, wiping his face.

I recount the story, down to me spitting at him, because I don't need to lie about it, ('You *spat* at him?') and I demand he's removed from the exhibition. He hasn't fucking earned it, anyway. He doesn't even have a Masters, and I went to the fucking *RCA*. You don't just get to mince out of fucking uni into fucking Hackney fucking Space.

'We can't take him out. I don't want him here either, but his uncle, Stephen Hart – lovely man by the way – he's a major donor. We can't… We can't pull Remy. We just can't.' Jamie shrugs.

'He just *threw* his *phone* at *my* work.' My jaw is clenched, I spray spit. She wipes her face. 'Look! You haven't even looked at it yet!'

Remy's phone lies in the middle of the floor, the length of the display boasting a huge lightning crack bursting from a spiderweb of shattered glass. My photograph has a matching wound on its frame: dead centre, a hole, with cracks erupting from it, all the way to the corners.

'Shit,' Jamie says. 'No one comes anywhere near that frame, in case the glass falls out.' She runs her hand through her hair. 'The photo doesn't look damaged, at least.'

The frame gets replaced later in the day with great fanfare. Uncle Stephen himself comes into the gallery, practically dragging Remy by the ear.

He makes the boy apologise to me. I accept, with my arms folded and my lips pursed. Uncle Stephen informs me that Remy has had a lot handed to him, and sometimes doesn't understand that larger work and larger gallery spaces are *earned*.

He's still fucking here, though, isn't he?

I'm less angry when Uncle Stephen makes a show of flashing his big fat wallet. He already paid for the new frame, but he wants to know how much each photo is worth.

I do some quick maths, and then I decide to take the piss.

'Three grand a piece.'

'I'll take the lot.'

'Oh.'

He goes on to tell me about all his kinky friends who would greatly appreciate these as gifts. He gives me his business card with a wink, and we chat while Remy pouts, and Jamie puts little blue stickers beneath each frame, indicating they've been sold.

'Tell me, Ms Sturges, do you like Japanese food?' asks Uncle Stephen. I toss my hair and look at Remy over my shoulder. I smile, with all my teeth, and giggle, and bat my eyelashes. Remy glares.

Uncle Stephen and I are going to the Sakurai together, on Saturday night. Not sure what makes me wetter: the threat of a £600 tasting menu, or the look on that little shit's face.

Hi Irina,
I know you haven't responded to my emails or texts in weeks but as my mum always says: God loves a trier.
I think I saw on the gallery's website that your private view is tonight, so I just wanted to say good luck and I miss you and I'm sorry for getting weird and freaking out, and I hope you'll consider replying to this.
I still think about you all the time.
Eddie.

REMY

After all the fuss with Remy, the day leading up to the PV is fairly uneventful. I drop into the gallery in the morning and make them rearrange the photos.

There's the one with the wine bottle, and one of Eddie from Tesco flicking the Vs with the bunny head on. There are two pictures in one frame, two close-ups of his bruised skin: a welt the shape of my hand on his thigh, set next to the ring of bruises around his neck. There's one of his lower back, and his butt with the tail fixed onto his underwear – it's the only image with my hands, one digging into his left thigh, one slipped into his underwear. I'm grabbing his skin hard, and you can tell. I've included one of Dennis, a close-up of the blood, his unfocused eyes half-open on the floor of my garage. Because you don't see Eddie from Tesco's face, you assume it's the same model, so it fits into the narrative.

The narrative they fucked up by hanging them the way they had.

The two-in-one photo should obviously be in the middle, but they put that first. I want Vs, grabbing, two-in-one, wine bottle, Dennis, but Jamie's hung it two-in-one, bottle, Vs, grabbing, Dennis. I make them move it. I make Jamie come downstairs and agree with me that this is better. She agrees, begrudgingly, and I leave for a solo brunch date.

It's a good day. I go to Selfridges with the intention of buying two new dresses – one for the PV, and one for my date. There's this designer lingerie brand I like a lot, who make really great ready-to-wear stuff – I head up to their concession. The salesgirls cut each other up to get to me first, when they see me looking at dresses.

The girl I get (the fastest, loudest girl) is a cute, curvy little brunette. She takes me to the changing room and brings me all the ready-to-wear they have.

I decide to buy this floor-length slip dress, like, the second I put it on. It's silk, plum-coloured, and split all the way up to the hip on the left side – it has this super dramatic lace cut-out from the right hip, curving around to the split. You can see your thighs, but your fanny's not out. There are lace cut-outs around the cups, too, and a pair of thin straps, which cross over my back.

'I *am* on commission,' admits the salesgirl, 'but you have to buy this.'

I agree. My nips are out, with the lace, though. I mention I'm going to my private view tonight, and I'd like to wear it out – does she have a solution for the exposed nipples? She pops out of the changing room, and comes back with a pair of pasties, which are black, metallic and heart-shaped, and I'm like, fuck it, go on then.

The next dress I decide on (after trying on a couple of things which are cute but too pyjama-y to get away with) is a black pencil dress. It's boned at the waist. There's a panel which runs from the bust to the hem down the centre (again, avoiding an exposed fanny) but the hips and the bum are sheer. The fabric is just thick enough that it's not obscene, but it doesn't leave a lot to the imagination. I love it. I'm a perfect hourglass in it.

I let the cute brunette sell me a couple of thongs to go with each dress (matching, and minimising VPL) and I'm done. I spend nearly a grand and a half, but... if you can't spend a grand and a half on dresses and pasties and knickers a day after some art collector drops 15k on your photographs, when *can* you?

I spend more money on dumb shit: new shoes, a handbag, perfume, lipstick and costume jewellery. I feel giddy and light, and I start drinking alone in my hotel room. I'm actually kind of drunk by the time I finish hair and makeup, and I treat myself to a rare photoshoot. My plum dress and I rack up more likes on Instagram than someone whose job it is to rack up likes on Instagram.

Flo is in with the first comment: *wig snatched, having a stroke, jessica chastain WISHES she could.*

I'm sure she does. Because I'm feeling extra as fuck today, I get a black cab to the gallery. I've forgotten to pull the tags off my new handbag and yank them off while I tell the cabby I'm a photographer, going to my private view. I've managed to stuff about a hundred business cards in the handbag, along with my purse and my phone.

'It's like a party, for when a show opens at an art gallery,' I explain.

'I know what a private view is,' says the cabby.

I bang through the doors of the gallery. No one turns to look at me, which is kind of annoying, because I had this image in my head of taking off my coat while everyone was looking at me, and people being like, *woah, who's that?*

No one looks at me but the attendant of a small, makeshift cloakroom. I hand her my coat. There's a boy in a waistcoat carrying a tray of champagne, and I wink at him when I take a glass. I find Sera, who is on the first floor. I haven't seen her piece yet, actually. Another film. It's her in Central Park, with some girl she's tying into *shibari* bondage while a crowd watches. She's all done up in fetish gear. It's a little lazy, to be honest.

I see her chatting with a dumpy woman in the corner of the room. Sera is wearing makeup today, and it takes years off her. Her lipstick is awful, though. It's the same colour as my dress, and it makes her teeth look yellow.

'I love your work,' I say.

'I love your dress, oh my God.' She looks at the dumpy woman, and points at me. '*Supermodel*, I told you, didn't I? Marnie?' I go to hand Marnie a business card, but she tells me she's the gallery owner.

'I know, take it.' She takes it. Sera makes a face at me. 'What?'

'Haha, honestly, her sense of humour, Marnie. She's *so* dry,' Sera says. She pulls me away, and leans in close. '*Please* don't get hammered,' she says. 'The dress is very *on brand*, but like… oh my God, your tits are basically out. I can see the wardrobe malfunction coming from a mile off?'

'What, are you my fucking *mam* now?' I snap. She rolls her eyes at me.

'I'm not going to bring this up again, but… just remember why you're here? If you look bad, *I* look bad, and I do want to move back to London, so…' She pats my hand. 'Behave, please.'

'Fair enough,' I say, with a shrug. I neck my champagne as soon as she turns around, and immediately pick up another glass.

I head back downstairs, drink more champagne, and stand by my photographs. Uncle Stephen comes over with a lecherous smile, and takes me by the waist over to some other red-faced old men, who collect art, or own galleries, and are amused and/or bewildered to receive my business card. Uncle Stephen laughs, and compliments my sense of humour, my *northern charm*.

He also drags me over to Cam Peters, who makes a weird dig about having to share the screening room with me and acts too grand to be here. He probably is, to be fair to him. I slip a business card into the pocket of his baby-blue suit – he doesn't seem to notice. I am whisked away to receive more champagne, and to be introduced to Laurie Hirsch, who is sharing the first floor with Sera. She's wearing a suit, and her hair is short, so I'm already sold. Even though I'm caught in Uncle Stephen's sweaty grasp, I wriggle free to tell her I love a butch girl. I tell her my phone number is on my business card, which I press into her sensibly manicured hand. She tells me she's married, and her wife is, like, two yards away.

'What she doesn't know won't hurt her.'

'Um, okay?' she says. I float back to Uncle Stephen.

While he does drag me around the gallery like a handbag,

he's surprisingly respectful. He hands me champagne, he lets me give out my cards, and he chuckles, like it's our little joke. He keeps his hand to my waist, or the small of my back, and never dips lower, even when we're in corners or side rooms and he could easily get away with it.

He leaves after an hour. I'm drunk and alone. I get pulled into photos with the other artists, with Marnie, and then I drift to the darkroom where my video is playing. I hit the bench with a thud and pop in the headphones.

I've watched this so many times now, I know where every little sound comes. Every twitch.

An older woman sharing the bench with me gives me a nudge. 'The way you've played with consent here is wonderful,' she whispers. 'Critical, bold, a wonderful actor, your boy. Discomfort radiates from the screen.'

It turns out she writes for the *Observer* – so there's at least one good write-up for me. I smile at her and empty my glass. Another materialises in my hand. My seventh? My eighth? Who knows? Eddie from Tesco snivels in my ear.

If he had a problem, he should have said something. I'm there on the screen. That's me. With the bottle, the power, a great big camera and bigger hair. I want to slip into the screen.

I feel hollow, but hot. I squirm where I'm sat, and I watch, and I watch, and I watch. I hear a bell, which makes me pull the headphones off and whip my neck around. No bell, just Remy.

He has lost the toothbrush moustache and shed his polyester skin, emerging in a fitted tartan suit, and no glasses. Lit in the soft glow of the film, he looks good. I imagine him shorter, and darker.

He sits beside me, tells me he's been watching me: with his uncle, with Laurie, with my business cards, and the silk of my dress clinging to my hips. He's sorry. He's seen my work, and he understands it now. He says he *gets the hype*.

He puts his hand on my knee, to test. I let him. I let him slip his hand past the dangerous slit of my dress and run his fingers along the inside of my thigh. He brings his lips to my neck, and his fingertips scratch at the delicate mesh of my new thong, suddenly hesitant.

He hadn't thought this through, had he? Poor thing. He looks like a frightened rabbit.

Do I get him right here? Do I smash my glass into his skull? *I don't know what came over him – he grabbed my neck, he put his hand up my dress.*

An excuse is bubbling on his tongue. I snatch his brand-new phone from his pocket. I invite him to my hotel room, tapping my number into his contacts, along with the hotel postcode.

'Give it half an hour before you come. I don't want to be seen leaving with you,' I say.

I do the rounds, the goodbye kisses. People are disappointed all the photos have been sold, but they are not surprised. I direct them to the photobook in the gift shop, my website. I dish out a fistful of business cards. Sera glares at me, and I leave a smudgy red kiss on her cheek.

'A few glasses of champagne really go to a girl's head, don't they?'

I leave.

In my hotel room, I wait, without my dress, but with the letter opener that came with Mr B's stuffed bear. I carry it with me. It's proof, isn't it? Tangible proof. I place it deliberately on the bedside table and play with a silk scarf I plan to use. It is red to match my lipstick, his insides.

He bursts through my door looking smug, just pleased as fucking punch, with no idea what's coming to him. He tries to kiss me. I tell him to take off his clothes and lie on the bed.

He asks me if anyone has ever told me I could be a model, that he'd *love* to take my picture.

I tie his hands together, above his head, then to the bed frame. He tells me I looked amazing tonight, and asks if I wore the dress with him in mind. I laugh at him. He keeps fucking talking, so I stuff a pair of socks into his mouth.

His wallet has fallen out of his trousers, and a fat baggie has fallen out of his wallet.

'Is that coke?' I ask. He nods. I have a bump, then another, and I straddle him. I stick a fingernail full of coke under his right nostril, and pinch the left shut. Greedily, he sniffs it. Then I slap him. I slap him harder, and harder, till his lip bursts. His eyes are streaming, and he can't get those socks out of his mouth.

I stop. I take photos on my phone. Blood drips down his chin. I smile at him. I ask him if he's okay. In what I think is some *attempt* at bravery (toxic, masculine bravery), he nods. I lick his chin, and regret it immediately. It's coppery, sickly, thick, and I gag, tasting blood and cocaine and champagne and bile on the back of my tongue.

His nipples are pink. I poke one with the letter opener, a tiny puncture mark which pisses blood, and he squeaks. I take photos. I prod and puncture his stomach. He has no muscle tone, no fat; he looks fragile and young. His belly wiggles, and flexes away from the sharp point in my hand, his skin sucking in, concave around his ribcage while I jab, and he bleeds. I cut a thin slice from his belly button to the dip of his collarbone. He is whimpering, and crying, now. When I ask if he's okay, he nods. He's still trying to hold face, where any woman would be screaming down the hotel.

Unless he's too afraid to scream.

I run the tips of my fingers through the blood on his chest, and I draw a smiley face on his torso. I slap him again. He starts coughing, so I let him settle.

I open the mini bar, and take out several small bottles of vodka. These won't do. I throw one at him, and it bounces off his skull and onto the bed. While it leaves a mean welt behind, it won't shatter, so I sit on the end of the bed and drink it.

When I squint, he reminds me of my boy – the ribs, the young skin. But his hair is too light, and too straight. He's too pale. He's wrong. And he'll be missed, and I don't have bin bags, or a meat-cleaver.

I can barely stand. Another dig at his mangled nipple elicits a high-pitched, piggy squeal. I slip, and nearly take it off. I'm dizzy – the room whirls. I am extremely nauseous. I try to take a few pictures, but I can't. Not now.

I stagger to the bathroom, leaving him in a puddle of his own tears and blood. I vomit into the sink. It lands with a splat. It's fizzy and almost clear – I didn't eat.

I slam the door and my knees hit the tiles of the bathroom with a thud. I vomit till I'm hacking and dry-heaving into the toilet, staring at myself in the water. My cheeks are streaked with mascara; there's lipstick all over my face and sick in my hair.

I've looked better.

I pull myself up off the floor, and knock my phone into the sink. I wipe off the vomit and look through the photos.

They are *perfect*. Each one is completely hypnotic. They're better for being on the phone, because it's more naturalistic, less staged; I can carry them with me everywhere.

I grab the sink. I stare at myself in the mirror. I stare at her. I press my forehead to the glass, and kiss her, smearing lipstick everywhere, slipping my fingers between my lips and coming, even though I'm numb with the drink and those bumps I didn't need but did any way.

The force of it makes me vomit again. I get to the toilet this time. I flush.

I crawl out of the bathroom. My scarf is on the floor, and the hotel door is wide open. He's gone, and so are his clothes. There's blood on the carpet and he forgot his cocaine.

I crawl on my hands and knees to kick the door shut, and crawl back to the bathroom. I force myself to vomit again. I stick my fingers down my throat till there's absolutely nothing left to throw up, then I crawl into the shower, forgetting to take the pasties and my underwear off before I switch the water on. I scrub my hair with the hotel shampoo, and sip the spray, and throw up again.

I sit there until everything stops spinning. I need to eat.

I manage to dress, and comb my hair into a ponytail, and get all the makeup off my face. I look halfway presentable – no one would ever know. I can just about walk in a straight line. And I see familiar, comforting lights. The yellow glow of a twenty-four-hour McDonalds, the hard, white light of a Tesco.

Tesco calls to me. There's a homeless man snoozing by the door, who I stop to assess for a moment. He is decent looking, I suppose, under the dirt and the straggly facial hair. I'm about to shake him awake when I spot the CCTV camera glaring at me from above.

I stand up straight and wave at the camera. I go into the Tesco and pick up bread, and crisps, and hummus, and croissants. I will regret having binged in the morning. I am delighted to see Eddie from Tesco, where he should be, behind the counter, smiling shyly, staring at my tits.

He's so beautiful. Even with glass hanging out of his eye, he's just adorable. I tell him, and he thanks me. He can't sell me a bottle of vodka at this time of night, but he'll give me cigarettes.

'Aren't you going to ID me?'

'No?'

'Cheeky cunt. You're lucky you just got away with the wine bottle, really,' I tell him.

'What?' The girl behind the counter blinks at me.

'Ah. Never mind, babe. Thought you were someone else.'

● ● ●

Yo yo yo eddie frm tesvo

In. Lnd atm bt whe i get home we can fuck again if you promis nott to be a little bitch about it

;lol

● ● ●

I wake up in my clothes, on top of the sheets, in a pile of crumbs. I wake up because my phone is buzzing, insistently, by my head.

Hey babe, last night was wavey. Really intense. Sorry for bolting – i'm schizy af when Ive had a bump (or two! Started at the gallery lol) & i'm just not into knife play. Plus, I dont really bottom or sub or whatever I am very much a top.

Went to A&E to get stitches and they told me i didn't
need any lol felt like a right bellend! Appreciate you
wanting to get a piece of me but watch what you're
doing with that little knife of yours ha ha ha!!! x

I really am sorry I broke your frame btw. I think i was
just intimidated by this incredibly naughty older woman
I wasn't expecting to see ;)

Hope you have fun with my uncle tomorrow i know he's
into some really weird shit lol x

I actually make a few attempts at a reply: I literally wanted
to kill you? I almost cut your nipples off? You went purple?
What about any of that read as safe, sane or consensual?

I hope he doesn't tell anyone. God, if he tells anyone he'll
be sorry I didn't gut him. Older woman. *Older woman.* Call
me that to my fucking face, you little bitch.

                    Lose this number. fuck off and die.

I block him, just in case.

I also have a bunch of texts from Sera, generally having a
go at me for being 'a cringey drunk bitch'. They're long, and
rambling, and sweary, and don't exactly read like the work
of a sober person.

                                        Chill out.

        You're acting like my fucking sponsor or something

                    Miserable posh cunt lmfao.

I look through the photos of Remy. They lack the same
interest they held for me last night. They're bad. They're
blurry. The white balance is off; they're overexposed or
underexposed or they're too yellow in the ugly tungsten

hotel lighting. I keep only two or three. Souvenirs, I guess. He's also not as cute as he was last night.

I have more texts. There's one from Eddie from Tesco where he calls me a *fucking reptile* and asks not to contact him again. I respond with a cheerful *okey dokey*, and it goes through, so he obviously hasn't blocked my number.

Scrolling up, I see that after I texted him I did send him a few photos of Remy. Oops.

I look at the photos again, the ones I didn't delete. I look at his purple face, his bloody chin and nipple, his swollen cheeks. I wonder what the fuck I have to do for people to recognise me as a threat, you know? It's like... am I even doing this shit? Have I even fucking done anything?

Like, do I have to snap the wine bottle inside him to get him to stop sending me sad emails? Do I have to cut his nipple off for him to realise he should probably ring the police? Do I have to cave his head in with my camera, rather than hit him the once? Do I have to crash his car? Do I have to smash a glass over the head of every single man I come into contact with, just so I leave a fucking mark?

GLASS

I spend almost a full twenty-four hours in my hotel room. I watch telly, I eat crisps, I vomit, and I shower again. I hear bells, and glass shattering, and I hear the sound of my own teeth.

Sera apologises for being a bitch. I'm like, *yeah*. I remind her I don't *need* her – I have private sales, and we *do* have galleries in the north. She just says she's sorry again, like she's so much bigger than me. Fuck her.

I pull myself together to leave the hotel again. It's the day of my big date with Uncle Stephen, and I decide to go for a light, salad-based brunch, after bringing up what I can of yesterday's carbs. My throat is raw. I don't want to eat on my own, so I go to text a friend then realise I don't have any of those. Sera is busy when I ask, so I'm just like… great.

I eat alone at the Breakfast Club, where I accidentally order a full English. I drown it in ketchup and brown sauce, and my stomach screams at me for filling it with carbs and grease and other *hard-to-digest* things, which I know are going to rip through my colon like a bullet. I feel like there's something sharp, and crunchy, in my mouth. Something *sharp*; I spit it into my palm, but all I get is a chewed lump of white bacon fat.

The waiter asks me if I'm alright.

'Never better,' I say. 'Just caught my breath.' He gets me a napkin, and I'm surprised he can work with that glass in his eye. I call Flo. I call her to ask her, when I do things, do they stay? Do they happen, and do they last?

She says she's a little worried about me.

'I'm serious,' I say, chewing my toast. 'It's like I do shit, and *nothing*... like, I do this awful shit, and I just want someone to... properly fuck me off because of it? Like, no texts, no emails, no crawling back, like... good-fucking-night Vienna, yeah?'

'Where did you get that dress from, on Insta? It looks *expensive.*'

'Are you fucking listening to me?'

'Yeah, you just sound mental. Are you on coke? Have you been on one since the PV or something? You sound cokey as fuck.'

'No,' I lie.

'Drink some water,' says Flo. 'I'm at work. I can't talk. And I'm back with Michael, by the way.' She hangs up. I knock over my coffee to see if the waiter will come and clean it, but he doesn't. I leave the cafe without paying. No one chases me.

That evening, I arrange to meet Uncle Stephen outside the hotel. I've got my coat on, and my red scarf, which is splattered with dry blood, but it's cold, and I haven't brought another. Uncle Stephen picks me up in a cab, and we drive to the Sakurai.

The basic makeup of his face is like Remy's, but redder, and flabbier. His hair is thick and silver, and his suit is sharp, tailored and extremely expensive.

'Did you make a pass at Laurie Hirsch?' he asks.

'Excuse me?'

'Laurie said you made a pass at her. She's married to my cousin's daughter – it came down the grapevine.'

'No,' I say. 'She's not exactly my *type*.'

'I didn't think so.' He rolls his eyes. 'She's such an attention-seeker.'

'Performance artists,' I say, with a shrug. We laugh together, at Laurie, at performance art. I kick the back of the driver's seat, and the cabby doesn't say anything. I kick it hard, as well. He just takes it. Uncle Stephen doesn't seem to notice.

'Cam Peters really came around to your work, in the end,' says Uncle Stephen. 'I'm sorry if he was a little sharp with you. He was *very* upset that he was sharing at first. I hardly blame him. No offence intended, darling, but he was the name there, wasn't he? Anyway, he *loved* your work. We've both agreed to pass your name on to our various friends at Tate Modern, the Serpentine Sackler, Whitechapel, et cetera.'

'I took Remy home with me, and I nearly cut his nipples off, and he literally texted me yesterday like we'd had a normal one-night stand,' I say.

'Oh, absolutely! I'd be excited too,' he says, smiling at me, like he hasn't heard what I said. 'You are a real *discovery*, aren't you? A little diamond in the rough,' he says.

'There's nothing little about me.'

'Of course, it's not a problem at all, really. I thought the business cards were *funny*, and anyone who didn't think they were just... They're of no interest to you, I promise. That *Marnie*.' Uncle Stephen shakes his head. 'She has wonderful taste – obviously – but what a *dour bitch* she is.' He pats my knee. His hands are huge and white, like underground spiders.

His hands are white, but his face is red.

The cab is expensive. The restaurant is in Chelsea. I lived in London for five years and never really *went* to Chelsea – like, I passed through it, obviously; I lived in Battersea. But only on buses, on foot. I never ate or drank there. I never went to a house there. I remember walking past a shop on the high street that only sold huge, ornate mirrors. They all cost thousands of pounds. I remember stopping, and pressing my face to the window, and seeing myself staring back over and over again, thinking I want one, but this city is *fucked*, isn't it?

'What would I do with a big mirror like that, anyway?'

'Hmm?' Uncle Stephen says.

We pull up at the restaurant: a white, neoclassical building. The sign is gold, and in kanji. Uncle Stephen takes my hand and helps me out of the cab.

The carpet in the restaurant is plush; it's hard to keep my balance in heels. The host wears a waistcoat, a shirt and a bowtie. His English is good, but his accent is thick. Uncle Stephen gives his name, and we're taken to a booth in the corner – his usual. The host takes my coat, and makes an O with his mouth, a tiny twitch of his eyebrows, before departing for the cloakroom.

'What *are* you wearing?' says Uncle Stephen. He sounds amused. He peers around me, at my back. I twig for the first time that he's taller than me, even with heels on. He's huge.

'It's expensive,' I say.

'I'm sure it was.' He guides me to the seat, with his hand in the small of my back again. 'It's stunning. But… well, the crowd is a little conservative in here.' He points out an older couple, who are looking at me. They look away when we look at them. 'This isn't a nightclub, you know?'

'I don't really care,' I say. I think.

He orders me a cocktail before I can order for myself, and a bottle of plum wine for the table. He talks about my dress more, with this tone like he doesn't mind, but I can tell he does. He just doesn't want people to think he's out with a call girl. I tell him I don't think he could afford me.

'I can,' he says. He laughs. I hate this. I'm just here for a free meal – he mentioned the Tate earlier. If I can just behave myself, for like an hour. He asks me to tell him about *The North* because he's never been any further up than Manchester. He's been to Edinburgh once or twice, but that hardly counts, does it? Because it's really just the London of Scotland, isn't it? How does it compare to London? Don't you feel hemmed in? Don't you feel like there are no opportunities? No jobs? No arts funding? No money? Do you have any restaurants like this? Isn't it *worth* taking a risk and living down here? Don't you miss the hustle and bustle? Sure, the rent is cheaper, but has your quality of life *really* improved? Did you move back for your parents? A boyfriend? Do you just like being a big fish in a small pond?

'Ah, well,' I say. 'You know. I hated it here, I hate it there. Whole country's fucked. Brexit, Tories, 'n' that.

Fucking service-based economy. There's the post-Thatcher government ghettoisation of the North but at least the wealth gap isn't rubbed in your face everywhere you go. I don't know what you want me to tell you. The rent is cheaper. There aren't any restaurants like this.'

That seems to make him sad – that there aren't any restaurants like this. When the plum wine comes, he tells me how it's made, and I don't give a shit. I just don't give a shit. It tastes like cough syrup, but it's obviously expensive, so I drink it, and I nod. And then I drink this awful cocktail he ordered for me. It has *yuzu* in it, and it's bitter as fuck, and I feel like I'm licking a lemon rind. I'd have been happier with a pint of fucking tap water.

Is he talking to me about his job now? I don't even feel like I'm here. I feel like he's talking to me from the opposite end of a long tunnel. I think he orders for us. I think I just agreed to the tasting menu. He asks me if I like the cocktail, and I shake my head, and he makes some comment about my palate, and I hear my teeth squeak together because I've clenched my jaw so hard.

'Excuse me,' I say. And I go to the bathroom. And I'm hyper-aware of a room full of Tories looking at my arse, and tutting, and assuming I'm a call girl because I suppose it is now a crime to wear a see-through dress to a posh restaurant. My fanny isn't even out. There's a panel. There is a fucking *panel*.

There's another woman washing her hands in the bathroom, who listens while I tell her this. She tells me she thinks my dress is nice, I think. She could have also just gone 'hmm', because I wasn't really listening to her, or looking at her, and then she was gone. I go into the toilet stall. I say stall; it's posh, so the stall is its own little room. The toilet has a heated seat and speaks in a perky Japanese accent. It sprays warm water directly into my vulva after I'm done pissing, and I go, 'Fucking hell!' loudly, because I wasn't expecting it. It also dries me off, with a little blast of hot air. And when I come back out of the bathroom, I'm aware I want to talk about the fucked-up talking toilet, but fucked-up talking toilets that spray water up your gooch without asking are probably just par for the fucking course here, aren't they?

Uncle Stephen tells me he complained about my cocktail, and got me a new one. The same one. I just don't think I like yuzu. And when he tells me it's unacceptable, with the amount he's paying them, looking genuinely perturbed, I am reminded of the iconic scene from *Keeping Up with the Kardashians* where Kim loses her earring. They are on holiday in Bora Bora, and Kim is swimming in the ocean wearing $75,000 diamond earrings, and loses one. She loses one, and has a complete meltdown, ugly crying, and sobbing, and then, ever down to earth, Kourtney appears from around a corner, baby on her hip.

'Kim, there's people that are dying,' she says.

'Kim?' says Uncle Stephen.

'You know, when Kim K loses her earring. And it's like… There's people that are dying.'

'Always good to have some perspective,' he says. The first course comes. It's sashimi. Uncle Stephen chastises me for taking a bite, rather than dropping the whole thing in my mouth. He eats loudly, reminding me of that bit in *The Return of the King* (the film) where Denethor is eating cherry tomatoes, and making Pippin sing for him. In this metaphor – allegory? – I guess I'm Pippin, which is strange because I've never identified much with the Hobbits before, and I'm actually a little annoyed that this is the position I'm in. Shocked to hear it comes in pints, and wondering if my simple Hobbit songs are good enough for these grand halls and their talking toilets.

He talks to me about his job while he eats. He's some sort of advertising thing? God, I don't care.

'Is this cocktail better?' he asks.

'I just… I don't like yuzu,' I say. He flags down the waiter.

'You'll drink a Bellini, won't you? Bring her a Bellini, a strawberry one, and make sure you use *champagne* not that Italian twaddle. I'll know.'

They bring me a Bellini, and the smell of champagne makes my gut curl. But I drink it.

'Tell me about you,' he says. 'I feel like we've only talked about me. I know you're a photographer, of course, but what else is there?'

'What else is there,' I say. 'I killed a boy, once.'

'Oh, did you?' Uncle Stephen chuckles.

'He was in the wrong place at the wrong time. We both were. And he was covered in scars,' I say. 'And I put his skull underneath this tree, but now it's gone. And it's like… There were no missing reports, or anything, so did it even happen? You know, like? Did it even happen?'

He laughs again, slapping his hand on the table.

'I love dark, northern humour, I really do. Do you like *The League of Gentlemen*?'

I do. So he talks about how he knows Mark Gatiss – did I know Mark Gatiss is from County Durham? He was in an excellent show recently. Do I like theatre?

'Didn't you hear me?' I ask. 'Didn't you hear what I did?' He laughs some more, and ignores me, and talks about theatre. I'm starting to feel a little frantic. I squeeze the champagne flute in my hand so hard that it shatters. My palm is filled with glass, and my hands are sticky with blood and bubbles.

I sit there, with my bloody hand, as he talks. I catch my reflection in my dinner plate, and there is glass in my eye, which I further inspect in the back of my spoon.

'Your lipstick is fine,' he tells me.

I lift my fingers to my eye. Nothing. I feel nothing. My hand is dry. My glass is intact. I stare at the glass, and my uninjured hand, and I blink. Uncle Stephen's face twists, and melts – he's his nephew, he is Eddie from Tesco, then he's my boy, lunging at me. I flinch. I crush the champagne flute into the side of his head, and a blood-curdling scream fills the restaurant.

They're all looking at me again. Uncle Stephen is Uncle Stephen again, and he is bleeding. My hand is bleeding. The waiters rush over, and they are so busy tending to him, they don't notice when I slip out of the booth. They whisper as I walk by, but nobody stops me, nobody wants to stop me. I even hear a man saying, 'Maybe they'll comp us,' and the blissfully unaware host hands me my coat, with a smile, when I tell him I'm going out for a cigarette.

I walk. I take off my shoes and walk barefoot on the cold, damp street. I hear a bell, jingling behind me. I walk till I can't feel my feet anymore, till it feels like I'm walking on a pair of fleshy sponges. I walk through Chelsea, down through Battersea Park. I wonder if anything will happen this time.

I pull out my phone and tap out a text to Flo.

Like 80% sure i just glassed my date

And then:

Lol.

I send her a line of shrugging emojis.

I spot a man on a park bench.

He is small and large. He is wearing an expensive wool coat, a ratty T-shirt and a polo neck. He is skinny and fat. He has his head in his hands. He's sniffing. He wipes his nose on his sleeve and rubs his eyes. I wave at him. I ask if I can sit down. I look at my feet. They're bleeding.

'Rough night?' I ask.

'Yeah,' he says.

I pick up my feet and inspect them. They are peppered with gravel and blood, and pieces of glass which I pluck out, one by one, with my fingernails.

'What's up?' I ask. He tells me a story I don't listen to. His lips are dusty pink in the moonlight, the streetlight. His skin is freckled, and brown and white and red and wet. His hair is dark and curly, and blond and straight. I run my bloody knuckles down his cheek, which is soft and peachy. I tell him he's going to be okay. I tell him not to worry.

I explain to him that nothing matters, and nothing lasts. Everyone forgets, and everything disappears. The things you do, the things you are; it's all nothing. Would anyone miss you, if you went away? Would anyone look for you? Would anyone listen, or even care, if I hurt you? If I put my hands around your neck and crushed your windpipe and chopped you up, would anyone find you? And if it's a no to any of these, did you even exist in the first place?

The man gets up, and tries to walk away, but I trip him. I sit on his stomach. I look into his face, and watch it melt from my boy, to Eddie from Tesco, to Will, to Lesley, to Remy, all with glass embedded in their eyes, all blood-spattered and knotted together. A rat king of boys in the face of this stranger, who is struggling and frightened.

'Have you ever modelled?' I ask him. He doesn't respond. 'Have you ever modelled?'

I take a business card out from the cup of my dress and put it in his mouth. I get up and walk away. I pass a homeless man with the boy's face, but I don't stop to look when he calls out to me. Am I okay? Do I need help? Where are my shoes?

I walk deeper into the park and arrive at the pond. I take off my coat and my dress, and get in. I expect to feel cleansed – to drop into the cold water and re-emerge with clean skin, filling my lungs with fresh air. But I'm just cold. I can feel a beer can by my elbow, and something soft under my feet. When I look down into the black water, I see the milky-eyed face of my boy, his head bobbing to the surface. I pick it up by the hair and find a knot of plastic bags and pond weed in my hand.

It isn't him. It never is.

ACKNOWLEDGMENTS

I have enormous gratitude for the staff at New Writing North. Without their generous Young Writers' Talent Fund it is highly unlikely this book would have been written. In particular I would like to thank Matt Wesolowski who served as my mentor, and whose expert assistance and encouragement helped take *Boy Parts* from a bloated short story to a fully-fledged novel.

I would also like to thank the staff at *Mslexia* magazine, where I was employed during the majority of the writing of this book, and which served as an excellent crash course in the world of UK publishing. It is perhaps worth noting that this novel was impulsively pitched by one of my 'Sock Puppet' accounts to Influx Press at a Mslexia Max pitching event I had organised, and was moderating. A testament to the adage that 'shy bairns get nowt'.

Which brings us to Gary, Kit and Sanya, the stalwart team at Influx, vanguards of independent publishing and a great bunch of lads, without whom none of this would be possible.

I am grateful to my parents, Ken and Wendy, and my extended family for their support – and am likewise indebted to an anonymous group of intellectuals known only as 'The K Hole Flirters' for facilitating much of the research that went into this novel. Additionally, I'd like to thank my earliest readers, among them my partner George. George's unconditional love and support was imperative to the writing, editing and completion of this book, and will be to all further projects. Unless we split up, in which case, what a massive gaffe this will be, eh?

ABOUT THE AUTHOR

Eliza Clark was born in Newcastle Upon Tyne and now lives in London. *Boy Parts* was written after Eliza received a grant from New Writing North's Young Writers' Talent Fund. She has been chosen as a finalist for the Women's Prize Futures Award for writers under thirty-five.

DON'T MISS
ELIZA CLARK'S
NEW NOVEL

PENANCE

A chillingly compulsive and brilliantly told story about a murder among a group of teenage girls

www.elizaclarkauthor.com
@fancyeliza